Detective Inspector Molly Watso[n] Police is twenty-nine, single, at succeed despite the efforts of her [ ] wants her out of the CID.

Back from suspension, she finds herself at the centre of the largest and most complicated letter bomb search and disarming operation ever known and then in charge of the Force Bomb Squad.

Pursuing international terrorists, she follows a trail of mayhem, rape and murder that leads to London where she meets her former lover, Detective Superintendent James Cranleigh-Smythe.

Things have changed, however. She soon discovers that he has joined forces with a devious MI5 agent and Scotland Yard are protecting senior Cabinet Ministers who, fearful of German domination of Europe, have committed a treacherous act that could cause numerous deaths and colossal destruction. Convinced that there has been a leak, they are prepared to go to any lengths to find and eliminate the suspect. The Superintendent believes Molly has information critical to his enquires but she refuses to betray a friend or deviate from her pursuit of the terrorists.

Following an armed siege and the taking of two American women students as hostages, Molly becomes the prime target as the story explodes into a surprising and dramatic climax.

***

Brian Windmill was born in Lincolnshire. He joined the Royal Navy when he was fifteen, leaving after eight years to became a police officer in the West Midlands. During his thirty-three years service he specialised in CID, serious vice, drugs and operations, rising through the ranks to become a commander at Birmingham, Wolverhampton and Dudley. He is now a full time writer and public speaker.

Also by Brian Windmill

DRUG SQUAD

BOMB SQUAD

A DETECTIVE INSPECTOR
Molly Watson Novel

Brian Windmill

Brandwell Books
Wombourne
England

Published by
Brandwell Books
39 School Road
Wombourne
Staffordshire
England
Tel/fax 01902 898259

First Published   1996
© Brian Windmill 1996

Printed in Great Britain by Redwood Books,
Trowbridge, Wiltshire.

A catalogue for this book is
available from the British Library
ISBN 0 9527317 0 3

1

She stepped out of the taxi and scanned the busy street, looking for the unusual. It was instinct now but when she joined the CID, eight years earlier, it had been the first rule she had learned. Not that it would help her today. She had broken the rules and her fate was in the hands of dark-suited bureaucrats at the Home Office Police Department.

A drop of rain caused her to glance at grey clouds scudding above an untidy forest of aerials on the top of the Headquarters building, a glass and concrete edifice towering above her.

Approaching the main entrance, she remembered previous visits. Her first uniform and the sergeant in the fitting room who *accidentally* let his fingers slip whilst measuring her inside leg; the hard hat that made her look like a jockey; a reprimand for being late on duty; a discipline hearing for shouting at a prisoner who had raped a little girl; commendations; promotions; and, finally, suspension because a corrupt Drug Squad detective sergeant had been killed whilst trying to escape from a trap she had laid for him.

She pushed through glass doors into the shabby, blue-painted lobby where in the past she had struggled with prisoners, pacified distressed victims, and humoured Saturday night drunks.

At the counter, she moved aside untidy piles of crime prevention leaflets and pressed the bell. No one appeared from the back office. She rang again, leaving her finger on the button.

Getting no response, she walked past a group of shaven-headed youths leaning nonchalantly against a wall and a line of Asian women sitting quietly on a wooden bench.

She glared at the security lock on the office door, aware the combination must have been changed many times since she last opened it.

Impatiently, she hit the buttons at random. The youths behind her sniggered and one of them called out three numbers. Late for her appointment, and ready to try anything, she pressed the buttons. The lock opened. 'Thanks,' she said, making her way through the door.

The lifts were being serviced. She used the stairs.

Slightly breathless, she reached the sixth floor and dashed into the Chief Constable's office.

A stringy sergeant in a starched white shirt made a show of studying his watch. 'Detective Inspector Watson,' he announced priggishly before leaving the room and closing the door behind him.

Oil paintings of self-important chief constables of the past, lined dark, oak-panelled walls and huge plants in sturdy ceramic pots filled the corners of the large room. It was rumoured that the Chief talked to his pot plants.

Grey-haired and distinguished-looking in full uniform, he sat behind a polished oak desk devoid of paper or any sign of industry. A remote and ambitious man, who had little regard for the welfare of his officers, he spent most of his time sucking up to local politicians in the forlorn hope that they might recommended him for a knighthood.

He studied his detective inspector, noting the rise and fall of her breasts and wondering how much the expensive green suit and matching accessories had cost. Tall and slender, with full, red lips and a pleasant, open face, she looked younger than her twenty-nine years. Rays of late October sunlight cut through the storm clouds and touched her short fair hair with gold.

'Sit down, please,' he said, waiting a moment until she had settled.

'Let me see - how long have you been suspended?'

'Eight months, fifteen days, sir.'

'Yes. Since your sergeant was killed...' He left the statement hanging in the air, hoping for some sign of remorse, an apology even; she had had enough time to reflect on her foolhardy and dangerous operation. '...Dont you have any regrets?'

'I'm sorry for his family. Sergeant Conrad brought about his own downfall,' she said evenly.

'Don't you accept *some* responsibility for his death?'

Her green-blue eyes did not waver. 'No, sir, I don't.'

'It was your case; you set him up.'

3

'I only did what was necessary.'

His brow furrowed and he glared at her. 'Do you mean to tell me, Inspector, knowing what you do now, you would have taken the same course of action?'

'Yes!' she snapped defiantly.

He coughed, deep in his throat; a sure sign he was annoyed. Damn the woman. What could he do with her? One of his best detective inspectors, she was a grafter who refused to accept defeat and rarely lost a case in court. When she was in charge of the Drug Squad they'd had fewer drug problems in Westhampton than any other city in the country.

He'd re-read her personal file and knew she'd had a rough start in life. When she was five years old, armed robbers had gunned down her parents in their East End off-licence, and she had been brought up in children's homes. At sixteen she had enlisted in the Royal Navy, leaving three years later because they wouldn't send her to sea. *This young woman is unsuited for peace-time service but I suspect she would be a formidable weapon in the event of hostilities*, her captain had scrawled across the bottom of the discharge report.

He tried again. 'Surely you've got something to say for yourself, Watson?'

'I made a full statement eight months ago, sir.'

'Oh, come on! I'm not the investigating officer, for Christ's sake. I put you in charge of the Drug Squad when everyone else said it wasn't a job for a woman.'

'I've done nothing wrong,' she said stoically.

4

'By God, Watson, you don't see it, do you? You're a menace. Your kind of coppering finished long ago.' He trumpeted into a large white handkerchief. 'The Police and Criminal Evidence Act is for real, not a party game for the legal people to muck about with.'

Her shoulders inched back but she showed no sign of being ruffled.

How could the bloody woman be so pig-headed? he wondered. With ten years service and no hope of a pension, she should be on her knees - pleading for her job.

He took a sheet of paper from the top drawer of his desk and winged it in her direction. 'Here, read that, I'll be back shortly.'

As he disappeared into the bathroom, she picked up the bonded paper and started to read:

Dear Chief Constable,

The accidental death of Detective Sergeant Conrad is regrettable. Fortunately, however, apart from ourselves and those directly concerned with the incident, no one is aware that members of the Metropolitan Police Special Operations Unit were engaged in an unauthorised and covert operation in your police area. I have decided, therefore - in the public interest - to take no further action against your Detective Inspector Watson.

Yours sincerely,

Sir Neil Raybold-Ardreen, C.V.O.

Permanent Under Secretary of State,

Home Office, London SW1.

She gasped, then read the letter again, her head in a whirl. She'd won; she'd got her job back. She wanted to cheer and laugh and cry all at the same time. It was over: eight months of not knowing; eight months without a future; eight months of pure hell.

The red telephone on the Chief's desk buzzed.

After a moment's hesitation, she brushed away a tear and answered it.

'Watson, Chief Constable's office.'

'Taken over the force, Molly or just passing through?'

She recognised the friendly voice. 'He's popped out for a minute, Graham. Where are you hiding yourself these days?'

'Control Room. Tell his nibs we've had an explosion at the Royal Mail Letter Office. Five dead and several injured. Your old boss, Detective Superintendent Davidson, is already on site.'

Turning a major incident into a disaster movie, she thought. Aloud she said: 'Pity the Royal Mail.'

The inspector in charge of the Control Room laughed. 'Welcome back, Molly; you've been missed.'

The bathroom door burst open and the Chief returned to his desk.

She put down the handset. 'Message from the Control Room, sir.'

He did not seem to hear her. 'What about the Home Office letter?'

'They had no choice.'

His brow furrowed. 'What do you mean *no choice*?'

'It's a political decision. The government of law and order would eat sand to prevent a public enquiry.'

'Twaddle. The Secretary of State's being extremely gracious.'

'He just wants everything hushed up. Am I getting the Drug Squad back, sir?'

'Certainly not. Report to Chief Superintendent Training at nine in the morning. In the meantime go to the stores and collect your uniform.'

'Uniform? I've done nothing wrong.'

His face reddened and he made no effort to conceal his anger. 'It's customary to address your chief constable as *sir,* and not customary for inspectors to challenge my decisions.' He paused, then raised his voice. 'Do I make myself clear?'

Realising she had gone too far, she could only nod.

'Lost your tongue?'

'No sir.'

'Have you anything else to say before I end this interview?'

'No - yes, sir. We've had an explosion at the Royal Mail. Five dead some injured.'

'What! Why in heaven's name didn't you say so earlier?'

Grabbing his silvered hat and leather-bound swagger stick from a small table beside his desk, he headed for the door.

'Come on, Watson. You might even be useful.'

2

Sirens screaming, a posse of motor cycles escorting a Jaguar shot over the red lights at Westhampton's city centre. Friday night commuters cursed and shuffled their cars into the kerb. Pedestrians, used to speeding police vehicles, kept their heads down and tried to keep dry in a sudden downpour. A traffic warden made herself small against the side of a battered Sierra, then slid a plastic-covered notice under a windscreen wiper.

In the dimly lit bar of the Queen's Hotel, a solitary customer stubbed out his cigarette. 'Hey! Joe,' he called to the barman. 'That stupid cow outside has just booked me. Can you fix it?'

Joe squinted into the shadows beneath an orange street light. 'Sure I can. She's quite tasty - if you like it close to the bone.' His face twisted in a conspiratorial grin. 'Only takes a couple of lagers.'

The stranger took a wad of notes out of his wallet. 'Here, buy the silly bitch a crate of the stuff and tell her where to shove that ticket.'

Accepting the money, Joe decided the man was in his mid-forties and he came from London or the Home Counties. Since lunchtime, he had stood at the bar and steadily worked his way down a bottle of Scotch.

Alert and on edge, he didn't seem to be the usual stressed out businessmen trying to drown his problems. More like someone on the run, Joe thought. Where were the CID? Most evenings at about this time they dropped in to cadge a few drinks before booking off duty.

He slid the money in his pocket. 'For that much, mister, she'll make the Kama-Sutra seem like Mills and Boon.'

The man smiled thinly and left the hotel.

In the back of the speeding Jaguar, Molly sat beside the Chief and contemplated her future. The thought of lecturing to a class full of disinterested, bleary-eyed bobbies, doodling on their assignment books and planning the next booze-up, filled her with dread. She'd rather be stuck in an office, shovelling paper from one tray to another.

The Jaguar swung into Stratford Road and braked sharply to avoid colliding with an haphazard line of emergency vehicles, beams of light from their blue and amber lamps chasing each other along the walls of the Royal Mail Letter Office. Silent, shirt-sleeved postal workers, recently evacuated from the premises and seemingly unaware of the rain, lined the pavements.

Weaving through ambulances, fire engines and police vans, the Jaguar stopped outside the main door. A constable, struggling to hold back the press, cleared a path for the Chief who dived through a battery of flashlights and into the building.

She remained in the car, still fretting about her impending move to the Training Department and trying to remember who was in charge.

Someone tapped the roof. 'Giving us a hand, ma'am? It's bedlam inside the Letter Office.'

Why not? she thought.

Getting out of the car, she saw that the roof-tapper was Bill Bannister, one of her former Drug Squad men.

She fixed her eyes on his shiny new stripes. 'Borrowed someone's uniform?'

'Promoted last week, ma'am.'

Bill Bannister; a sergeant. Twenty-six, married with two young children, he was a big, fair-haired, blue-eyed man. All smile and muscle, he was also a push-over for any woman who showed the slightest interest. After a shaky start in the Drug Squad, he had proved to be her best and most loyal detective.

She shook his hand. 'Congratulations, Bill. You'd better show me around. Just keep well away from people with frost on their hats.'

Obviously pleased to be back with his former boss, he powered his way through the mob of pressmen and led her into the foyer.

Passing empty, glass-fronted offices, they entered a wide corridor and stopped at a door guarded by a uniformed constable.

He stood to attention and saluted. 'Good evening, ma'am.'

After so many long, miserable months away from the job, she wanted to give him a big kiss. Instead she made the standard police reply: 'All right, officer.'

'The *Secondary Sorting Office*,' Bannister said in the low, reverent voice of someone entering a cathedral. '...Where the explosion was.'

Feeling very small in the hangar-sized room, she craned her neck to look at the rows of fluorescent tubes marching beneath a high ceiling spanning letter racks, ducting, conveyors, mail chutes and an impressive array of mechanical sorting equipment. In the distance, she could see open mailbags hung in metal frames and above them large white boards bearing the names of towns or postal districts. In the aisles between rows of letter racks and sorting machinery, four-wheeled skips lay on their sides, mail scattered about them.

She moved forward slowly, Bill Bannister at her elbow.

They passed the end of the letter racks and the floor space opened out. In front of them, near to the hanging mailbags, was an expanse of shredded paper and blackened canvas. At the far side of the room, a group of men, some in uniform and others in suits, stood attentively around the Chief.

'I thought we were avoiding them?' Bannister said.

'I've changed my mind,' she replied truculently. 'If the Chief didn't want me here he should have left me at Headquarters.'

Bannister chuckled, a comforting sound she hadn't

heard for a long time. 'He just likes to be seen sharing his smart motor with a classy bird.'

'Cut it out, Bill. He's sending me to Training.'

She stopped and Bannister bumped into her. 'Christ! he exclaimed, suddenly noticing the carnage in front of them.

Three bodies lay amongst the tattered and scorched remnants of mailbags and their contents. Two more were slumped against a wall, pools of arterial blood darkening the concrete floor. The fingers of a severed hand still clutched a small bundle of letters. Other hands and booted feet were spread over a wide area.

It was always the same, she thought sadly, too many hands and feet. The air conditioning had been shut down and the smell of burnt flesh suddenly hit her nostrils. She held her mouth and gagged, somehow preventing herself from being sick. No matter how much gore and splintered bone she saw, it never got any easier.

Noticing Bill Bannister's ashen face, and convinced he was about to pass out, she grabbed his arm and held it firmly. 'Take deep breaths and count to six.' He did so, his large chest straining against the silver buttons of his new uniform.

'Feeling any better?'

He nodded and gave her a weak smile.

'Can you spot the seat of the explosion?'

Eyes avoiding the scene of death, he shook his head.

'Beneath the ceiling.'

He looked up. The heating pipes directly above the

12

London 2 district name board had been flattened. 'I didn't think of that, ma'am.'

'Now you'll never forget it.' She stepped over part of a leg and went down on her haunches to examine a small, blackened circuit board. 'Letter bombs,' she breathed.

'Inspector!'

She looked up and saw Detective Superintendent Davidson bearing down on her. Short and fat, his once-red hair was now a sparse halo of grey and only his bushy red eyebrows brightened up an otherwise plain and podgy face.

'You're not supposed to be in here, Miss Watson,' he blustered. 'And you've definitely got no right to interfere with the evidence.'

She winced inwardly, hating the egotistical, ignorant man. It was common knowledge he only kept his job because he would have been a disaster in any other post.

Her boss when she'd been in charge of the Drug Squad, he'd trapped her in an empty office after a Christmas CID binge and tried to grope her. When he ignored her protests, she'd smashed her knee into his groin.

After that incident his attitude towards her changed and he'd done his utmost to get her thrown out of the Department.

'The Chief said that you're to forget about training for the time being,' he went on. 'He needs everyone down here and wants you to liaise with the Royal Mail people. Use the offices inside the main entrance and do whatever's necessary.'

'You're standing on someone's small intestine,' she said quietly.

Crying out, he jumped back and looked down at a pool of blood and gut. Quickly regaining his composure, his eyes narrowed. 'I suppose you think that's funny?'

'Only trying to be helpful, *sir*.'

'Yes, I'm sure,' he sneered, glancing at Bannister. 'Remember this, Miss Watson; you may be back in the police force but you'll never worm your way back into the CID. Keep out of my way and out of this investigation. Divisional CID and Regional Crime Squad will handle the enquiries - real detectives.'

'How would you know?' she said, turning her back on him and heading towards the exit. Immediately behind her, Bannister tripped over his feet in his eagerness to distance himself from the furious CID boss.

Molly stopped and took stock of the pandemonium in the foyer. Frantic relatives of the dead and injured, pressmen and union leaders, were all demanding to know what was happening. At the centre of this melee, a tall, solidly built man in his late fifties was calling for order.

She gave Bannister a meaningful look and he started to clear a path through the mass of people. Pleased the natural telepathy between them was still working, she followed him until they reached the man in he centre of

14

the room.

'Are you supposed to be in charge of this circus?' she shouted up at him

'I'm the manager of the MLO,' he shouted back.

'What's that?'

'Mechanised Letter Office; who's asking?'

'Police Liaison.'

His once-handsome face darkened. 'Can't you see I'm busy?'

'I've come to help.'

'Good, then leave me be, woman.'

'Inspector Watson to you.'

The MLO Manager glanced at Bannister's uniform, then shook a thick finger at her. 'Now you listen to me; evacuation procedures, fire-fighting and everything else was fine until your heavies stormed the place and fucked it all up. We've got dead men in the Secondary Sorting Office and they'll be a few more if we don't move our arses and isolate the mail.'

'What mail?'

'All the bloody mail. At least six million items in this building and that's only for starters.'

'What do you mean?'

'There's mail at local delivery offices, post offices, in letter boxes, on station platforms and stuffed inside vans, lorries, trains and aeroplanes.' He bent closer to her. 'Westhampton is a central distribution point and mail from all over the country pours in and out of this place every working day of the week. Tell me,

15

Inspector, how many bombs d'you think we have in that lot?'

She looked around the hot, stuffy room, the enormity of the problem becoming clear to her. 'Bill,' she called. 'Get me the crowd's attention.'

Concentration showed on his face for a moment, then he fished in his pockets and produced a police whistle. He blew on it, his only reward being a cloud of trouser fluff. He tried again and was more pleased with his efforts. Voices lowered and people turned towards him. After the fourth whistle, he had everyone's attention.

She stepped onto a stool and raised her arms like the Pope. 'I'm...' she hesitated for a moment, '*Detective* Inspector Watson, police liaison.' The crowd edged closer. 'We have received information that a number of letter bombs are in the room above.'

There was a shocked silence. Then, as one, the crowd glanced fearfully at the ceiling, turned, and stampeded out of the building.

Bill Bannister followed the last person to leave and fastened the doors.

She faced the manager and held out her hand. 'The name's Molly, my sergeant here is Bill.'

'Bert Tallis,' the manager replied, shaking her hand uncertainly. 'You'll do, I suppose.'

She pointed at the empty offices. 'We'll have to commandeer some of those rooms.'

He looked her in the eye. 'I started as a sorter in this

16

place thirty-seven years ago. Good men were murdered here today and they were my friends; you'll have everything you need.'

She smiled sympathetically. 'Thank you, Bert.'

Bannister, polishing his police whistle on the arm of his jacket, ambled across to them. 'It's called the *Metropolitan* and was designed in 1834 to be heard for a distance of two miles,' he offered. 'It was my Grandad's and I carry it for luck.'

'Let's hope it works,' she said, her mind working furiously as she worked out a plan of action.

He put the whistle into his pocket. 'Grandad never picked up his police pension; he fell into the river after a wedding party and was drowned.'

She snapped her fingers. 'Right, Bill, start setting up an incident post, please. We need at least half a dozen BT lines and furniture for the same number of bums. I'm going to tell the Chief and his hangers-on they should have their tete-a-tete somewhere else. This building is still full of unsorted mail and they're probably standing in a minefield.'

'Think of the vacancies, ma'am.'

3

'Davidson!' warned Bannister, a moment before the Detective Superintendent filled the Incident Post doorway.

Eyes squinting in the strong light, he took time to spot Molly. 'That stupid PC you've stuck outside asked to see my bloody warrant card, Miss Watson.'

'This is a classified area,' she replied evenly.

He glowered at the busy scene around him.

Office staff lowered their eyes; not wanting to be part of the antipathy between their new boss and the head of CID.

They were crammed amongst an assortment of borrowed office furniture and equipment; answering telephones, setting up filing systems, preparing duty lists, mapping out areas containing suspect mail, and a myriad of other essential tasks. On a table in the centre of the room, document trays surrounded a computer, its printer spewing paper into a cardboard box that had once held smoky-bacon crisps.

Davidson looked through glass partitioning at a small group of shirt-sleeved men in the next office. 'What's going on in there?'

'That's the Royal Mail Information Centre,' she

replied. 'They're dealing with staff problems and *where's my mail?* enquiries. Bert Tallis, the MLO Manager, is in charge.' Davidson gave her a sideways look but he was too insecure to ask what MLO meant. She went on: 'The small room across the passage will be the exhibits store and the office next to it - the one with the sink - we'll use as a laboratory for the initial examination of bomb material.'

A PC carrying an armful of boxes collided with Davidson's back. 'I wish you'd find some other fucking door to lean.....' Belatedly realising who he was talking to, he dropped the stationery onto the table and scurried out of the room.

Someone stifled a laugh.

'Where did he get that lot from, Miss Watson?' Davidson asked.

'*Inspector*, if you don't mind.'

His bushy red eyebrows twitched. 'Answer the question.'

'Force stores.'

'At ten o'clock; on whose authority?'

'Yours - it's an emergency.'

'What else have you done in my name?'

'Details of the incident have been broadcast on the Police National Computer. Motorcyclists are waiting at Junction 3 of the M5 to escort a bomb disposal unit. Forensic at Birmingham are providing a search team. The Dog Section is on the way and the Press Office are setting up a news desk at HQ.'

19

She leaned forward to allow a PC with a handful of urgent messages to pass behind her. 'The Casualty Bureau is on line and swamped with calls. Traffic have thrown cordons around this building, local delivery offices, post offices, mail vans, and any other place where mail is being held. Transport Police are isolating mail on station platforms and mail trains that have been shunted into sidings.'

'Is that it?'

'No. East Midlands Airport have grounded Royal Mail night flights until further notice. Emergency services have been up-dated. A paramedic ambulance and a fully crewed fire appliance will remain outside this building until further notice. Hospitals have been warned to have emergency medical teams on standby. The Technical Support Unit is available at HQ if special equipment is required.'

Davidson spoke with a loud voice, making sure everyone heard him. 'Detective Superintendent Dunn has set up a Major Enquiry Office at Divisional HQ. You and your staff are not to interfere with his enquiries, *Miss* Watson.'

She clenched her fists, sharp fingernails digging into her palms as she struggled to contain her anger. 'Everything we've done is on the Major Incident Log, she said in a tight voice. 'Searching the mail and liaison with other agencies will be coordinated by me from this office.'

'For the moment,' he said. 'How many

unexploded bombs d'you think we're dealing with?'

'You tell me, *sir*. We've six million items of mail in this building and a similar amount left here during the last twenty-four hours.'

'That's a bit much, isn't it?'

'The Royal Mail sorts and delivers fourteen billion letters every week.'

He moved further into the office, pushed aside the boxes of stationery, and settled on the edge of the table. 'Did the explosions occur in mail collected today?'

'We're not sure.'

'What do your pals next door say?'

'They're working on it.'

'I should hope so...Tell me, where's everybody you've called out supposed to congregate - the bar of the Dirty Duck?'

'Force Headquarters is the rendezvous point. Heads of departments have been told to report here for a conference at seven in the morning.'

'I am invited, I take it?'

'You're the chairman. We're meeting in the management suite on the third floor; well away from the mail. I wouldn't want you to be blown up, *sir*.'

'I'm sure you wouldn't, Miss Watson. Is there anything else?'

'Forensic and a team of explosive boffins will be attending the conference. Birmingham's Anti-Terrorist Squad offered their services but I didn't think you'd want a big force telling us how to do things.'

21

His annoyance showed. He had transferred from Birmingham City Police on promotion to his present post and hoped to go back there as an assistant chief constable one day.

'Explosion at Dinsall Delivery Office - some injuries!' called out a constable.

She reached for her coat. 'I'll go with you.'

Davidson smiled sardonically. 'No you won't, Watson, you're non-operational.'

Shaking with anger, she lowered her arm.

His grin widened, fuelling her frustration. 'See you later - *miss*,' he called over his shoulder.

Emotionally drained, she sank into her chair, only the presence of her staff forcing back the tears.

Half an hour later, she wrapped her hands around a mug of hot chocolate thoughtfully provided by Bill Bannister. What a day. Eight months in the wilderness for stopping one of her Drug Squad sergeants who had falsified statements, stolen drugs and planted evidence, and now this; letter bombs and non-stop action in a place that was a complete mystery to her.

Bannister broke into her thoughts. 'What was it like, ma'am; being suspended?'

'The pits.'

'How did you fill in your time?'

She sipped her chocolate. 'Bit of this - bit of that. I suppose I moped about a lot at first. Then something happened and I pulled myself together.' He looked at her over the rim of his mug. '...It was Holmes,' she said, a lump in her throat.

'Your little dog?'

'He was run over.'

'You live in a cul-de- sac.'

'It only takes one car. Luckily, he didn't suffer, it was very quick.'

'...And that pulled you together?'

'I was broken hearted; it was my way of coping. I got out my old walking boots, packed a rucksack, and was off the very next day. I did two long-distance walks in one - over five hundred miles.'

Bannister whistled through his teeth. 'Where?'

'The Pennine Way and then the West Highland Way in Scotland. It was in the Spring. I shall never forget Loch Lomond and Rannoch Moor. There'd been a late fall of snow and I was walking under brilliant blue skies so that it was like Switzerland.'

'What about your antique collecting - the crested china?'

'W H Goss...I went to a few sales and an auction in London at the start but soon lost interest.'

Bannister picked up the telephone and she went to the rest room.

'Message, ma'am,' he said, when she returned. 'Wouldn't give his name - mentioned a blagging at Lloyds Bank'

'Go on.'

'He said: *The letter bombs are only the beginning: a*

diversion to keep MI5 chasing their tails. Then I lost it -
just before the line went dead. Like one of those old war
films. You know, where the hero's sending a vital
message from behind enemy lines and the Nazis storm
into the loft and shoot him up. I couldn't get the end bit.'
   'Try.'
He sat down. 'I'd only be guessing.'
'Give it a go, it's important.'
He sat down and tapped his Biro on the desk, as if
sending Morse Code to himself. 'Something like,
They're moving south to take out the town.'
It didn't make sense but she nodded, to herself
mostly. It must have been Mad Mick from her Crime
Squad days. She had arrested him for an armed robbery,
then done a deal with him. A word with the judge had
kept him out of prison and he'd helped her to lock up a
team of top class villains. With the money she squeezed
out of the insurance company, he'd gone to Northern
Ireland and opened a betting shop.

'Who was the caller, ma'am?' It was after midnight and
only Bill Bannister was with her in the Incident Post.
On the Drug Squad, his hair had been long and he
had dressed like a hippy. In his smart uniform, with
short hair, he looked much younger, she thought. 'Give
that message limited circulation, Bill.'
   'Protecting your sources or keeping the CID in the
dark?'
She gave him a meaningful look; wondering, not for

24

the first time, whether he knew her too well. 'Get one of your girlfriends at HQ to quietly check out Michael Joseph Rewan. He's thirty-fiveish and has loads of form. I want to know where he's living or the address of his business. Have you ever been to Northern Ireland, Bill?'

'No, ma'am, but I think I can find it.'

She smiled; he was a good man to have on her side. 'I thought you promised Liz you'd pack the job in after the Drug Squad fiasco?'

'I did, and I did.'

'What happened?'

'Couldn't settle. I missed the action and the lads.'

'And Liz?'

'She was brilliant. In fact, she was the one who talked me into coming back.'

'Any regrets?'

'No, especially not after the promotion. Liz was really chuffed about the stripes. She's told all the relatives I'm bound to be at least a chief constable.'

'Still fancy the CID?'

He studied his hands before he spoke. 'Liz might get a bit shirty about that.'

Molly was sure she would. Liz had given him hell when he was working all hours on the Drug Squad. 'I haven't had time to tell you before, Bill,' she said. 'I've got permission to keep you as my office manager for the duration. Get whatever staff you need to keep this place going twenty-four hours a day. It'll be hard work but the overtime's guaranteed.'

'Good,' he said enthusiastically. 'How long?'

'I'm not sure. Plan for a week, at least.'

He pulled a block of A4 across the desk but she laid a hand on his arm.

'Not now, Bill. Go and tell Liz what you've been up to. I'll wait for the night crew.'

He glanced at his watch. 'Thanks, I think I will.'

After a moment's silence, he coughed in the back of his throat. She looked up, noticing that he'd coloured slightly. 'It's good to be working with you again, ma'am.'

'You to,' she replied. 'We're going to get the evil swines who killed the mail sorters.'

Surprise showed on his face. 'Davidson's stuck you in this place and said you're to keep out of the enquiries. There's no way you can catch the bombers.'

'Want to put money on it?'

4

The Incident Post night shift had taken over and some of
the lights and equipment had been switched off. Two
PCs and a busty computer operator talked quietly, filed
reports and smoked filter tips.

Bert Tallis walked into the office and sauntered up to
Molly's desk. 'Time you packed it in, missus.
Tomorrow isn't going to be any easier.'

Her hackles rose, no one called her missus. 'I didn't
ask for your advice.'

'Sorry, just trying to be considerate.'

'Nannying I don't need.' He shook his head wearily
and made a move towards the door. 'How are things
with the Royal Mail?' she asked quickly, wanting him to
stay. He looked back at her, seemingly unsure what to
do.

'I need to know,' she said desperately.

He shrugged his shoulders and slumped into a chair.
'It's a mess. Mailbags all over the place and everyone
convinced that chunks of the city are about to vaporise.
Persil washes whiter will be given the supreme test
tomorrow.'

'What's the latest from Dinsall?'

'A canopy over the loading deck collapsed and half a

27

dozen workers are picking glass out of their heads. Fortunately, none of the injuries were serious.'

'Thank God for that. How many explosions were there?'

'One, I think. A heap of mailbags was set on fire.'

She scribbled on the message she had been reading and dropped it into the out tray. 'I'm staying here tonight. No point in rushing home if I've got to be back before dawn.'

'What will your old man say about that?' Tallis asked, eyes on the computer operator as she bent down to empty an overflowing paper basket into a plastic bin bag.

'There's no such animal,' she replied with a faint smile, trying to make up for her earlier abrasiveness. 'Thanks for your help, by the way. It must have been difficult for you.'

'A real shit of a day,' he growled. 'If sleep was on the cards, I'd sod off home.'

Feeling restless, she stood up. 'Seeing as how we're both night-owls, why don't you take me on a tour of your magic roundabout?'

'Why not,' he said, waiting until she had put on her coat, then following her out of the Incident Post.

She raised the collar of her sheepskin. It was cold and damp in the Secondary Sorting office. Over-awed by the confusion of equipment and machinery, she looked around her. 'Bert, go slowly, this place is a mystery to

28

me and I need to know how it works.'

'And I need to know the size of a letter bomb?'

'I'm not sure. We were shown mock-ups on my senior CID course but they must have advanced since then. At a guess, I'd say they'd be about the size of a thin paperback.'

'What we would call *packets*,' he said, leading the way towards the sorting machinery. 'They come in so many different shapes and sizes the brains haven't developed machinery capable of sorting them automatically yet.' He glanced down at her. 'Pretend you're a postal packet and I'll take you through the system.'

'I'll try not to blow up.'

'Register Mail Office,' he muttered as they passed a room with barred windows.

'Then why are the doors wide open?'

'Because while you were drinking tea in the Incident Post, my people were working their guts out emptying it; over five million quids worth. It's now at the Severn Street Sorting Office in Birmingham.'

They stopped at red and white plastic tape that cordoned off the area around the seat of the explosion.

Tallis stared at the chalked outlines of five bodies. 'I thought this place would've been crawling with coppers in white overalls by now.'

'The scene's been photographed and videoed,' she replied. 'We're waiting for the plan drawers.'

'And then?'

'Boffins examine and remove bomb fragments. Scenes of Crime and Forensic teams carry out a fingertip search of the whole area.'

'*Boffins?*'

Explosives experts from the Defence Research Agency at Fort Halstead.'

He rubbed his square chin. 'When will you get around to searching for more bombs?'

'As soon as we know what kind of explosive device we're looking for.'

'People are screaming for their mail.'

'At least it will stop your posties shoving junk through my letter box.'

He gave her a hard look. 'You coppers have no idea, have you? Stop this place and you stop life itself. Something affecting everyone in the city and goodness knows where else, is stuck in here.'

Not wanting to fight him, she nodded in agreement. 'I just don't want to see any more of those chalk marks.'

He led her out of the building onto a raised loading bay. Switching on floodlights, he exposed a mountain of mailbags stacked up in front of a row of red vans backed up to the bay. 'This is where it starts and ends,' he said.

They went down a short flight of steps and walked across a large yard to the exit gate where a solitary constable stamped his feet to keep his circulation going.

'Glad you joined?' she asked him.

'I've started to count the stars,' he grunted. '...If my relief doesn't come soon I'll probably freeze to death.'

She smiled. She'd liked night duty. There was less formality and a closer bond between members of the Unit. It was as if they were the only people left in the city and it belonged to them.

'Why Westhampton?' Tallis asked as they returned to the three-storey Royal Mail building.

She shook her head. 'Until we find and disarm a letter bomb I couldn't even guess.'

'Who do you think planted them?'

'I wish I knew.'

'Oh, come on!' he retorted angrily. 'You know as well as I do - it's those murdering bastards from the IRA.'

5

Alone in her Earl's Court flat, Gina Jones sat at a crowded dressing table and studied her face in the oval mirror, slender fingers tracing the outline of her sensuous lips. Rich men fought over her now and she could afford the most expensive make up. But it hadn't always been like that. She remembered the small stone cottage in Armagh and the door-mat existence of her ma whose only purpose in life seemed to be waiting on smelly, foul-mouthed men armed with Kalashnikovs.

Memories flooded back. The urgent tapping on the kitchen window in the middle of the night. The latch lifting as her ma let them into the house. Whispered conversations; sometimes laughter, sometimes curses. But always the clink of glasses and the rattle of dishes as her ma cooked them a hot meal. At dawn they would slink out of the back door and disappear over the fields, like foxes returning to their lairs.

Using Max Factor, Gina disguised the faint shadows beneath her large brown eyes. The telephone came to life but she ignored it. She knew who it was and enjoyed making him wait until she could sense his frustration melting the lines. She'd soon learned how to make men kings and how to make them grovel; this particular man was a Member of Parliament.

She exercised her eyes and brushed back a mass of red Irish hair. 'You beauty,' she whispered. 'You could have any man in London.'

But the mirror did not reflect the ugliness inside; the thirst for revenge and the all-consuming hatred of the Brits who'd murdered her pa.

It was ten years ago. He'd set gin traps during the evening and returned at first light to collect his catch, leaving her and her ma at the end of the lane to watch out for the gamekeeper or an army patrol. A woman and child were also less likely to be searched during the journey home.

Soldiers lying in wait for gun-runners, saw her pa ducking below the hedges. She could still hear the brief rattle of gunfire across the meadow, see the birds rising from the hedgerows, and feel the choking in her throat. Screaming uncontrollably, she raced across the fields and found her pa lying face down in the mud, a brace of rabbits at his side.

Months later, she gave evidence in court at the trial of the soldiers. Standing on a pile of books so the judge could see her in the witness box, she told the court her ma's testimony was the truth. Her pa had only been carrying a stick when he was killed and had never owned a gun.

On a table in the well of the court, lay a single-barrel shotgun she'd never seen before. The soldiers claimed her pa had been carrying it and they shot him in self-defence. The judge believed them and they were acquitted.

That night, head resting on her tear-stained pillow, she had sworn on the Holy Bible, that the Brits would regret their lies and her pa's murder.

He would be proud of me now, she thought sadly. She'd learned quickly and done everything her republican masters asked, even though she rarely understood the information she obtained for them.

On her seventeenth birthday they'd sent her to London where she'd lost her accent to order and trained at a business college. She was then taken on by a top secretarial agency, soon gaining a reputation in the plush offices of Westminster for her good looks and the after-hours extras she provided for certain, well-placed clients. Some of them asked her to be their private secretary but Controller insisted she remain with the agency. He needed to be able to place her in Government departments where she could be of most value to the Cause.

Now, twenty-five years after beginning the latest armed struggle for a united Ireland, the IRA had declared a ceasefire and an intention to pursue their objectives by peaceful, democratic means through Sinn Fein, the Republican political movement.

Surprisingly, instead of sending her home, Controller gave her what he described as her most important job. He even promised a bonus of twenty thousand pounds if she was successful.

Cultivating her parliamentary friend and working harder than she'd ever done, she managed to pass to Controller the current addresses and whereabouts of all the high ranking Brits he was interested in.

Early on Saturday morning, he said, many of them would die.

6

'Ready for the first lesson according to the book of
Tallis?' asked the burly MLO Manager, standing beside
Molly on the loading deck. 'Mail collected from pillar
boxes and post office counters is taken by small vans to
local delivery offices then transferred here in bigger
vans.' He picked up a mailbag and lifted it towards a
metal hook hanging from a chain conveyor.

'Stop!' she yelled. 'They haven't been checked for
explosives.'

'Just testing,' he said without conviction, gingerly
lowering the bag. 'The conveyor carries mailbags up to
the Primary Sorting Office on the second floor where the
letters and packets are tipped into a *segregator*. Come
on, I'll show you.'

Pleased to be back inside the building, she followed
him up two flights of stairs. 'This is where the packets
are separated from the letters,' he announced, leading the
way towards a grey painted machine as tall as himself.
He tapped the inside of a large, stainless steel cylinder.
'Spins like the missus's washer. Letters are whisked
through slits in the side, packets fall to the bottom of the
drum and trundle along to the far end where they drop
into an *alt*.'

'A what?'

'Auto-level trough. They've got sprung bottoms to save the workers' aching backs. Most people call them skips.'

'And the letters?'

He picked one up. 'D'you see the row of blue dots along the bottom of the envelope? They're phosphor and they glow under ultraviolet light. Clever machines read them and sort the mail into nine hundred different destinations at thirty-four thousand letters an hour. It was a struggle to do eight hundred an hour when I started.'

'And they still used stagecoaches?'

'And there were no smart-arsed women detective inspectors.'

She smiled to herself, warming to the straight-talking manager.

They moved on to three massive wooden desks. He brushed his fingers across ancient ink stains and a rough carving of a heart enclosing the name *Lillian*.

'An old flame?'

'Yes, I married her. This is where the packet stampers work.'

'Lucky they weren't blown to pieces.'

'So were the next lot.' He led the way to another machine and they climbed up a metal ladder. 'After they've been stamped, the packets are thrown onto a band feed conveyor and brought up here to the *packet sorting machine*.' She gripped a rail and looked down at a honeycomb of dinner-mat sized holes, each marked with the name of a postal district.

He went on with his commentary. 'Sorters throw packets into those holes and they drop onto enclosed conveyors running under the ceiling of the Secondary Sorting Office; the floor below us.'

She looked down at the mass of packets frozen in situ when the sorting machinery had been switched off. 'If any letter bombs are found inside the conveyor underneath that lot we've got problems.'

Assuring Tallis that she now understood the workings of the Primary Sorting Office, she then followed him down a flight of steps to the Secondary Sorting Office, the scene of the explosion.

He rubbed his bloodshot eyes. 'Good men died here today - and for what?'

She glanced at the scorched metal frames and the charred remains of the mailbags hanging from them. Above the work station, the black and white name board was strangely untouched by the disaster.

'Where's *London 2?*'

'Mayfair, St. James - posh places.'

'Perhaps the bombs were meant for *posh* people,' she said quietly, still trying to make sense of it all.

He gave her a fatherly smile. 'I can see why they made you an inspector. Packets from the enclosed conveyor drop through nets into skips which are taken to the different districts. Sorters stand in a half-circle around the frames, take packets from the skips, then chuck them into the appropriate bags.' He lowered his voice. 'Which is exactly what the sorters were doing when they were killed.'

'And then - if there hadn't been an explosion?'

'The mailbags would've been labelled, time stamped, tied and sealed.' He pointed at a trapdoor in the wall. 'After that, they'd have been hefted down that chute, back to the loading bay where it all began.'

'Why are so many mailbags piled up around the chute?'

'I should have guessed that you wouldn't miss that.' He scratched his stubble irritably. 'Some gormless pillock forgot to open the trapdoor at the bottom. Because the mailbags were heavy, it took us an hour to open the bloody thing.'

'At least it stopped some of the mail getting out.'

'You could say that,' he admitted with a tired sigh. 'D'you think there's any chance of a brew, Inspector?'

'Molly...I think we're going to be seeing a lot of each other during the next few days.'

'That might be difficult,' he said, slowly, as if searching for the right words. 'I talk in my sleep and the missus is the jealous type.'

Julia, the computer operator, met them at the door of the Incident Post. 'Mr Davidson called while you were away, ma'am. The Chief will be attending the conference and he wants you to make sure there's a

39

shorthand typist available.'

She checked the time: it was one-thirty on Saturday morning. 'I'll rub my magic lamp.'

Tallis found a chair. 'Ask the genie to put the kettle on while you're at it.'

Taking the hint, Julia left the office.

Heavy footsteps advanced down the corridor and pressed khaki marched into the office. 'Captain Standish and Sergeant Grant, Explosives Ordnance Disposal, Hereford,' the taller of the two soldiers announced in a clipped, Sandhurst voice.

Sitting at her desk, she gave the Captain her full attention, admiring his strong features, short, jet black hair and dark, intelligent eyes. A trim moustache seemed to emphasise his military bearing.

'Take a seat,' she said. 'Would you like a hot drink?'

The sergeant moved to the back of the room.

Captain Standish sat down. 'Great idea. We've travelled from Hereford in one hour forty-three minutes.'

'Congratulations...I'll break out the chocolate biscuits.'

Tallis found the energy to laugh. 'Don't mind her, mate. It's been a long day.'

If the Captain was offended, he showed no sign of it. 'Tell me what's happened?' he said pleasantly. 'I have a lot of catching up to do.'

It was three o'clock when the soldiers left.

'Thoughts?' she asked Tallis.

Eyes closed and half asleep, he roused himself. 'I don't know whether they're brave or barmy - both, I suppose. The Captain's a bit over-the-top but he hates the IRA and that's good enough for me. The sergeant seems a decent sort.' He smiled at Julia. 'And he's definitely got plans for you, my girl.'

'I like men, not boys,' she retorted, bouncing out of the office.

His eyes followed her. Five foot nothing and just out of her teens, everything about her, including her thick-rimmed glasses, seemed to be brown and round.

'What about you...Molly?' he asked. 'There must be easier jobs for women these days.'

She gave herself time to think. 'I could trot out the recruiting brochure garbage about being dedicated to the creation of a more caring society, I suppose. But, to put it simply, I get a buzz out of helping people.'

'The one's who are always complaining, or those who hate the sight of you?'

'Mostly, people are good. I'm talking about the victims. The people who come to us every minute of every hour of every day.'

'Is it a woman's job - coppering?'

'Men have managed it for over a hundred and fifty years, what's so special about them?'

A knee joint cracked as Tallis rose to his feet. 'Well, I'll say this for you, you seem determined enough.' He walked to the door and stopped. 'Good night, Sherlock. I'll see you in the morning.'

She spoke briefly to the night crew, found the holdall someone had dropped off for her, then headed towards the washroom.

The green suit she'd worn for her confrontation with the Chief was now a wreck and she wondered what the smart Captain had thought of her appearance. How could he have known what a hideous, topsy-turvy kind of day she'd had?

7

Specialists and heads of departments sat around the mahogany table of the Management Suite; only the chairman was missing. It must have been a long time since he'd been up at seven o'clock in the morning, Molly thought, glancing across the room at the shorthand typist who was nervously sharpening her pencil.

Davidson slipped into the chair beside her. 'The Chief can't make it, Miss Watson,' he said. 'He's on his way to the Home Office to give them a personal account of what's happened here.'

After the introductions, she began the meeting with a situation report.

The Captain spoke next, rattling off bomb data and search practices with machine gun precision.

When they broke for coffee, Detective Superintendent Davidson mumbled a few words of apology, then dashed off to make a breakfast television appearance.

She took over the Chair and tried to resolve a heated discussion on the best way of dealing with what the Captain insisted on calling *IED's* - improvised explosive devices - and everyone else called *letter bombs*. It was eventually agreed that no searching of the mail would take place until they knew what kind of letter bombs they were dealing with.

After the conference, she returned to the Incident Post. The only person working was an overweight constable with a telephone clamped against one ear and a finger stuck in the other. Everyone else seemed to be engaged in a slanging match as police and letter office staff argued their differences.

She picked up a metal tidy bin and crashed it to the floor, startling everyone into silence. 'Out! Out of this office, now!' she shouted, stopping Tallis before he could move.

When the room had cleared, and only the two of them remained, he stepped away from her. The colour had drained from his face and his whole body shook. 'Who the hell d'you think you are?' he demanded angrily. 'You can't treat Royal Mail managers like a bunch of yobbos.'

'If they act like yobbos, they get treated like yobbos.'

He rubbed a hand along his heavy jaw, a habit she was already familiar with.

When he spoke his voice was quieter but it had lost none of its malevolence. 'Now you listen to me,' he began. 'This building controls the whole Westhampton City Postal District; one thousand square miles of it. We also employ over two thousand people.' He moved closer to her. 'Widows and orphans are screaming for help and workers are demanding their wages. If we can't get to our records and the safe, the whole fucking system collapses. This letter office isn't a miracle of self-perpetuation,' he continued without taking a breath. 'It needs love and attention or the lights go on the blink, the heating starts to sulk and all the bloody machinery packs in.'

She opened her mouth to speak but he raised his voice and went on before she could utter a word. 'And there's the world outside. You know - that place where people live, eat and fornicate. Pillar boxes are boiling over. Vans full of yesterday's mail are parked in the streets. People have been evacuated from their homes and want to get back to their own beds.'

He took a deep breath. 'I don't know whether you've bothered to poke your nose out of the door lately but the street outside is jammed solid with fire engines, police cars, ambulances, television crews and gawking sightseers. Traffic, like everything else around this bloody place is totally, completely and irreversibly fucked up!'

Normally a man of few words, his considerable weight sagged onto the edge of a desk.

She had stood still throughout the tirade, her face giving no clue as to her thoughts. People outside the office waited for her to hit back.

They were disappointed. He was right. She needed to take a grip of the situation.

'Sergeant Bannister!' she called, waiting for him to return. 'Bring the staff back in here and shut up these damn telephones. Then get me the superintendent in charge of Personnel, Les Rankle at Traffic, and whoever's running Communications these days.'

When everyone was back in the Incident Post, she stopped the first man to pass her desk. 'Fetch me a hot drink and a plate of bacon sandwiches from the canteen, please.' She caught Tallis's eye. 'Fancy some breakfast, Bert?'

He stiffened for a moment, then relaxed, as if the fight had gone out of him. 'Yeah, okay,' he said. 'What about the Finance Manager?'

'He can buy his own breakfast.'

'Access to the records and the safe?'

'Whatever he needs, just keep him out of this place.'

Later in the morning, she was working her way through dozens of reports when Bannister interrupted her.

'Traffic Warden Hotchkiss is in the office across the way, ma'am. She's asking to see you.'

'Tell her I'm busy.'

'I already did.'

She threw down her pen; she hated paperwork anyway. 'All right, Bill, keep this place going, please.'

The traffic warden was hunched up in a chair, hands on her temples as if she was suffering from an acute attack of migraine.

'Meryl! You look awful,' she cried. 'Whatever's the matter?'

The woman stared at the chewed remains of her fingernails. She was shaped like a bent broomstick, her sparse, greying hair tied tightly in a bun. Plain and without humour, she terrorised the motorists but the draconian order she imposed on the streets contrasted sharply with her private life. She was lonely and vulnerable, giving herself cheaply to any available man, then seeking refuge in the bottle.

Meryl had sought her help before. On a summer evening, many years ago, she had found her squatting on the kerb outside the Rose & Crown, singing 'Land of Hope and Glory' at the top of her squeaky voice. Her breath had reeked of gin and she was surrounded by what, at first sight, looked like cartridges but turned out to be spent lipstick cases.

Picking up Meryl's handbag, she had pushed the drunken woman into a taxi and taken her home, looking after her until she sobered up.

The evening paper solved the mystery of the lipstick cases.

City Centre Cars Daubed with Double Red Lines, ran the news item. **The authorities do not know whether it is a protest against illegal parking or prostitution.**

'We're determined to find the RED PHANTOM,' said the Mayor.

Since that night, Meryl had sent her a card every

Christmas, always writing the same message on the bottom: *God bless my savio*ur, *may you find true happiness.*'

She held Meryl's hand. 'Come on,' she said kindly. 'What's up?'

'I need your help, ma'am.'

'I'll do what I can.'

Meryl whimpered, like a kitten in distress. 'It's the first time.'

'What is?'

She sat up, finding her voice. 'The Queen's Hotel, ma'am. Yesterday evening. A car was parked outside on double-yellows.'

'Go on.'

'I booked it but the barman asked me to scrap the ticket.'

'And did you?'

'Yes, ma'am; I marked it *spoilt*.'

'Why?'

'Well, me and Joe - that's the barman; we're kind of friendly.'

Molly wondered if she had missed something. 'Is that it?' she asked.

'No, ma'am. Joe said later that the driver of the car was up to no good. He'd been drinking in the Queen's all afternoon and kept his eye on the window, as if he was waiting for something to happen. After the explosion at the Letter Office, he scarpered straight away.' Meryl lowered her voice. 'I think he must've had

48

something to do with the bombing, ma'am.'

She was suddenly interested. Could this be another lead, something she could tie in with Mad Mick's information?

The traffic warden reached into a uniform pocket, then handed her a copy of a parking ticket.

8

Gina Jones did not know about the explosions at Westhampton, even though Davidson had featured prominently on television, warning people not to open suspicious looking postal packets.

Curled up in a giant sized bed at a luxurious Eaton Square apartment, she'd been sleeping off a long night of heavy eating, hard drinking, high stakes gambling and finally, the least demanding of all, perfunctory sex with Sir Peter Tordone, MP.

Rolling onto her back, she stared at the moulded plaster ceiling. Saturday at last. Today she would finally avenge her pa's murder and go home, her London assignment over. Some of the bombs must have reached their targets already.

She cursed Peter for not having a television, radio or even a telephone in his apartment. It was his refuge, he'd told her several times. She wondered how many other young office workers he'd coaxed, tricked or bullied into the big bed and decided that, knocking shop, would be a more apt description.

An ugly man with thick rubbery lips and greasy skin, he reminded her of a toby jug her ma kept in the pantry for her odds and ends. His wife and four children lived in leafy Hertfordshire and he frequently complained of the boredom and futility of life as a lowly back-bencher. *Lobby fodder,* he moaned; *kept hanging about for that bloody Division Bell.*

According to him, the other members of parliament were shallow, inadequate people who spent a great deal of their time totting up inflated expense claims or boasting about their latest fact-finding junket to exotic, far away places. Those who had *done the world* settled for the House of Commons bar, drinking northern beer with self-opionated lobby correspondents bent on uncovering the latest scandal they could sell to the tabloids.

She usually stayed at the apartment on Tuesday and Thursday nights but Controller had insisted she also slept with Peter on Friday this week. Knowing she would be returning to Northern Ireland later today, she hadn't objected, persuading Peter to stay in the City for an extra night by promising him a special treat he would have traded a year's salary for.

He was singing in the shower and his voice grated in her ears. She was sick of bedding old men. She wanted a man of her own age. Someone with smooth skin, taut muscles and boundless energy. Someone interested in all-night discos. Tomorrow, back in Armagh, she'd put on her best gear and find out where the action was.

She sat up, resting her back against the satin bedhead. Was it all a dream? Had everything at home changed during the two years she'd been away? Now

51

that her city life was coming to an end, she was starting to feel nervous. She'd had a great time in London, earning fantastic money and making lots of friends; influential men mainly, some of them mega-rich.

She'd been ordered to get close to Peter because he was a member of the Security Services Committee, with access to classified addresses.

Finding a way into his confidence, which really meant his bed, had been easy enough. Sent to his office to clear a backlog of letters, she'd stayed on after the rest of the staff had gone home. Most of the night had been spent sitting on Peter's lap or bent over his desk studying the carpet pattern whilst he grunted and groaned behind her.

He emerged from the bathroom fully dressed and looking like a country squire in a brown tweed suit and brogues. Embarrassed by his flabby figure, he rarely allowed her to see him naked or even partly clothed.

'Did you hear the big bang, my dear?' he asked.

She swept back her red hair. She'd heard it, all right. But it couldn't have been a letter bomb because none of the addresses she'd given Controller were near to Eaton Square.

'What bang?' she asked, wide eyed and innocent.

'The noise down the street. It might have been an accident, I suppose.'

'Or someone knocking off the bank,' she said, irritated by his plummy voice.

He went into the kitchen and she listened to the

sirens of the approaching emergency vehicles. She'd no way of knowing a Royal Mail van was wrapped around a pseudo nineteenth century gas lamp, its back doors lying in the middle of a road now resembling Park Avenue after a ticker-tape parade.

Peter returned to the bedroom and placed a tray on her lap. Breakfast in bed was something she always enjoyed but today the sight and smell of sausages, eggs and bacon made her feel faint. Closing her eyes, she gripped the sides of the tray until her hands steadied and her breathing became easier.

'I say, old girl, are you all right?'

She shook her head. 'I must have overdone it last night,' she lied.

'You get some sleep, I'll wake you up in an hour.' He took the tray from her. 'I'll still have time to catch my train to Hertfordshire.'

But she didn't sleep. She trusted her instincts and knew something was wrong. Why had Controller made her spend Friday night with Peter? The night before she was due to go home.

Controller had always been a mystery to her, she didn't even know what he looked like because they'd only spoken over the telephone. His voice had surprised her at first; she hadn't expected him to be a Brit. Cold and business-like, he was also sarcastic, talking to her as if she were a backward child when she questioned his instructions. She hadn't complained because he was her boss and she'd wanted to please him.

She thought of Armagh and the green fields beside the river where she'd played with her bothers. Despite London's attractions, she now realised she wanted to go home more than anything else in her life.

But first she must return to her apartment and collect the cash box which guaranteed her future security; there would be nothing else from the IRA after she'd picked up her final pay check and the bonus they'd promised her. The black box was stuffed with money and jewels given to her by rich men; some left discreetly under the pillow, some stuffed into her handbag during the excitement of a big win at the casino.

An hour later, she put on her stylish new travelling suit and arranged her hair so that it tumbled over her shoulders in a glorious profusion of natural curls.

Pleased with her appearance and feeling full of life, she skipped down the stairs to join Peter in the black and white tiled hallway with its huge rubber plant and polished brass umbrella stand.

'Something in the post?' she asked cheerfully, bending forward to see what he was holding.

'It looks like a pressy',' he replied, a thick brown packet in one hand and a letter knife in the other. He smiled at her and sliced into the top corner of the envelope. The silver blade cut through tinfoil, activated an electrical circuit and detonated high explosive which blasted away his skin, ripped red flesh from white bone and drove the knife deep into his body.

9

An hour after Sir Peter Tordone's death, Constable Raybould dropped a message form onto Molly's desk. She took time to watch him walk away and wondered if he ever pressed his trousers or polished his shoes.

The telephone buzzed and she tried to reassure an irate caller. How could he know of the frantic activity all around her and the flood of technical and logistical problems swamping the Incident Post.

'Two of the boffins need a fast car and motorcycle escort to Fort Halstead, ma'am,' a second constable called out. 'It's in Kent.'

'I know where it is, thank you.'

'Sorry, ma'am,'

'There's no need to be. Who are you?'

'Twenty-eight, ma'am.'

'Your name?'

'PC Blissett, ma'am.'

'Get onto Traffic and organise an escort, please.' She watched his face crease with anxiety; he'd only left training school a few days ago. 'If they argue, tell them you're speaking on behalf of the Super,' she added, remembering the confusion of her own first few weeks in the job.

Her caller rang off and she stared at the handset for a moment, trying to remember what his problem had been. An earlier message came to mind.

'Birmingham have been on again,' she called out to PC Raybould. 'When the man in charge of their Anti-Terrorist Squad arrives show him around but keep him out of the restricted areas.'

Blissett strained to make himself heard above the office din. 'Ma'am! They've stopped searching at Dinsall. A suspicious package has been found on the loading deck. Joe Grant, Army Bomb Disposal, has gone to check it out.'

She acknowledged him with a raised hand, then answered her telephone. 'Yes, sir. Yes...yes...yes. Four-thirty. No, sir, of course not.'

She put down the receiver and cleared her throat. 'Does anyone know where Sergeant Bannister is?'

Raybould looked up from his desk. 'He's gone for some nosh. Said he'd been smelling your bacon sarnies all morning, ma'am.'

She answered the telephone again, then got on to the Captain, asking him to go to the post office in South Road. It had been evacuated because a packet was giving a positive reaction to a squaddie's electronic sniffer.

'Another mail order, bloody alarm clock,' he groaned. 'That's the third today.'

Bannister cast a shadow over her desk. Dressed in jeans, his fashionable blue shirt was unbuttoned at the top, showing off his chunky gold necklace so that he

56

looked more like the Drug Squad detective she remembered.

'Have you been after me, ma'am?'.

'Yes, Bill. The Chief wants me at a press conference at four-thirty. I'd be grateful if you'd take over for a while. I also need to nip home for a couple of hours.'

'Of course, ma'am.' He glanced down at his jeans. 'I was hoping to escape from this place. Davidson's CID teams have drawn a blank.'

'Have you managed to see the barman of the Queen's yet?'

'Next on my list.'

Blissett replaced him in front of her desk. A lean, highly strung man, his left eye twitched every time he spoke. 'PC Raybould said I was to tell you this required your urgent attention, ma'am.'

She started to read: **I am a leading member of the Westhampton Conservative Club. A green dumper truck with *long live the IRA* painted on the side has just passed and I want it stopped.**

She dropped the message and laughed out aloud so that everybody looked at her, seemingly convinced she had cracked up under the strain. But they were wrong. It was pure joy, the realisation that she was back amongst the hurly-burly and the mickey-taking of the job that was her whole life and which, until recently, she thought she'd lost.

'You can tell PC Raybould that if he doesn't watch it, *he'll* end up in a dumper truck.'

The telephone buzzed again. 'I've already told you,' she said to the Dog Section sergeant, 'until we know what we're looking for, it's pointless searching. Give them some extra bones; they'll need plenty of stamina during the next few days.'

She looked around the office. 'Has anyone seen Bert Tallis lately?'

'He's probably in the Travellers,' a passing Royal Mail worker offered.

The Travellers Rest was mock Victorian; dark wood fittings and furniture, frosted lampshades, dirty-looking lace curtains and old library books glued to corner shelves.

Bert Tallis was perched on a high stool at the bar. She sat next to him, helped herself to salted nuts from a miniature guz-under, and ordered fresh orange juice.

He insisted on paying. 'Everybody's working their balls off up there. How long can they keep it up?' he asked.

'They're enjoying themselves. It's a welcome break from the monotony of endless, unsolvable burglaries and waste-of-time domestics.'

He grunted, deep in his throat. 'You're the one who's enjoying it.'

'Just glad to be back.'

'Holiday?'

'Resting, as the actors say.'

'Never heard of a police inspector out of work.'

'Call it a sabbatical then,' she said sharply.

He studied the froth on his beer. 'Bit edgy, aren't we?'

'Sorry, Bert.' She picked at the salted nuts. 'Call it frustration. The people who killed your friends are still on the loose and I should be going after them, not stuck in your Letter Office.'

'If it makes you feel any better, I'm pleased you're here.'

She smiled. 'That's not what you said yesterday.'

'Things grow on you - I had a pet alligator once.' He emptied his glass and slid it along the bar. 'Your round.'

'Sure you want another? I'll need you at the press conference this afternoon. Somebody's bound to ask awkward Royal Mail questions.'

'Make it a pint.'

'Ah! Found you, gaff - ma'am,' said a relieved PC Blissett, his nervous twitch in overdrive. 'The sergeant sent me. Davidson's in the Incident Post, shouting about someone stopping the Head of Birmingham's Anti-Terrorist Squad going into restricted areas. He didn't say it was you, ma'am.'

'He will.' She handed him some money. 'Here, get yourself a drink.'

Tallis passed her another orange juice. 'What is it between you and this Davidson chap?'

She held his eyes for a moment, tempted to tell him of the bigotry, hassle and pressure the CID chief had subjected her to since she rejected his advances. But in her heart she knew it would be pointless - prejudice had to be lived to be understood.

She didn't have her expected bust-up with Detective Superintendent Davidson when she returned to the Incident Post. He had laid into Bannister, threatening to reduced him to PC if he saw him in the office dressed like a hippy again.

The Captain was waiting for her, however. 'We don't need a bloody audience,' he said.

Accustomed to dealing with belligerent men, she was not unduly concerned by his attitude. It was his blazing eyes that fascinated her, she thought they were beautiful. 'What's the matter?'

'A big-footed copper from Birmingham has tramped all over the evidence and I expect you to do something about it. I want him out - yesterday!'

'Don't you bark at me, Captain. Your responsibility is explosives. I decide who enters this building and who doesn't.'

'Then keep your pals out of my way,' he said, turning on his heel and stalking out of the office.

Answering the telephone, she gestured for silence and started to scribble on a note pad. When she had finished, she sent for the Captain and leaders of the search teams.

They arrived within minutes but none of them spoke, her expression warning them the news was not good.

'I have received an urgent message you should all

know about,' she began as soon as they had settled. 'Two devices have exploded in Belgravia.'

'London 2 District,' Tallis interrupted.

She referred to her notes. 'The first explosion occurred at nine-thirty this morning in the back of a Royal Mail van being driven along Buckingham Palace Road, near to Victoria Station. The van was reduced to scrap and the driver's in hospital. The second explosion, thirty minutes later, was in an apartment nearby.' She lowered her voice. 'An MP was killed and a young woman seriously injured. Scotland Yard are working on the assumption that the bombs were in packets posted yesterday in this city.'

A boffin was the first person to speak. 'The young woman might be able to tell us something useful.'

'If she lives.'

'It seems that five IED's exploded in this place and four at Dinsall,' the Captain said. 'I should say three must have been in the back of the van and one at the apartment, making a total of thirteen - not a logical number.'

'A baker's dozen,' suggested Tallis.

The Captain shook his head. 'Whoever put these beauties together had a science background and would think in multiples of ten.'

'Are you suggesting that we're looking for another seven letter bombs?' she asked.

'Possibly. And they might be in this building, on the way to selected targets, or lying in someone's front porch. Of course, if you want to be really pessimistic, there could be another seventeen, twenty-seven, or whatever seven you like.'

It was four-fifteen when she found a vacant seat at the back of A Division's canteen. She never enjoyed the ballyhoo of press conferences but it amused her to watch senior officers preening themselves for their few minutes of public exposure. She was also pleased when the Chief by-passed Davidson to ask her for an up-date on the situation at the Letter Office.

The Chief, scheming for a bigger force and the knighthood that went with it, never missed an opportunity to appear on television. The Royal Mail Area Manager sat on his right and a top Union Official was on his left. An accomplished speaker, the Chief soon reduced both men to bit players.

She admired the way he dodged the difficult questions whilst emphasising his leadership skills at a time of crisis. He also sought to convince the viewers that one of the smallest, ill-equipped forces in the country was at the forefront in the use of modern technology and more than capable of responding positively to acts of international terrorism.

During question time, he strenuously denied the existence of any evidence which might involve the IRA.

'If it was the Republicans, would this mean an end of the ceasefire and would the Government order troops back onto the streets of Belfast and Londonderry?'

pressed a particularly difficult interviewer with flowing, blonde hair and long, skinny legs.

He beamed down at her as if she were his favourite person. 'You should have listened more carefully to the previous answer, my dear.'

'Who did it then?'

The Chief raised his eyes to the ceiling in a practised gesture of exasperation. 'In due course, young lady, you will be told.'

The cameras were switched off and senior officers crowded around the Chief to congratulate him.

Molly slipped out of the back door, then hurried across the car park to her XR2 Fiesta.

Thirty minutes later, she drove into the small South Staffordshire village of Coovers Wood. It was too dark to see the old church on the sandstone outcrop above the village but street lights reflecting on the duck pond gave her the feeling of peace and tranquillity she never experienced anywhere else.

Passing the grocer's shop, she crossed a small ford, then turned into a short cul-de-sac of Georgian style houses built on the site of an old water mill.

Her house was at the end of the road, behind a beech tree, and separated slightly from the other houses. She herself had often felt apart from her neighbours. They were too polite not to speak or pass the time of day, but she always sensed a social distancing because of her profession and the more subtle isolation of a woman who was not married, mothered and domesticated.

She loved her home and it constantly reminded her of Ishbel Plowwright, the fine lady and lonely widow who she'd lived with when she first joined the force. Ishbel had left her the money to buy the house and it had been Ishbel who had taught her dress sense and an appreciation of the finer things in life, so that her deprived upbringing was now less obvious.

She parked on the drive and glanced at the borders of wallflowers framing the front lawn. The only advantage of her long suspension had been the amount of time she was able to devote to her home and garden. The door brasses shone and the house was still warm and welcoming. During her years in the CID it had been a neglected bachelor pad with an empty fridge and dusty drapes.

She warmed a bowl of soup and dunked yesterday's crusty bread whilst flicking through her mail. The kitchen was her favourite place because she could sit at the table and see the fields and low wooded hills beyond her back garden. Tonight the hills were black silhouettes in a cold, starry sky.

Holmes, her King Charles spaniel, big-eyed her from the framed picture on the wall and she felt a pang of sorrow. She'd missed him more than she'd imagined possible and sometimes at night, sitting alone in the lounge, she was sure she heard him scratching on the patio window to be let in.

After her meal, she took a long, hot shower then

packed enough clothes to last for a week.

She set the answerphone and burglar alarm, then locked up the house.

The drive back to the crowded, polluted city where she earned her living seemed very quick because her mind was full of the seemingly insurmountable problems still to be faced.

10

Molly walked into the Incident Post. The air was thick with blue smoke, waste paper baskets overflowed, plastic cups were filled with cigarette ash and half eaten sandwiches littered the desks. Satisfied everyone was doing their best to cope with an ever increasing workload, she fought off a natural urge to start shouting and get the place cleaned up.

'Am I glad to see you, ma'am,' said Bill Bannister, sweat beading his brow and biro smudges on his nose. 'I'm not cut out for pen-pushing.'

'Do you good,' she smiled, feeling better after her brief visit home. She hung up her coat, then started to tackle a tray full of enquiries.

Bert Tallis soon joined her and they went through the incident log, the trailing print-out curling around their feet as they checked that all the mail still to be searched was under guard.

Only the night staff remained in the Incident Post when Tallis led her to the fourth floor and the Head Postmaster's large, en-suite office she had decided to use as her sleeping quarters until the operation was finished.

He opened the cocktail cabinet and poured large measures of Scotch before they made themselves comfortable on the leather-covered settee the Royal Mail provides for its most senior executives.

Reluctantly, she answered the telephone. It was the Captain reporting that the scene of crime search had been completed and all exhibits were on their way to Fort Halstead. She thanked him and invited him to join them for a night-cap. Much to her surprise, he accepted.

When he first arrived, the atmosphere was strained but the Head Postmaster's Scotch broke down the barriers and they were soon arguing about the problems of searching for an unknown number of letter bombs in such an enormous amount of mail. The Captain stressed that it would be the biggest mail search undertaken anywhere in the world.

'What's the percentage of packets?' he asked Tallis.

The MLO manager held a silver table lighter to the thick cigar he had taken from a carved box on his boss's desk. 'Difficult to say, we distribute a lot of advertising stuff these days.'

'It should be stopped,' she murmured.

Tallis's cigar glowed. 'I told you before; it's good for business. When do we start the mail search?'

The Captain answered. 'Boffins at Fort Halstead will work through the night until they can tell us something about the IED's.'

He turned to her. 'When's the next conference'?'

'Ten in the morning. Depending on what the boffins'

say, we can start searching the mail at two pm.'

'That's it then,' said Tallis. 'I'm off.'

She looked at him in alarm. She had not expected to be left alone in the middle of the night with the Captain.

'See you tomorrow, cobber,' he called after Tallis.

She quickly moved from the settee they had been sharing, and sat in a vacant chair.

'I don't bite,' said the Captain. 'let me replenish your glass.'

Obediently, she held it out. 'What makes you think I care?'

'You do. You look like a skittish virgin trapped in a tub full of footballers.'

'I'm used to being alone with men,'

'Really?'

'Yes.'

'I suppose you're one of those radical feminists who go on about *gender* all the time, as if sex was a dirty word.'

'No I'm not. I'm an old fashioned girl who believes we should bring back the age of chivalry.'

'But accept the independent, professional working woman?'

'Why not, for heaven's sake? I've proved I can do my job as well as any man. The trouble is, I have to keep on proving it.'

'What's it like, being a woman in the police?'

She sipped her drink. 'Do you really want to know, or can't you think of another chat line?'

He laughed. 'Christ, don't you ever open the shutters? You should loosen up a bit. No one's going to steal your job, your bank account, or your cherry. We've all got our own demons to fight and our own problems to fret about. No one wants to enter the closed world of Molly Watson uninvited.'

She drank more whisky. 'I'm not sure what you're on about and I'm too tired to argue.'

'Go on,' he urged, 'tell me about life in the fuzz; sexual harassment and all that crap they print in the papers?'

She thought for a moment. 'It's different now than when I first joined, but it can be just as devastating. It's more subtle and therefore more difficult to deal with. Some of the new girls don't even recognise it at first. They even laugh at snide remarks about themselves. The men who do this are experts who could easily qualify for masters degrees in practical psychology. They're the cunning interviewers who always get coughs from prisoners and can stand in the witness box, looking like saints of virtue, whilst lying through their teeth.'

'Who are these men?'

'Oh, I don't know.' She sipped her whisky. 'Yes I do. The influencers; the senior PCs and the sergeants. We only have a few of them, but the harm they cause is enormous. Mostly, they've got a grudge; wives are giving them hell, or they're sex starved.'

'Ordinary, everyday bullies?'

'Yes, we have our share of those.'

'What do they do, these tormentors of the opposite sex?'

'Things you would probably find funny or insignificant. Snide remarks in the locker room, squelching sounds when women march, sly whistles, dirty talk meant to embarrass. Touching. At first you think it's accidental. Hot hands in strange places as you're struggling with an unruly crowd or trying to pacify a prisoner. Hands which should be around your waist when you link up for public order training *accidentally* too high or too low so that someone's grabbing at your left tit or tearing out your pubics.'

He laughed again, spilling his whisky.

'See!' she said. 'You *are* sexist. You think it's a big joke.'

'No I don't,' he protested. 'It's the way you tell 'em.'

'Sexism ruins people's lives,' she went on. 'Women who would have become good coppers, given half a chance, are driven away.'

'Because of an occasional grope, snide remarks or name-calling? If they can't take that, they shouldn't be in the job.'

'Would you put up with it - *squaddie - soldier-boy*?'

'I'm an officer.'

'*Pig - snotty.*'

'Perhaps not.'

'And I haven't even started yet. How about a condom in your salad sandwich, cling film covering the

70

bottom of your loo, or your pocket book stuffed with dirty pictures which drop out when you're asked to produce it in court. I could go on for days. A young woman with only a few weeks service walked into the canteen one night and found the walls were covered with pictures of vaginas - fifty of them.'

'Did she complain?'

'When the sergeant eventually got off his back side to check out her story, the pictures had disappeared and he wouldn't believe her.'

'What would you have done in her place?'

'Ignored the pictures. No reaction from the victim, means no fun for the boys; they want to hear you scream.'

'You said it was worse when you joined.'

She looked into his dark eyes, still uncertain why he was asking so many questions. 'The men were suspicious of us. Half of them felt threatened and the remainder hoped the night shift was going to be home from home; except the billiard table or the back of a patrol car would replace the bed. In fact, it was the policemens' wives who opposed equality. In the old days, car crews would pop home for a break during the night. They don't any more, not if they're sharing a car with a female partner.'

'And were the men threatened?'

She stretched out her legs and closed her eyes for a moment. 'Some convinced themselves we were only promoted because of the Government's policy of advancing women through the ranks.'

'Were you?'

'A small proportion, I suppose. At one time Police Committees were keen to curry favour with the Home Office by appointing the first woman chief constable. Now it's happened, the novelty's worn off. It's what the liberal press call *tokenism*.'

'And the men who thought they were going to get their leg over every night?'

'They were mostly disappointed. The desperate ones returned to freebies from the pro's.'

He poured the last drops of whisky into their glasses. 'What about you personally?'

'You ask too many questions and it's late.'

'It's the best time to talk; *truth time* my girl always called it.'

She looked him in the eye; he hadn't mentioned a girlfriend before. 'Training school was all right. Some of the girls got into a mess by sleeping around but they would have ended up the same wherever they'd worked. Some of the married ones were the worst. They'd spent years locked into kids and kitchens and suddenly they were let loose amongst hundreds of virile young studs.'

'What about you?'

'Like the majority, I wanted to pass the course and get a good report. I could have men and sex afterwards. There was a group of us. We went to dances and things and we let the fellas buy us drinks but we made up our own rules of engagement and stuck to them. And it worked. Most of the group ended up near to the top of the class. We still meet once a year; one is already a superintendent.'

'Any awkward moments?'

She smiled. 'I've got you, Captain. You're just a no good voyeur after the smut.'

He yawned. 'You might be right. But I think it's more than that. I've had one hell of a year and I'm enjoying the moment. Just relaxing and listening to you talk; it's therapeutic.'

'Thanks. If my CID boss does gets rid of me, I'll be an Aunt Sally.'

'Did he have a go at you?'

'Once, in a drunken, fumbling, old man sort of way. I've fantasised about dropping my pants in his office and watching him have a coronary.'

'Now you're getting interesting,' he grinned. 'Tell me more?'

'There's not much. I could fill a book with other policewomen's problems but they bring a lot of it on themselves. One of our probationers slept with the training sergeant because he told her it was the only way she was ever going to be appointed. Another was afraid of walking the streets alone at night so she made herself available to the car crews and never had to.'

'Is that it?'

'What do you want? The chief inspector who made a young probationer perform oral sex as an alternative to dismissal for losing her police radio, or the woman attached to the Vice Squad who was persuaded to spend the night in the Rape Victim Interview Suite with a ponce.'

'How did they manage that?'

'They told her it was the only way they could get him to tell them about a million pound drug scam?'

'What did the Vice Squad get out of it?'

'They'd got in the beer and chips, and had watched her performance through the one-way mirror we use when rape victims are being questioned. It was also on film.'

'Did she complain?'

'Not after they mentioned the video. She's a Traffic inspector now.'

'And the young probationer who lost the radio?'

'Married, two kids, and still in the job...So is the chief inspector.'

'Sounds like everyone's at it?'

'I told you, it's only a few; most of the men are great. It's just that every now and then you come across one, or sometimes a pair of them, who shouldn't be allowed out on the streets. Any woman could fall foul of them, no matter how careful she was.'

She glanced at her watch, wondering why she didn't feel tired. 'It's time you went, before *this* policewoman starts screaming rape.'

'Tell me how you dealt with sexism, then I'll go quietly?'

'I was brought up in a tough school - from the tender

age of five. In the children's homes and later the Wrens, you had to fight your corner or you would end up being used and abused in all manner of soul-destroying ways. When I joined the police force it didn't take me long to sus' out the dangers. I never let a man get away with anything; not once. Pretty soon, they stopped trying.'

'So - you're a hard case?'

'Not really. As I say to the women probationers, men are bound to try and score if they're given half a chance. It's simply a matter of *drawing the line* so they know how far they can go.'

'And your line is like the wall of China.'

'Is that what you think?'

He looked at her for a moment, then took hold of her hand. 'I've been through the mill myself and learned to read people. In my eyes I see a caring, sensitive person who's built a very brittle shell around herself.'

She took back her hand. 'You hope.'

'On reflection, perhaps it's as thick as a dinosaur's egg.'

'Go away,' she said with a sleepy smile. 'I've never talked like this to a stranger before.'

'What do you mean, *stranger*? We've known each other for a whole day.' He stood up and looked down at her. 'I've enjoyed this last hour, Molly. I would like to know you better.'

'It's the rarefied atmosphere. Chatting up a police inspector in a building full of bombs must be new, even for a hard-headed army captain who faces death every working day.'

He looked at the prints of country scenes lining the walls. 'I'd forgotten about the outside world. It's as though we've been in some kind of time capsule together.'

She laughed. 'They used to say *desert island.* If that's your best line, get out of here and don't bother to come back.'

He put on a hurt expression. 'Call it innocence and inexperience.'

'And I'm Winnie-the-Pooh.'

She let him out of the door. 'Good night, Captain.'

11

Molly had only been asleep for a short time when the Head Postmaster's extension woke her up.

'What is it, Julia?' she asked the night computer operator.

'Message from Fort Halstead, ma'am. One of the boffins wants to speak to the *man* in charge.'

'I'll be right down. Contact the Captain, please. Tell him to get over here sharpish.'

Accustomed to being called out of bed in the middle of the night, the Captain soon joined her in the Incident Post, then spoke to the boffin at Fort Halstead.

'Right,' he said, slamming down the receiver. 'Each IED contained six ounces of Semtex and micro-chip, printed circuit TPU's.'

'...*TPU's*?'

'Time power units. There are two in each IED. The first is a time-delay circuit which enables the couriers to post the packets and get well away before they become live. The second circuit supplies power to the anti-handling device which, when broken, activates the detonator.'

'When did the circuits become live?'

'They don't know yet. Probably at the time of the first explosion. They're suggesting that at least one of the anti-handing circuits had already been broken in Bert Tallis's packet crushers.'

'So the situation was reversed. When the time-delay circuit became live at least one packet exploded and set off the others?'

'You've got it.'

'Is Semtex used solely by the IRA?' She already knew the answer but his closeness made her feel uneasy and it was the first question that came into her head.

'No,' he said earnestly. 'Most terrorist groups use the stuff these days. It's a commercial explosive and therefore not too hard to come by. It's also malleable and safe to handle - as long as you keep it well away from an electrical charge.' He paused, then added: 'Six ounces is more than they usually put inside a postal packet - these things are designed to kill.'

'Anything else?'

'Technical stuff mainly but you may be interested to know that the same TPU's have been used in Northern Ireland.'

'IRA?'

He nodded.

'Were we the target or was it people living in London?'

'You never know with those devious bastards. This place could be what they call an *economic* target.'

'I don't get it, the IRA are supposed to have laid

down their arms.'

'And I'm the Queen's uncle,' he replied savagely. 'They'll never give up violence, it's part of their culture.'

'Do you know something?'

'Only that recruiting and firearms training have increased since they declared their so-called cease fire.'

She noticed that the neat scar across his right cheek went white when he was angry and for some strange reason she wanted to run a finger along it. 'Can we start the mail search?'

'Yes, but I shall need more men; men who can hump heavy mailbags all day and won't panic every time something starts to tick.'

'Special Patrol Group; men and *women*,' she replied curtly, trying to match his abrupt, military way of answering questions. But it didn't seem to come off; how could a slept-in track suit compete with bulled-up khaki?

'It's vital we find an unexploded IED as soon as possible,' he said. 'We need a physical description to give us an edge; something to distinguish IED packets from all the rest.'

'How about a sticker: *If this packet fails to explode please return to the IRA Army Council, Dublin.*'

'You like him a lot, don't you, ma'am?' Julia said after the Captain had left.

'There's room for improvement.' She sat at her desk

79

and wrote down a list of names which she then handed to the computer operator. 'Warn this lot to attend the conference at ten in the morning, please.'

Julia glanced at the wall clock Raybould had plundered from the Personnel Office. 'It's the middle of the night, ma'am. I'll get a right earful from some of these; they're mostly gaffers.'

'No later than six thirty then. Call Davidson first and give him my regards.' She lifted her sheepskin coat off the hook behind her desk. 'I can't sleep now, Julia. I'm going to have a nose around the sorting offices. I need time to let it all sink in and this will be my last opportunity.'

'You should get some rest, ma'am. It's spooky down there.'

'If I see any ghosts, I'll holler.'

She felt small and vulnerable as she entered the Primary Sorting Office, its monstrous machinery making strange pinging noises as metal continued to contract. Water unaccountably gurgled in cold heating pipes. Above her, in the dark shadows of the rafters, something moved. Was it a bird or a bat? Julia was right, she should have gone back to bed.

Telling herself not to be so stupid, she looked around, still bewildered by the seemingly impossible task that lay ahead. How many more bombs lay hidden in the mail? And how the hell were the searchers supposed to find them? Simply opening a mailbag could be fatal.

She dropped onto her haunches and peered at a cluster of packets scattered around a skip which had been knocked over in the panic following the explosion.

The light was poor but she could make out addresses and recognise some of the stamps. But what was she looking for amongst such a variety of shapes and sizes? Something unusual, she supposed; like a Customs and Excise officer deciding which person or bag to search.

She moved on, examining packets wherever she found them, getting colder and more disillusioned by the minute. It was hopeless. And this was only part of the problem, there must be hundreds of thousands, perhaps as many as two million packets, in the building or elsewhere in the City.

Rubbing her hands and deciding she'd had enough, she headed towards the door.

Light reflecting from the drum of Bert Tallis's segregator caught her eye. She stopped. '*This is where the packets are separated from the letters*,' he had said.

'I must be daft,' she murmured, turning back and slowly picking her way between stamping tables and sorting machinery to the segregator.

She could see brown and white packets lying along the bottom of the polished drum but there was nothing unusual about them.

Walking around the machine, she then looked into the drum from the opposite end. Resting on the lip, like coins balancing over the edge of a fair ground cascade machine, was an untidy group of packets, some of them bulky, others paper thin. One of the bulky packets had a row of three stamps; stamps she had never seen before.

Being careful not to touch any of the mail in the skip below the drum, she inched forward and examined the end stamp, the only one completely exposed.

The colour of new mown grass, the eighteen pence stamp showed the Queen's head and in the top left hand corner there was a small star-shaped symbol beneath a crown.

Holding her breath, she leaned closer and squinted at the stamp. Her heart started to pound. She blinked, steadied herself, then checked again. Inside the small, star-shaped symbol there was an open hand - the *hand of Ulster.*

12

Livid with rage, the Captain backed Molly into a corner behind the segregator. She could feel his breath on her cold cheeks.

'You could have got yourself killed!' he shouted.

'I was only...'

'I'm the explosive expert around here.'

Her hackles rose and she pushed hard against his chest. 'You couldn't find a bomb if you were sitting on it,' she screamed, dancing clear of him. 'And in case you'd forgotten, I'm in charge of this building.'

He closed in again. 'Down here you're in charge of shit. This is *bomb alley* - my territory.'

She stood her ground, her eyes bright with defiance. 'I found the flaming thing, didn't I?'

'You just got lucky.'

In the passage outside, the constable guarding the door and Julia hung on to every word.

'Any bombs would've gone off by now,' the constable whispered.

Julia moved closer to the partly open door. 'It's quiet. D'you think he's clouted her?'

'Other way around, more like.'

'She's coming,' gasped Julia.

The door burst open and her new boss dashed past, flattening her against the wall.

'Are you all right?' asked constable.

'Apart from tin-shaped tits,' Julia replied, using both hands to pump them back into shape.

'What happens now?' asked the constable in a husky voice.

'God knows, I'll go and see what she wants.'

'I'd rather face the All Blacks.'

'He'd no right to shout at her like that; she's got to stand up for herself.'

'A good man is what she needs; something to slow her down a bit.'

Julia blinked through her glasses. 'Is that all you macho bastards can think about? You make me sick, the lot of you.'

Returning to the Incident Post, she looked at the still figure seated at her desk, the sheepskin coat wrapped tightly around her.

'You should get some sleep, ma'am.'

She stared at a spot on the wall. 'There's not much chance of that, Julia. Did you hear us?'

'Some, I went to see what all the fuss was about, ma'am.'

Still boiling up inside, Molly shrugged off her coat and paced the office. 'I tried to tell him I hadn't disturbed the flaming mail but he wouldn't listen.'

The telephone buzzed and she answered it.

'Himself,' she said, replacing the handset. 'It's a letter bomb, all right. There's a pair of them close together. He wants us to send for his team.'

'Did he say he was sorry for shouting at you?'

'He'd choke first.'

'They should give you a medal, ma'am.'

'My notice, more like. Give Sergeant Grant a call please, Julia. I'm going upstairs. If I can't sleep I can rest.'

She did fall asleep but was soon woken up by a worried looking Bill Bannister.

'The Chief's been on the blower, ma'am. I said you'd ring him back.'

'On a Sunday morning; what's the time?'

'Eight o'clock.'

She put on a pair of loose trousers and a blue cotton top, knowing it would be hot in the Incident Post.

Bannister had thoughtfully left a cup of tea and a piece of toast on her desk.

She returned the Chief's call and was pleasantly surprised when he thanked her for finding the letter bombs. 'I've spoken to Captain Standish,' he said. 'I want you to forget you ever saw the Northern Ireland stamps. Do I make myself clear?'

'Yes, sir,' she replied, carefully replacing the handset. He'd called to silence rather than to congratulate her. But why? Gulping down her tea, and absentmindedly eating cold toast, she set off for the Primary Sorting Office.

In a pool of bright light close to the segregator, she could see two bulky packets, each one lying inside a thick metal box.

The Captain approached and she sensed a change of mood. When he spoke, she was sure of it.

'Good morning,' he said pleasantly. 'We're getting ourselves organised.'

'Good morning. Can you break off for the conference?'

'Afraid not. Would you mind putting them in the picture for me?'

'Without mentioning the stamps?'

He glanced at the metal boxes. 'The Government's *gagging* department's been at work. There's nothing they wouldn't do to protect the peace process.'

'If it *was* the IRA, surely they wouldn't be daft enough to use Northern Ireland stamps?'

He shrugged, the gold stars on his epaulettes catching the light. 'The paddy factor's saved more lives than St. John's Ambulance Brigade.'

'Perhaps they were so confident it was a kind of *up you* card.'

'Far too subtle for those donkeys.'

She read the names on the printed labels of the packets. 'Zobari and Freidman, don't tell me they're now targeting Jews?'

'Whoever they're after, I must get on with the disarming,' he said brusquely.

'Is there anything you need?' she asked, feeling she was being dismissed.

'Peace and Quiet. And make sure this place is sealed tight. If I see a rat, bat, bird, or a careless bobby, I'll shoot them.'

'How long will the disarming take?'

'Four hours - eight hours - a day. It doesn't matter. Safety is more important than time. Tell Bert Tallis to send me an engineer on stand-by and I'd like a couple of cops as runners. You can set them up near to the door; well away from me and my men.'

'Refreshments?'

'Suit yourself, just keep everyone out of my way.'

Christ, she thought. How could she get through to this arrogant, moody, pig of a man? She noticed the film of sweat on his brow and wanted to wish him luck. Instead she turned and walked away.

The Chief opened the morning conference by announcing that *his* Inspector Watson had found two letter bombs at four am. Around the table, she saw the raised eyebrows. *What the devil was the damned woman doing in the Primary Sorting Office at that ungodly hour?* she guessed they were thinking.

At the Chief's request, she described the packets - without mentioning the stamps - and read the letter bomb report which had recently arrived from Fort Halstead.

A general discussion followed and the Chief approved further press, radio and television warnings to the public.

Detective Superintendent Dunn talked at length about his co-operation with the Post Office Investigation Branch but complained about the lack of information from the Incident Post. She didn't show her annoyance, she'd been expecting some kind of attack. They needed a scapegoat to explain away their lack of progress.

Chief Inspector Black, a thin man with a prominent Adam's apple, informed the conference the woman injured at Sir Peter Tordone's apartment was his research assistant.

'Is that what they call them these days?' asked a voice at the end of the table.

Davidson intervened. 'Why were the packets addressed to Zobari and Freidman, and who the hell are they?'

'We're not sure why,' replied Black. 'One is the director of a Government Quango and the other is the head of a city bank.'

The Chief asked him how the bombers could have obtained their home addresses.

'*Who's Who*,' he replied. 'The trick is to know when they will be at home and, more often than not, *which* home.'

'Has anyone claimed responsibility?'

'No, sir. It could have been any terrorist group. The Animal Liberation Front even; letter bombs are their favourite weapon.'

Davidson laughed. 'Don't be daft, man. They're a bunch of half-hard, green-wellied lefties.'

The Chief spoke. 'Are you saying it's the animal rights people, Mr Black?'

'No, sir. I'm suggesting we keep an open mind.'

Bert Tallis was the last speaker. He described the Royal Mail's current problems and gave details of the temporary sorting system he had set up at the Town Hall.

Winding up the meeting, the Chief concluded that the identity of the terrorist group responsible for the letter bombs had not been established. Furthermore, he believed the explosions at Westhampton had occurred because of the terrific pounding the packets were subjected to in Bert Tallis's sorting machinery and the real targets were Jewish VIP's living in London.

Chief Inspector Black had a final word, suggesting Friday posting for Saturday morning delivery was significant: it was the only time London commuters were at home to receive their mail.

As everyone trooped out of the conference room, the Chief handed Molly an envelope.

Later, in the foyer, Inspector Jones, a rugby-playing Welshman and head of the Special Patrol Group, shook her hand. 'Welcome back,' he said. 'And thanks for calling out the elite; we like to be where the action is.'

'Don't I know it,' she said with a forced smile. She

was still seething over Dunn's complaint about receiving no information from the Incident Post. 'Are you sure this place is secure, Dai?'

'A bonsai tree bug couldn't get in here,' he replied. 'Not without your PC's the red disc.'

'Ah,' she said, glancing at the lapel of her coat.

'Try him,' challenged the SPG inspector as they approached Blissett, standing beside a board containing rows of red discs hanging on brass curtain hooks. The first seven discs of the top row were missing.

'Who's in the Letter Office?' she asked Blissett, playing for time.

He checked the numbers in his book and read out the names. 'Captain Standish, Sergeant Grant, two squaddies, Mr Grubb - a Royal Mail engineer, PC's Jenkins and Graham - SPG.'

Removing disc number eight from the board, she pinned it onto her coat.

'Ma'am,' Blissett croaked, suspecting he was being tested. 'You can't have a pass until I've seen your warrant card.'

She glared at him. Didn't the stupid man realise it had been taken from her when she'd been suspended?

A sudden thought crossed her mind and she dug into her shoulder bag until she found the Chief's envelope. Tearing it open, she took out a familiar leather wallet. Inside the worn cover was a photograph of a younger Detective Inspector Watson, the force crest, and the legend **Police Warrant Card.**

13

It was mid-afternoon. The mud-splattered Rover, looking as if it had just completed the Round Britain Rally, stood alone at the back of the service station car park. It was close to the perimeter fence and the casual observer might have thought it was abandoned. Cooped up inside, however, were four men wearing rough navvies clothing and big boots. Needing a shave and gutted with fatigue, they had left Armagh in glorious sunshine on Thursday morning and now it was Sunday. The excitement of their departure and the heady prospect of active service on the mainland had gone. They were far from home and each man had his own doubts about the next operation.

Jimmy Coster, restless in the front seat, looked at the man behind the wheel.

Head back and apparently asleep, Sean McKindon, a steam-roller of a man with dark, Romany good looks, was in his late twenties. Until recently, Coster had only known of him by reputation. He was regarded as one of the most successful fighters in the IRA. Kids in the back streets of Belfast, playing their games of blowing up the Brits', yelled *Super-Sean* with the fierce pride they reserved for heroes.

Danny, his younger brother, slept on the back seat.

Next to him was Mahmoud, the Arab who had joined them shortly before they boarded the ferry at Belfast.

Coster, twenty-eight, slender and light enough to be a jockey, moved the drivers's mirror to comb his short, brown hair which was prematurely highlighted by streaks of grey. He then fingered the stubble on his square chin and checked for tiredness lines around his striking blue eyes. Vain and good looking, he normally spent a lot of time pampering himself.

Restless, he turned on the car radio.

'Great,' Sean grunted, rubbing sleep out of his eyes.

Coster increased the volume. 'We've got to know what's going on, for fuck's sake.'

Sean looked with distaste at the mess of food wrappers and cigarette ends littering the car. 'It's a stinking pig-hole in here.'

Danny yawned noisily and complained that he was hungry.

'What's fucking new?' asked Coster.

Sean glared at him. 'If you don't shut that filthy mouth of yours, I'll ram it down your scrawny throat.'

'No you won't,' Coster retorted. 'You and your fat brother need me.' He glanced over his shoulder at Mahmoud. 'And why is he here? Come to that, why the fuck are any of us here; the war's supposed to be over?'

Sean moved his head from side to side, loosening stiff neck muscles. 'The boss will tell you when he arrives - it's the best deal you'll ever get.'

'I'm hungry,' Danny repeated.

Glancing over his shoulder, Sean picked up Mahmoud's nod and ordered everyone out of the Rover.

Making sure that the doors were secure, he led his active service unit across a wide expanse of empty tarmac and into the service station restaurant.

Once inside, they each picked up a tray and stood in a line, waiting to be served by a spotty-faced youth wearing a baseball cap.

Sean chose a table in a corner of the smoking section. It was partly screened from the rest of the room by an island of plastic palms. Only a few customers occupied the other tables. Students drinking out of cans, day trippers having a late lunch, and the usual scattering of loners reading the Sunday supplements.

It was the three men at the back of the room who attracted Sean's attention.

Torn anoraks, shabby jeans and dirty trainers belied the easy, seemingly effortless discipline of the surveillance trained. Certain he hadn't been followed onto the car park, Sean decided someone must have tagged the Rover with a tracking device.

Coster interrupted his thoughts. 'She needs a good shafting,' he said, leering in the direction of a thin, fragile-looking woman barely out of her teens.

Sean leaned closer to him, as if about to carry out his recent threat. 'Keep your mind on the job,' he hissed. 'After Friday you can have as many women as you want.' He looked up in time to see the men who had been watching them file past the end of the table. 'Follow them,' he said to his brother.

'I haven't had any grub yet,' Danny protested, knife and fork poised over his plate.

'Do it. And make sure they don't see you.'

Stuffing a whole sausage into his mouth, Danny moved off.

'You shouldn't have brought him along,' Coster said.

Sean looked up from his meal. 'He's the best shot in Northern Ireland.'

'Yeah, yeah,' Coster said. 'And I'm Sylvester Stallone.'

Danny, back in his seat and reaching for a bread roll, reported that the three men had driven off in a Ford Escort, the front seat passenger using a radio or mobile telephone.

Sean kept his thoughts to himself. He was even more convinced they were Special Branch or MI5.

Coster, having gone to the shop, returned to the table with a newspaper.

Sean snatched it from him and read the headline: **Letter Bomb Kills MP - Mystery Woman Seriously Injured**. A separate article gave details of Sir Peter Tordone's outstanding political career, describing him as a staunch supporter of Israel. Lady Tordone said her husband had been under considerable

94

stress and the young woman was helping him to cope with his enormous work load.

'That'll stop those bastards at Brigade from moaning about the cock-up at Westhampton,' Coster said.

Sean was still reading the paper. 'Shame about the woman.'

Coster sneered. 'You going soft in the head or something? He was knocking it off. No wonder the stupid cunts can't run the country - they're too busy fucking it.'

14

Molly entered the Primary Sorting Office.

'All right, ma'am,' one of the SPG runners whispered loudly, warning the small group of men at the door of her presence.

'All right,' she replied quietly.

Carefully feeling her way through a maze of sorting machinery and letter racks, she approached a distant pool of light and the army Bomb Disposal team.

'Bang!'

Startled, she looked down at the Captain, seated on a tool box.

'Just making sure you knew where you were putting your copper's feet.'

'Thanks,' she replied shortly. A few metres away, a pair of squaddies lay face up on a sheet of canvas, smoke from their cigarettes snaking into the bright lights above them. 'They'll set off the sprinklers.'

'We could do with a shower.'

She sat on a stool next to him and looked at a confusing array of complicated-looking equipment and the tangle of multi-coloured electrical cables encircling the segregator. On the floor, balanced between two house bricks in front of an X-ray machine, was a brown manila envelope bearing Northern Ireland stamps.

She glanced at the Captain, expecting to be asked to leave.

He showed her an X-ray film. 'See the bar sticking out of the Semey?' he asked. 'It's the detonator. The two wires at the top are connected to printed circuits and if we don't cut them simultaneously, we're dead.'

Sergeant Grant appeared from the surrounding gloom and the Captain spoke to him. 'I'm going to the bog to reflect on life and all its mysteries - see you in twenty minutes.'

Grant peeled off his uniform jumper and brushed back a mop of ginger hair. 'Best laxative in the world, this game, ma'am.'

'Is he always so precise?'

'It's what we're paid for. *Precision and logical thinking,* as the manual says.'

'Don't you get frightened, Joe?'

'Every time. Without fear you wouldn't last long in our business.'

'What about your wife?'

'She thinks I'm in the Veterinary Corps. He picked up his jumper and showed her the badge with its colourful cartoon cat. 'We take our code name and call sign from *Felix.* Legend has it, he had nine lives.'

'Has your Captain used up his allowance?' she asked casually. 'He doesn't seem to be a happy man.'

Grant looked around him and lowered his voice. 'He hasn't much reason to be. The IRA killed his girlfriend.

Good Irish Catholics aren't supposed to fraternise with enemy officers.'

'What happened?'

An SPG man put two steaming mugs and a plate of ham rolls on the top of a small generator. 'With PC Raybould's compliments,' he said before going over to the squaddies.

Grant bit into a roll and waited until the SPG man was out of hearing before answering her question. '...We're not sure. His girlfriend was seen talking to an old lady who got into her car. She probably asked for a lift or something. Later that evening the burnt out wreck of the car and the melted fragments of a granny mask were found on waste ground. It took longer to find the driver. They'd laid her face down on a Belfast tombstone. Every hair had been burnt off her body and the word **traitor** was branded on her back. The pathologist said it had been done with cigarettes - while the Captain's girl was still alive.'

She was silent for a few moments. She was used to dealing with the evil things people did to each other but now it seemed closer; personal even.

'The Captain was on the mainland at the time, doing secret work for MI5,' Grant said.

Deep in thought, she twisted her mother's engagement ring around her finger. 'How does he live with it?'

'By having only one thought in his mind - *revenge*. He keeps badgering the Army to let him go back over the water. They were only too pleased to send him here, which is why you've got the best ATO - *Ammunition Technical Officer* - in the regiment.'

'What was he doing for MI5?'

'God knows. When I asked him about it, he threatened to throw me out of the mob if I ever mentioned it again.'

'Has his girlfriend's murder affected his work?'

Grant vigorously rubbed his bare arms. 'The men in white coats carried out all the tests and declared him fit for duty, but he's not right. We did a job on the Welsh hills recently; crashed aircraft from World War II. We were sharing the same tent but he thrashed about so much in his sleep I had to move in with the truckie.'

She stood up. 'I shouldn't think he's ideal material for the Number One of a bomb disposal team.'

'You can't take away his skill or his courage,' Grant said, pulling on his jumper. 'Before it happened he was the most laid back man in the army, everyone wanted to work with him.'

She nodded, to herself more than the Sergeant. 'Anything you need, Joe?'

He hesitated only for a moment. 'I'd be grateful if you'd do one thing for him, ma'am. Make sure there's a bottle of Scotch handy.'

The Captain re-joined them before she could answer. 'Your turn, sarge,' he said. 'When you get back I'll start again and keep going until the job's finished.'

'What's next?' she asked the Captain, seeing him in

a new light and wondering what his girlfriend had been like.

'More X-rays. Pin-point the wires to the detonator. Disrupt the circuitry with the Pigstick.'

'*Pigstick?*'

'See the Wheelbarrow?' He gestured towards a tracked, remote-controlled inspection vehicle. 'It's the attachment on the front. Should leave a hole about the size of a fifty pence piece. There'll be plenty left for the fingerprint people and the Fort Halstead explosive boffins to work on.'

She glanced down at the innocent looking postal packet. 'Just be careful,' she said with feeling.

A cruel smile crossed his lips. 'Don't you worry, I've got a few scores to settle before I die.'

15

'Davidson rang from home, ma'am,' Bannister said when Molly returned to the Incident Post. 'He wants an up-date.'

'It's tea time and it's Sunday, I'd hate to interrupt his cucumber sandwiches.'

Bannister chuckled. 'Fish and chips more likely. Bert Tallis has been on twice; after his vans.'

'Tell him he can have them - if he searches the mailbags first.'

Remembering an earlier request, she gave Blissett some money, telling him to buy a bottle of whisky and to give it to Sergeant Grant.

Two hours later, she learned that the letter bombs had been made safe.

Slipping into her coat, she was about to leave the Incident Post, when Bannister intercepted her.

'Call for you, ma'am,' he said gravely.

She took the handset from him. As she listened, her grip tightened until her knuckles turned white. There was an intuitive hush in the office and everyone looked at her, sensing the news was not good.

'Something up, ma'am?' Bannister enquired as she

put the telephone down.

Feeling she was about to throw up, she glanced at the door. 'Take care of things for me please, Bill,' she replied, pushing past him and hurrying out of the office.

When she arrived at the Primary Sorting Office, the Captain was slumped in a chair surrounded by his hard helmet, plastic visor and protective clothing. The Wheelbarrow had been moved and the arc-lights now illuminated a table covered with the remains of gutted letter bombs.

'Present from Felix,' he said wearily.

She sat on a chair next to him and stared at her shoes.

'What's the matter?' he asked. 'You look as if you've given ten pints of blood.'

'Another letter bomb explosion.' She looked up. 'London again. An Under Secretary of State at the Foreign Office, his wife, their two year old daughter, and a baby son have been murdered.'

'When?'

'Mid-morning. They'd been on holiday in Canada and had returned on the night flight from Calgary. It happened soon after they got home. Mum died on her way to the hospital, the others were killed outright.'

'Anything else?'

'What more do you want?' she cried angrily. 'They're dead aren't they; a whole family wiped out in one go.'

'Information?'

'I didn't ask; I needed some air.'

He picked up PC Blissett's bottle of Bell's and poured two drinks, handing one to her. 'Empty it.'

She obeyed, the fiery liquid scouring her throat. For some reason she felt she needed to suffer. Perhaps it was guilt. Could she have stopped the letter bomb reaching London?

The Captain refilled his mug but when he held the bottle over hers, she stopped him.

'I thought I could handle this kind of thing,' she said sadly. 'They say all cops become insensitive, uncaring bastards in the end.'

'I don't believe that,' he said gently. 'If you didn't care you wouldn't do the job.'

Sergeant Grant, full of confidence after a successful dis-arming, marched over to them.

'Have you seen the guts of an IED before?' he asked her. She shook her head. 'All you need is a power source, a timer, a detonator, and the stuff that does the damage,' he went on.

Forcing herself to concentrate, she looked at the letter bomb parts. A flat piece of wood had been laid across the table, separating the contents of the two packets. 'Semtex?' she asked, indicating two blobs of dark orange substance that looked like something she wouldn't tread on.

The Captain answered her question. 'Yes; with an explosive velocity of eight thousand metres a second.'

She stared at the other bits and pieces, mostly held together by clear epoxy resin and attached to backing boards with brown sticky tape. 'It doesn't look much for something so deadly.'

'Like all good booby traps,' said the Captain. 'Simple in design and activated by a normal action, such as starting a car or opening a letter. As long as the bomb maker knows the habits of his target he can't fail.'

She gestured towards a row of small batteries. 'How long will the power last?'

'They oscillate on a frequency of one point five-five Kilohertz. Assuming there are two batteries in each packet, they have sufficient current to activate the detonator at any time during the next twenty-five days.'

It was midnight when Bannister finished talking to one of his female admirers in the Criminal Record Office.

'More bad news I'm afraid, ma'am.'

'Go on.'

'The body of Michael Joseph Rewan was found in a car park off Belfast's Shanklin Road on Saturday morning. He was bound and gagged and had been tortured. Death was caused by blows to the head with a blunt instrument.'

Shocked, but not surprised, she saw his face with its cheeky grin. He'd given her a lot of information but it was his quiet charm and self-depreciating Irish jokes she would always remember. 'Mad Mick,' she said with a heavy sigh. 'He may have been a rogue but he didn't deserve that.'

Leaving Bannister in charge of the Incident Post, she made her way up the stairs to the Head Postmaster's suite.

She took a long, hot shower, then slipped into her track suit and curled up on the settee. Too upset to sleep, she was soon pacing up and down the room.

'Yes?' she shouted, in response to light tapping on the door.

'Can I come in?' asked a male voice.

She yanked open the door. The Captain, holding a full bottle of whisky, fell forward in surprise, staggered across the room and collapsed onto the settee.

Taking the bottle from him, she helped him to sit upright.

His grin was wide and drunken and when he spoke his voice was slurred. 'Thought...you'd like a dr...ink,' he managed, struggling to connect tongue with brain. 'Me and me old buddy...Joe bloody Grant...bless 'im. We've survived another one. N...ot that it bloody-well matters.'

She stopped him from falling off the settee. 'And now you're going to pickle your kidneys for posterity,' she said, not sure whether she wanted to shout at him or cradle him in her arms.

'Ah...come on, Moll' Don't be such a wet arse. You're one of the team now. Let's have a little dr...inkies.'

'Only if you have something to eat first,' she replied as he sank sideways onto soft leather and closed his eyes. She removed his tie and shoes, and made him comfortable before covering him with a blanket.

'Gormless gorilla,' she murmured, putting on her trainers and setting off in search of food.

In the canteen, a PC wearing an apron and seemingly enjoying his new role in life, cut her some ham sandwiches. She asked for more and he gave her a puzzled look; only SPG officers ate half a loaf at one sitting.

The Captain was still asleep when she returned. She decided to leave him.

Finding a space at the end of the settee, she helped herself to a large measure of his Scotch, then settled down to watch the late night film.

Half way through, she felt a hot hand travelling up her leg. 'You're a real good pal,' said a sleepy voice beneath the blanket.

She smiled to herself, the whisky having relaxed her somewhat. 'Not that flaming good,' she said, moving his hand away. 'Go to the bathroom and wash out those things you call eyes. Then we'll get some food inside you.'

He yawned, scratched his bristles, and pulled himself up. 'Right, ma'am; at the double, ma'am.'

'Let's have a ball and cheer up this bloody awful planet of ours,' he said half an hour later, having washed, shaved and eaten most of the sandwiches.

'A short time ago I didn't think you'd wake up for a week.'

'Was I that bad?' he asked contritely.

'I've seen worse - in the drunk cell.'

'Sorry.'

'I think I can understand.'

'Understand what.'

'What you've been through.'

The muscles of his jaw tightened and he was serious again. 'You're not talking about the IED's are you?'

She shook her head.

'That bloody sergeant, I should get rid of him.'

'He's the best friend you've got.'

They were silent for a few minutes and she wondered if she should ask him to leave.

'What about you?' he asked.

'You had enough of me last night.'

'Bill Bannister said you're single and unattached.'

'What else did he tell you?'

'Mostly, it was very good. I don't think he knows it, but he's got a crush on you.'

She laughed. 'I've always run him ragged.'

'Some men like that. Don't you ever get lonely?'

'It's what I'm used to. As I said, I was an orphan.'

'Was it hard - being an orphan?'

'Not really, there's millions of us.'

'You should get yourself a man.'

'I've had men. It's just that I'm no good at lasting

107

relationships. I always make a mess of things or choose the wrong flaming model.' She wasn't sure why she was talking to him like this and put it down to the drink. Or was she stressed out? Days of non-stop action, following months of enforced idleness. Somehow, she didn't seem to care any more.

'I shall marry and have a family. It's something I dreamt about when I was cooped up with hundreds of other kids in the institutions. Especially at Christmas. I'd gaze at the cards for hours; happy families sharing presents around the tree or someone's dad in a ridiculous paper hat slicing up a fat turkey. I promised myself that my picture would be on a Christmas card one day.'

'Is the dream still there?'

'More so. Thanks to my neighbours at Coovers Wood, I get quite broody sometimes.'

'Coovers Wood?'

'A little village about thirty minutes drive from here. The church is over a thousand years old. The locals tell you about the site of an old monastery and an ancient spring that's supposed to have healing properties.'

'Have you supped the waters?'

'Not likely; they've been poisoned by farmers' nitrates.'

He laughed. 'You can't have everything. When this lot's over, you'll have to show me around.'

'I'd need to know more about you first.'

'Me? I'm just a whacked out old soldier who wants to rest his weary head on your soft, sweet bosom and close his eyes.'

'No one sleeps on my tits.'

'That's better, Moll',' he said softly, 'you're a real cracker when you smile.'

He edged along the settee.

'And you're half cut,' she said, enjoying his closeness.

'Do you want me to count to ten or walk along the straight white line?'

'You couldn't even *see* the line?'

'Blow in the bag?'

'I doubt whether you could find your mouth.'

He reached over and kissed her, gently at first, and then more urgently.

Afterwards, she couldn't remember why she hadn't stopped him. Neither could she work out how her track suit and pants ended up behind the settee.

But she would never forget his hard, thrusting body and the stupendous orgasms that seemed to go on for ever.

16

Coster, now on the north side of the motorway, stood under an oak tree at the edge of a wood and looked across the car park towards the lights of the service station. It was a cold, damp night and a full moon hid behind a bank of dark clouds.

He'd seen several women park their cars close to the perimeter fence before going into the main building. Which one would come back first?

He drew a drivers' knife from the holster strapped to his leg and ran his finger and thumb along the razor-sharp blade.

Hearing someone approach, he tensed. A car passed. In the beam of its headlights he saw her. She was the smart, executive type with the briefcase and mobile phone. About thirty, he decided, admiring her long legs as she got into the BMW. She adjusted the illuminated vanity mirror, freshened up her lipstick and touched her hair into place.

Watching his prey closely, he waited.

She switched on the ignition.

He dashed forward, opened the off-side rear door and threw himself into the car. She started to turn her head but his hand clamped over her mouth and he yanked her backwards. 'Now, cunt,' he breathed, holding the knife to her throat. 'Do exactly what you're told and you won't get hurt. Piss me about and I'll slice your fucking head off.' He twisted the knife slightly, drawing blood. Eyes large with fear, she stared back at him through the rear-view mirror. He eased his grip and told her to drive into a narrow lane at the back of the car park.

A short distance down the lane, he made her turn into a rough track between the trees. 'Stop!' he yelled. She braked sharply and he scrambled out of the car to open the driver's door. She tried to cling onto the wheel but he gripped her long her hair with both hands and yanked her out of the car. Managing to stay on her feet, she kicked at his shins and clawed at his face. He cursed and hammered his fist into her stomach. Gasping for breath, she doubled up. His other fist smashed into her nose. Blood spurted over her suit and she fell to the ground, curling up into protective ball. His heavy boots thudded into her back.

Whining, she scurried away from him on all fours. He laughed hysterically, prodding her bottom with the toe of his boot to make her go faster. Soon becoming bored, he brought back his foot and kicked her as hard as he could between the legs. Screaming in agony, she rolled over and over in a desperate but futile attempt to escape from her tormentor.

She crashed into a tree.

Like a boy happily tormenting a fly, he laughed,

raised his foot, then stamped on her head.

She lay perfectly still and he feared she was dead.

Cursing his clumsiness, he knelt down and felt her neck, fingers slipping in warm blood. He wiped his hand on the shoulder of her jacket and tried again, pleased when he detected a faint pulse; he needed her to be alive.

Grabbing an ankle, he dragged her to a clearing in the wood.

The moon appeared from behind the clouds. Her skirt was around her waist, showing white thighs. His breath shortened and he turned her onto her back. A small animal screeched and there was a threshing sound in the wood; a fox making a kill, he guessed.

Distracted, he remembered the car and hurried back to it; driving it deeper into the trees.

He returned to the clearing. The woman had gone. Relishing the thrill of the chase, he took a pencil torch from his pocket and searched for her trail.

Minutes later he found it. She had dragged herself along the ground, flattening the undergrowth. He listened. Moisture dripped from the trees and a fresh wind rattled the branches. Dropping on to all fours, he followed her trail, stopping when he heard a twig break.

He directed his torch at what he thought was a rock. It moved - it was the heel of a foot. Then he heard another sound, a quiet sobbing. The excitement boiled up inside him and became almost unbearable. He parted the ferns in front of him. She was lying on her stomach as if trying to make herself at one with the ground. The soles of her bare feet were covered with blood and her tights were in tatters. Cat-like, he inched closer.

She turned, her tear-stained face ghostly pale in the moonlight.

Then she saw him and her mouth opened in a strangled, soundless scream of terror. Leaping forward, he pushed her face into the decaying leaves.

Sean McKindon wound down the window of the Rover and threw out a dog-end. It blew away on the wind which also carried the monotonous melodies of the restaurant tape.

Where had his explosives expert got to? Coster must be back for the midnight pick-up. He'd complained he needed space and air after being cooped up inside a crowded metal box for four days.

Now he wished he'd kept Coster with him. They'd all felt the strain of smuggling the letter bombs past the Liverpool Dock Police, then posting them at Westhampton. Why should he treat Coster any differently? He hadn't strolled away from the car like a man seeking room to breathe and solitude; more like someone with urgent business to attend to.

'You shouldn't have let him go,' Mahmoud said, his soft voice at odds with his fierce black eyes. He was thirty-something and he reminded Sean of the proud, black-robed Tuaregs; the nomadic desert warriors he had read about at school. 'Coster has no respect and is dangerous,' Mahmoud went on. 'In my country I would shoot him like a rabid dog.'

Without warning, Coster clambered into the car, his arms laden with polystyrene cartons. 'Grub's up,' he said cheerfully, reaching over his seat to pass hamburgers and portions of chips to the men in the back.

'Where the hell have you been?' Sean demanded.

'Getting my head right,' Coster replied through a mouthful of food.

'What's that supposed to mean?'

'I told you, I needed fresh air. I've been on the north side of the motorway. Then I got cleaned up.'

The light in the car was poor but Sean could see that Coster had shaved. He could also see long scratch marks on the right side of his face. 'Water cold, was it?'

Coster swallowed a mouthful of hamburger. 'It's those cowin' throw-away razors. I should sue the makers.'

'Your boots are covered with mud and grass; they didn't get like that in a car park.'

'I saw a fox and followed him into the woods,' Coster replied sullenly.

Sean didn't believe him. There had to be another explanation for his long absence. 'If you've done anything to jeopardise this mission I'll throttle you with my own hands,' he threatened.

Danny collected the empty cartons and threw them out of the window. 'That's just what I needed, Jimmy.'

Turning, Coster ruffled his hair. 'Jimmy takes care

of everybody,' he said, eyes avoiding Mahmoud.

'That's it!' Sean called urgently as the lights of a nearby Transit van flashed twice.

Exactly five minutes later, Sean and his team left the car and boarded the Transit.

At one am four men wearing the active service unit's jackets alighted from the Transit van and climbed into the Rover.

Shortly afterwards, the car moved off and joined the south-bound motorway. A small Ford with a high powered engine emerged from behind a camper van and followed it.

'That's the blokes who were watching us when we had our dinner!' Danny exclaimed from his observation point at the back of the Transit. 'Their car's got a special suspension - like a racer.'

'Aren't we a clever boy?' Coster mocked.

Danny dropped the spy hole cover and sat on the bench seat, alongside the other members of the unit.

A man seated opposite them introduced himself.

'Lagan!' cried Coster. 'That's an Irish bleeding lake.'

He smiled. 'A name given to me by the Metropolitan Police. It amuses me to use it.'

Sean strained to see him under the dim overhead light. Could this puny, uninspiring individual really be the Mainland Commander who had duped the Brits for so long?

'The Rover was tagged,' Lagan said. 'MI5 should have had you on their screens since Armagh.'

'Why weren't we fingered then?' asked Sean.

'They were hoping you would lead them directly to me.'

'Do they know about the next target?'

'No. We did have a minor problem with a bookmaker from Carrickfergus but it was resolved before any harm was done.'

Coster stood up and faced Lagan. 'I've got a problem, mate. There's peace over the water and I'm into fuck knows what with Rambo here, his fat, idle brother and an Arab who gives me the shits. Brigade conned me into this lot and unless you tell me what it's all about I'm buggering off.'

Mahmoud started to rise but was waved down by Lagan. 'You're no longer a republican soldier fighting for the Cause, Mr Coster. You're a mercenary; a hired gun.'

'Like shit, I am,' Coster retorted, always suspicious of men who called him *mister*. 'I don't take...'

Lagan interrupted him, his voice so low it was almost a whisper. 'One more stupid remark like that...' he glanced at Mahmoud, '...and your contract will be terminated.'

Coster looked at the McKindons, as if hoping for their support. Slowly, he sat down.

'A lot of money is being paid for our expertise,' Lagan continued. 'By someone who appreciates our ability to strike at the very heart of London whenever we want to.'

He looked at the three Irishmen in turn. 'If this operation is successful, each one of you will receive five hundred thousand pounds, to be paid into numbered off-shore accounts.'

Coster glared at Sean. 'You knew about this.'

'Some.'

'And that's why you brought your useless brother along, isn't it?'

Lagan intervened. 'Are you with us, Mr Coster?'

He took a moment to consider his options. '...Yeah, I suppose so.'

'Good, now let me tell you about our friend, Mahmoud. He's here to observe and report back to his masters. If he doesn't get home to tell of our success we will not be paid.'

Mahmoud said nothing. He had been educated at Jerusalem's Bir Ziet University and he hated his crass, ignorant companions. They stank, squabbled about unimportant things, and ate like pigs. They had no heart for their cause and were not prepared to die for their country. Not like his brave friend, Saleh Abdel Rahim Al-Souwi from QalQilya who strapped explosives to his chest and had killed so many enemies of Palestine.

Mahmoud looked forward to the day when he would be free of these uncouth men. When he would become a hero of his people, kill many infidels, and attack a world-famous symbol of British power.

117

17

It was six-thirty on Monday morning. The night staff had left the Incident Post, the telephones were still silent, the message pads blank.

Always an early riser, Molly was alone, trying to catch up with her paperwork. But she couldn't get the Captain out of her mind. She already felt close to him. It certainly wasn't his charm that attracted her; he'd been pig-ignorant most of the time. Perhaps it was a barrier he used to stop people from seeing the real man inside the uniform.

Whatever it was, he'd been different last night - when he sobered up. Strong and decisive, he was also kind and sort of vulnerable; a lost soul looking for a friend. After their torrid love making, he'd talked long into the night.

She sighed. She needed someone she could share her innermost thoughts with; someone she could love. But could it really be the pompous, no-nonsense Captain who was so easy to hate? Love and hate were supposed to be bed-fellows and she knew her relationships would always be stormy; life had made her a fighter. Perhaps she was her own worst enemy; always picking up lost causes and trying to change them. The Captain

Standish's of the world usually had so many problems, a saint couldn't help them.

The door crashed against the wall and Bannister bowled into the office.

'All right, ma'am?'

'I was a minute ago. Did Liz kick you out of bed?'

'Fancy a cup of tea?' he asked, searching for clean cups.

He's got something important to tell me, she thought, giving him the briefest of nods.

'I've seen Joe, the barman at the Queen's Hotel,' he called across the office. A short time later he placed a steaming cup on her desk. 'The man in the bar paid him fifty quid to stop the parking ticket.'

She sipped her tea, wishing he wouldn't make it so strong. 'How come Joe's so free with his information?'

'I happened to mention that assisting the bombers would be conspiracy to murder.'

'Tell me about the man in the bar?'

'Mid-forties. Dark, receding hair. A very average sort of bloke, according to Joe. He did say the man drank Scotch and spoke like a BBC news reader.'

She stretched her legs under the desk. 'What was he doing in Westhampton?'

'He didn't say, ma'am. But Joe smelt drink on him when he first showed. He must have been in a boozer somewhere in the city.'

Bannister dropped his head back and let the sugar from the bottom of his cup drip onto his tongue, a habit

119

that always irritated her.

'Oh, yes, ma'am. I knew there was something else.'
He banged his cup down on the desk. 'I've checked out
the car - it's on false plates.'

Her next interruption came two hours later: the Chief
called. 'What do you think, Watson?' he asked
immediately. 'Are we going to find any more letter
bombs?'

'I don't know, sir. We've got to search every packet
in the building as if it's lethal.'

'And how the dickens long is that going to take? The
Home Secretary keeps pestering me. He's worried in
case the IRA are blamed for this lot and the Prime
Minister's peace initiative goes down the tubes.'

'Two, possibly three days, sir. If we find no more
bombs, that is. Every one we trace means another hold
up while it's dis-armed.'

'Hum! Do your best, Watson. I'm relying on you.'

She put down the receiver. *I'm relying on you* was
certainly better than *you're a menace* of three days
earlier.

After a quick breakfast, she made her way to the
Secondary Sorting Office. It was full of activity, men
searching for the letter bombs moving about with great
care and speaking softly.

She wandered over to a converted fork-lift truck.
The driver sat behind a metal shield and peered through a

thick glass viewer.

'What do you think about the *Tomcat*?' asked the Captain as he arrived at her side.

She gestured towards the Felix badge on the arm of his uniform jumper. 'You're all cat mad.'

'We do tend to prowl around late at night,' he said softly.

'And get up early.'

'So that nobody knows where we've been.'

'Or with whom.' She felt confused and unsure of what was going on between them. Did he really care about her?

'Ready, sir!' called out the driver of the Tomcat. The Captain gave her the briefest of smiles then waved his soldier on.

The Tomcat trundled past them towards a pile of mailbags. Mechanical arms attached to the end of its jib grabbed a mailbag, raised it head high, then released it. The mailbag hit the concrete floor with a thud and police helpers held their breath. Nothing happened. They'll soon be as blase as the soldiers, she thought.

As the dust settled, a squaddie dressed in protective clothing moved forward and opened the top of the mailbag. It was then raised into the air once more but this time it was tipped over so that the packets and letters cascaded out, like fish from a trawler's net. Again there was no explosion.

The Captain gave a positive-sounding grunt. 'Bleep, our electronics man, has already done a sweep of the bags. Now he'll do the same over the loose mail.'

Watching him systematically work his probe back and forth across the packets, she wished she'd told the Chief the search would take weeks rather than days.

When the electrical search was completed, two police dog handlers with their German Shepherds took over.

The first dog shot forward, nostrils twitching furiously and head moving from side to side as he touched each item of mail with the tip of his wet nose.

'Dogs are expendable,' the Captain whispered, leaning close to her.

She stepped away from him. 'I know a lot of dog lovers who wouldn't agree with you.'

The second dog was young and more excitable than the first one. Dashing forward, he lost his footing so that he slipped and slithered all over the mail.

'Style's different,' she observed dryly as the hapless animal was put back on his lead and hauled away by an embarrassed handler.

'At least we know those packets are safe,' commented the Captain.

'It all seems a bit Heath Robinson to me,' she said. 'Haven't you got anything better for searching packets; airport X-ray machines, for instance?'

He lowered his voice again but this time he kept his distance. 'We have, actually. But there's a technological war going on and the boffins are reluctant to display their latest gimmicks. They'll only wheel out the silver if the lives of royalty or the privileged few are in danger.'

'The next time we find a bomb I'm going to send it straight to 10 Downing Street,' she said angrily.

He laughed. 'That should do the trick.'

Chaos reigned in the Incident Post but after three days it was more controlled; like the kitchen of the Ritz at lunchtime.

Bannister sat behind a growing pile of paperwork. Around the office walls, duty rotas, overtime records and tea money lists fought for prominence amongst search schedules, HQ memos and safety regulations. Raybould's pigeon pictures and Blissett's pin-ups added personal touches.

Tallis, now a chain smoker, ambled into the office. 'They've turned my sorting office into a bloody circus,' he complained. 'There's a forklift truck doing figure of eights and dropping bags of mail like a mechanical monkey trying to break coconuts. And dogs as big as bears have cocked their legs at everything standing upright - including me.'

Bannister called for silence. 'Message from Special Branch, ma'am,' he said. 'Another letter bomb explosion in London. A Middle East ambassador has been killed.'

She felt her stomach turn. How many more? The office was silent as everyone digested the news.

Raybould answered his telephone. 'They've found another bomb!' he called out, writing down the details. 'Near to the scene of the first explosion. The letter offices have been cleared.'

She glanced at her watch: they had been searching the mail for just three hours.

Later in the afternoon, Bannister, on his way out of the office, stopped at her desk. 'Anything from the Met, ma'am?'

'Not a lot, Bill. Special Branch say that the Foreign Office man, the one killed before the Middle East ambassador, had been doing a job in Saudi Arabia.'

He made a move towards the door. 'I'm beginning to think there's more to this lot than the Irish problem, ma'am.'

'Mr Tottles's on the blower,' Blissett called across the office. '...The Headmaster of the Grammar School. His kids are going wild because their A Level results are stuck in this place.'

'Call from Dinsall,' bellowed Raybould. 'Something's ticking inside a mailbag.'

'Message, ma'am,' said Julia. 'A firm of stockbrokers are complaining that thousands of cheques are stuck in the post.'

A PC appeared at the door of the office. 'Sorry to barge in, ma'am,' he said, red-faced and unsure of himself. 'But we have an unhappy greengrocer in the foyer. His fruit is going rotten and the SPG won't let him get it out of his store because it's inside the cordon.' The PC took a quick breath. 'There's also a Traffic Warden Hotchkiss - say's she knows you, ma'am - who wants to cone off Stratford Street, Calais Road, Jarrock Street and Rodney Street.'

'The Chief's on this line,' Blissett yelled. She took the receiver from him.

'I hear you've had another one,' the Chief said.

'Another what, sir?'

'Are you being deliberately obtuse, Watson?'

'No, sir,' she sighed. 'We've found a suspect packet and there's been another letter bomb killing in London.'

'Oh my God, that won't do the Prime Minister's ulcer much good.' She kept her thoughts to herself and waited. 'Never mind,' the Chief went on. 'It makes what I am about to say to you even more important. I've put you in charge of the force Bomb Squad.'

Wondering if her ears were playing tricks, she struggled to control her voice. 'We haven't got a bomb squad.'

'Yes we have - congratulations.'

Nerve ends tingling, she stalled. 'I don't understand, sir?'

'The Home Office have been on. They wanted to know who was running my Bomb Squad. I told them of your appointment *last Friday*.'

The picture suddenly became clear to her. Rather than admit that he didn't have a bomb squad he'd created one - back dated to the day of her interview. 'I thought the Home Office wanted me out of the job, sir?'

'Different department. Fortunately they rarely speak to one another.'

'I know nothing about bombs.'

'That's never stopped you before, Watson,' retorted the Chief, clearly agitated by her questions. 'I can only spare you one sergeant, by the way.'

'Sergeant William Bannister,' she replied without hesitation as it dawned on her that not only was she back in the CID, she'd been given her own department.

'Don't let me down, Watson,' the Chief said. 'I expect you to nab those bloody terrorists.' He rang off and she sat back, her mind in ferment. The office was quiet and everyone was watching her. They didn't need to be police personnel to know something unusual had happened.

Raybould broke the silence. 'What about the ticking parcel at Dinsall, the next generation's exam results, the stockbroker's cheques, the greengrocer's rotten bananas, and Frau Groobenfuhrer's parking restrictions?'

She pulled herself together; if the Chief could make field promotions, then so could she. '*Acting Sergeant* Raybould,' she said briskly, 'you sort it out.'

18

It was seven hours since the third letter bomb had been found by a police dog.

'Molly,' said Tallis, sprawled on a chair in the Incident Post, 'why is it something as basic as an animal's nose has beaten the army's fancy detection equipment?'

'Ask the dog,' she suggested.

He puffed at his cigar. 'What's the Captain playing at? He's had a couple of packets to practise on.'

'You're so smart,' she snapped. 'You disarm the flaming things. People are risking their lives down there.'

'Edgy females,' Tallis grumbled, rising from his chair and stalking out of the office.

She twisted her mother's ring around her finger. The Captain must be getting tired, and tired men made mistakes. In his case it could be fatal.

Catching hold of Blissett as he tried to walk past her desk, she gave him some more money and told him to buy another bottle of Bell's.

At the far end of the Primary Sorting Office, the Captain was sitting at a small work bench. The third packet was smaller than the previous two and the circuit was a mess.

He selected a miniature chisel from his leather tool case and checked the X-ray film. Holding the blade over the right hand corner of the envelope, he paused for a moment, waiting for his hand to stop shaking. When it did so, he pressed down, cutting out a small triangle.

Returning the chisel, he selected a tool with a long, narrow blade, similar to a surgeon's scalpel. Inserting the blade into the open corner of the envelope, he gently sliced along the edge, glancing at the X-ray as he did so. Just short of the Ulster stamps, he stopped cutting.

Heart thumping against the walls of his chest, he laid the tool on the bench and sat back in his chair.

Silently he cursed himself. He should have destroyed the packet with a controlled explosion. Taking unnecessary risks was contrary to all his training and experience. It was his hatred of the IRA that had impaired his judgment and drove him on; the gut-wrenching need for revenge.

Leaning forward, he studied the X-ray, tracking through the maze of wires for the hundredth time. He then inserted the long-bladed tool into the same corner as before but this time he slit open the bottom of the envelope.

His next break was longer. He had come to the most dangerous part of the dis-arming.

He rubbed clammy hands on his trousers, paused for a moment, then held the envelope steady with the thumb of his left hand. Taking his time, he prepared himself mentally to raise the right hand bottom corner of the envelope and expose the innards of the IED.

Tension gripped his throat, the muscles of his belly knotted and his head hurt so much he thought his skull would burst. He saw Joan's face and was tempted to take the easy way out. 'Not now,' he said under his breath. 'Not now.'

Fighting cramp in his forearm, he gripped the tip of the brown manila flap between the thumb and forefinger of his right hand. Slowly, he peeled back the front of the packet, ignoring the sweat stinging his eyes as he exposed time-power units, batteries and resistors, all encased in clear epoxy resin. A maze of coloured wires, crossed and re-crossed the white backing board. Muslin tamping covered the Semtex and the detonator.

He waited until his hands steadied, then pinned back the front of the envelope with the head of a small hammer from his tool case.

His sergeant approached him. 'You're due for a breather now, boss.'

Eyes locked on the IED, he shook his head. 'I'm going to crack this bastard. One of the detonator wires is trapped behind the Semey and I've got to tease away the tamping to get at it.' He leaned further over the work bench. 'Out of the firing line, Joe.'

Reluctantly, Grant left him and returned to the boundary tape.

'He won't give in until he's cracked it, ma'am.'

Never good at standing still for a long time, Molly

moved her weight from one foot to the other. 'He doesn't look too good.'

'This one's a real swine.'

'He shouldn't be anywhere near it, should he?'

'No, ma'am.'

'I thought it was always safety first?'

'So did I.'

The Captain picked at the tamping around the explosive and its detonator. Muscle spasms raced along his arms as he pulled the soft white material clear.

Red and blue wires curled out of the exposed end of the detonator. He could follow the blue wire to one of the time-power units but the red wire disappeared under the backing board. He had to release more red wire if the the pig-stick was to cut both wires simultaneously.

He eased a section of red wire out of the binding tape, knowing too much pressure would break the delicate solder connection to the tin-foil anti-handling strip in the top corner of the envelope.

Gripping the top of the detonator, he carefully lined up the two wires. Tremors ran down his back and he realised he was about to lose control of his hands. Releasing the detonator and the wires, a fingernail snagged the red wire, jerking it upwards. He held his breath and waited for the end.

Nothing happened.

'Thank God,' he gasped. It was not death he feared, it was death before he found the men who had murdered his girl.

He stood up and staggered away from the work bench. Grant, soon at his side, guided him away from the still-active IED.

Later, in the Incident Post, she took a call from Grant. 'We've done it,' he said cheerfully. 'Pigstick sliced through both wires - minimal damage.'

Thanking him, and relieved the Captain was safe, she called out the search teams, making arrangements for them to work through the night.

When there was nothing else she could do, she went to the canteen and ordered her first cooked meal for three days.

She was content to eat alone and for some time afterwards sat with a cup of tea, idly flicking through the evening newspaper but not reading it. Her mind was elsewhere. She had moved on from her worries about the Captain's safety and their relationship - if there was any.

It was the new job that needed her attention now. How the hell was she going to catch the bombers? All she had to go on at the moment was Mad Mick's call and the man from London who spent the afternoon in the Queen's Hotel. Davidson wouldn't help her. He'd make sure his enquiry teams kept their distance, probably by telling them she was after their jobs.

She wasn't completely on her own; she had Bill Bannister. Not always the brightest of men, he was nevertheless loyal and very keen. What she needed now was a break, a decent lead she could follow. Once she was on the bombers' trail, nothing would stop her.

She took her empty plate to the counter. 'Thank's for the best piece of steak I've had in a long time.'

The balding constable in the once-white apron stuck out his chest. 'You should marry me, ma'am.'

Still smiling as she returned to the Incident Post, a plan of action formed in her mind. She increased her pace, tonight the Bomb Squad would be an item; tonight she would begin her enquiries.

19

Molly popped her head into the Incident Post. 'Cover for me until the night shift turn up please, Bill. I'm going to see an old friend.'

'And you're not leaving a forwarding address for Superintendent Davidson?'

'Right.'

It was a cloudy night but the moon appeared briefly as she picked her way along a road strewn with rubble left by the demolition gangs. Once a market town, Westhampton was changing yet again and a variety of small shops were being knocked down to make room for a shopping mall.

Further on, she walked past a Portland stone building that was once a church. Now it was a supermarket, its concrete car park covering the hallowed ground where past generations had buried their dead.

It started to rain but she didn't mind; she liked walking in the rain.

The Four Feathers was in a cul-de-sac of terraced houses at the back of the Queen's Hotel. She stepped into a dark doorway opposite the public house and watched the licensee usher late drinkers down the steps before closing the door and switching off the bar lights.

Making sure no one else was about, Molly crossed the road and walked up a covered entry at the side of the licensed premises.

Through the back window she could see Bernadette O'Brien sitting at her living room table. Shoulders hunched under a garish red cardigan, she was counting notes. Bernie didn't believe in cash registers that stamped the time of sale on the till roll and were incapable of making adjustments for spillage, tips and wrong-changing. Bernie's starting to show her age, she thought, remembering the younger woman in outrageously short skirts and revealing low tops.

She was inside the living room before the older woman had a chance to cover the money.

'Watson! You nearly gave me a fucking heart attack.'

'Serves you right, you should be more careful.' She closed the curtains. 'It might be the real thing one of these nights.'

'Naff off. With my contacts the yellow bellied bastards wouldn't dare. If it's a drink you're after you could've tapped the tranny like the rest of 'em do.'

'I came to see you, Bernie.'

'You know where it is, pour me one while you're at it.'

She went to the sideboard and ran a hand over half a dozen bottles before deciding on the Bell's.

Handing Bernie a Scotch, she sat beside her. The room was a shambles but it was as warm and friendly as an old coat. She had cried in this room when she'd lost her first case and she got drunk after convicting her first rapist.

'Any of the local CID about?'

Bernie slid her money box under the sideboard and sat back in her chair, feet resting on a crate of beer. 'I never see the buggers on Sunday anymore,' she replied, pulling a loaf of bread across the table and cutting off a thick slice. 'Fancy a bunghole sandwich?'

She shook her head.

Bernie laughed. 'Still looking after the best figure in town. It's women like you who show us all up.'

'I take care of myself.'

'No you don't. You got yourself suspended over that slimy cretin, Sergeant Conrad. Now you're in the shit with super-creep Davidson.'

'I love you too.'

'Don't get your arse in your hand with me, Molly Watson. I'm the best friend you've got, even though you upped and left me without a word.'

She'd stopped visiting the Feathers when too many detectives, after free drinks, had started to use it. 'I'm at the Letter Office; organising the bomb search.'

'Only until the men bastards fuck you off. A woman to them is someone who lies on her back and takes it with a smile. Your trouble is you want to be on top all the time.'

'We have equal rights now; it's the law.'

'Arseholes! That piece of mumbo jumbo just makes them more crafty with it.'

'The detectives like me.'

'Like fuck, they do. They put up with you. Give me another drink before I die of bleedin' thirst.'

She poured a large measure. 'What do you recommend?'

Bernie laughed, showing brown, gappy teeth. '*What do you recommend*! Come off it. Use your fanny and those other gadgets they can't keep their mucky maulers off. Get yourself a man and attack from the inside. Screw him stupid and make him believe he's doing the business.'

'I came for information, not a lecture, Bernie.'

'I've told you what you want, girl.'

'I need your help.'

'That's exactly what you're getting.'

'Were there any strangers in here last Friday?'

'They're out to get you, Molly.'

She sighed. It had always been like this. As if they were speaking some kind of code. No answers, just questions and statements and Scotch and patience and more Scotch, until she got what she came for. Many a morning she hadn't remembered the journey home, only the information.

'I'm back in the CID,' she said.

'Hard shit.'

Feeling the warm glow of the whisky, she shook her head. 'You've got a lovely bed-side manner, Bernie, you should've been a shrink.'

'What else d'you think a fucking landlady is?' She

coughed and banged her chest. 'See to the drinks, a detective with an empty glass worries me.'

'I need your help, Bernie.'

'Yeah, I heard you the first time.'

'A lot of people are dead and many more will join them if the devils behind the letter bombs aren't locked up.'

'What can you do, holed up in a bloody office?'

'I told you, I'm back in the CID - in charge of the Bomb Squad.'

'So, wonder-woman Watson is going to show them how to do it again. Fuck me, girl, don't you *ever* learn?'

'I'm after the slime who posted the letter bombs and I need to know if a stranger was in here last Friday.'

'Any idea what he looks like?'

'Mid-forties, receding hairline, medium everything else. London accent, throws his money about and drinks your poison.'

Bernie's face screwed up in pain as she lifted her feet off the box. 'Ever had gout?' she gasped.

Feeling sympathy for her friend, she shook her head. 'Is it very bad?'

'Fucking awful. She carefully placed her feet on a worn rag rug. 'What was it you asked?'

'The stranger?'

'Yes,' murmured Bernie. 'There was someone in the bar last Friday lunchtime who fits the bill. He was with a student from the University. They were in the corner of the bar, heads together. Seemed to me that the kid was

137

flogging his ring or something.'

She could hardly believe her luck. 'Can you remember anything special about the man?'

'Now you mention it, his left hand was mostly stump: three fingers were missing. He held his glass with his thumb and little finger; in my business you notice these kind of things.'

'Is that all?'

'What the hell do you want for Christ's sake, a fucking dog tag with his name and address on it?'

'Anything about the student?'

'The man gave the kid a bag. One of those holdall things. It looked heavy and there were Pepsi cans on the top. That's what convinced me the kid was on the game.'

She emptied the remains of the Bell's into their glasses. 'Did anyone hear what they were talking about?'

Bernie scratched her pot belly. 'Ernie the Ears might have; he misses fuck all.'

'Can I see him?'

'If you can find him. He's one of those courier blokes, jetting all over the place.' She lowered her voice. '...Mostly drugs, if you ask me.'

'When's he due back?'

'Don't know.'

'Great! That's all I need; a vital witness on safari.'

'Tough shit, if he turns ups I'll give you a bell. Just leave off your bloody questions, I've had a pig of a day.'

She took hold of Bernie's hand. 'Thank you anyway. When all this is over we'll have a night on the town and you can tell me how to snare a good man.'

Bernie's laughter became a chesty cough. '...There's no such fucking animal. They're all selfish, rotten bastards - that's why we love 'em so much. Now get your arse out of here before I call the cops.'

A little unsteady on her feet, and overwhelmed by a feeling of melancholy, she let herself out of the back door. She would have to visit the Feathers more often. Bernie was almost family, the only family she had.

20

Refreshed after her walk through the city, Molly returned to the Incident Post.

Bannister, showing signs of a long day, was waiting for her.

'I thought you'd have been tucked up in bed by now, Bill,' she said, hanging up her coat, then sitting down at her desk.

'Had to know you were all right, ma'am.'

Eyes narrowing, she looked him. Was he treating her like the *little woman*?

He raised his hands in mock surrender. 'I'd have done the same for one of the lads.'

Now he's reading my mind, she thought, wondering if having him in her new squad was such a good idea. 'Anything I should know about?'

'Not really, ma'am. I've sent the night shift to get some nosh while it's quiet.'

'Where's the Captain?' she asked casually.

Bannister glanced at the whisky bottle sticking out of a tidy bin. 'He asked the same question about you. He was in here with Joe Grant. They're now on a tour of the nightclubs - with *Acting Sergeant* Raybould.'

A frown crossed Bannister's tired face. 'Am I being

sent back to Division, ma'am?'

She decided to tell him about his transfer, knowing she should have done so earlier. 'Raybould has your job because you're now a detective sergeant in the Westhampton City Police Bomb Squad. Welcome to the force's finest, as the Americans say.'

Too startled to do anything else, he accepted her hand. 'What Bomb Squad?'

She smiled, recalling her own reaction. 'It's just you and me at the moment. The Chief expects us to catch the letter bombers.'

He jumped out of his chair. 'How, for Christ's sake? CID, Regional Crime Squad, Special Branch and the Anti-Terrorist bods haven't even had a sniff.'

'We've achieved the impossible before.'

'Dealing with drug traffickers and con artists; these bastards are mass serial killers.' He dropped back into his chair. 'I can't do it, ma'am. Liz said she'd leave me if I ever worked for you again.'

'Women say a lot of things when they're worried about their men. Tell her that the expenses, car allowance and overtime will take her to Bermuda for a month. Think about it, Bill. If we get it right, we can lift the bombers.'

'And if we get it wrong?'

'We can't be worse off than we were yesterday. Both of us faced with years in the cloth; you working endless shifts and me trying to train the untrainable.'

He squirmed in his seat and she imagined his brain

going through the same movement. 'Can I leave if it doesn't work out, ma'am?'

'Give it to the end of this job, Bill. Then see how you feel.'

Still looking uncertain, he took a message from his pocket. 'I've just remembered, this came while you were out. The Office Manager of a Murder Enquiry Room at Gloucester thinks he might have something for you.'

She took the message from him. 'Do our CID know about this?'

'No, ma'am.'

'Good.'

She called Gloucester and started to make notes.

When she had finished they covered three sheets of A4.

'Was it useful?' Bannister asked, his skill at reading upside down having given him the key words, *motorway service station, businesswoman, rape, murder, Irish suspect.*

'Yes,' she replied, tidying up her notes. 'We may have got our third lead.'

'Third?'

'Mad Mick's tip off, the man in the Queen's and Four Feathers, and now the Gloucester incident.'

Bannister looked baffled. 'What's rape and murder in Gloucester got to do with our bombers?'

'During Sunday afternoon four men were seen in a mud-splattered Rover at the back of the Gloucester motorway service station car park - south side.

At eight o'clock that evening a lorry driver noticed there were only three men in the car.

Half an hour before midnight a cleaner saw a man at the restaurant leaving the gents. He had long scratch marks down the right side of his face and she found blood all over a washbasin and on the floor.

A few minutes later the same man, who spoke with a hard Irish accent, purchased four take-away meals.

At first light on Monday morning a boy, walking his dog in the woods behind the North side car park, found the mutilated body of a woman.'

'North side?' queried Bannister.

'There's a footbridge. Later, a car park attendant found the four food cartons where the Rover had been parked.'

'What was the cause of death?'

'Strangulation. She'd also been badly beaten, raped and cut with a sharp knife, according to the pathologist.'

'It's a bit thin,' Bannister murmured. 'But if we're on the right track, then one of our happy band of murderers is also a raving psychopath.'

'You told me once you liked a challenge.'

'I'm not a bloody masochist. Where are the men now?'

'I don't know; their car was last seen heading south.'

His eyes widened. 'Exactly what Mad Mick said. *They're moving south to take out the town.*'

'But where, and what does it mean?'

'Rape...' pondered Bannister. 'According to the last

CID course I attended, terrorists are mostly fanatical killers programmed not to deviated from their primary objective.'

'Maybe, but it only takes one head case to ruin a slick operation.'

'D'you think the man from the Queen's is with them, ma'am?'

'I doubt it. He was probably one of the organisers, making sure the letter bombs had been posted and were on the way to their targets.'

She thought for a moment. 'Yes...and I bet that's why he left in such a hurry; he was going to tell whoever's behind the operation there'd been some kind of a cock up at the Letter Office.'

Bannister sheepishly pulled another message out of his pocket. 'Sorry, ma'am, we've also had a call from Chief Inspector Black, Special Branch. He said the woman in the MP's apartment in London has a badly burned face but otherwise she's okay.'

She sighed. It was the second piece of vital information he'd forgotten to give her since she'd returned from the Feathers. The worried look in his eyes told her it wasn't his memory that had gone; it was his courage. He was psyching himself up to tell Liz about his transfer to the Bomb Squad.

'Did he say anything else about the woman?' she asked.

'Yes, ma'am. She's Gina Jones, nineteen years and a temp who had been working in several Whitehall offices. Her security clearance is suspect and she's believed to have contacts with the IRA.'

'Can we see her?'

'Mr Black says she's in hospital and MI5 are guarding her like the Crown Jewels.'

Snug under her warm coat, she lay on the Head Postmaster's settee. But she couldn't sleep. If the men in the car at the service station were the bombers, which town were they heading for?

She heard footsteps outside the door, followed by a knock.

'Moll'!' called a familiar voice. 'Let me in - please.'

She hesitated only for a moment. 'You've had too much to drink.'

'I need to see you, Moll'.'

'A good night's sleep is what you need, go away.'

A few minutes later she opened the door.

The Captain had gone.

21

'How were things at home,?' Molly asked Bannister during a short coffee break on Tuesday morning.

'She's not talking to me.'

'Is that bad?'

'Like the weather, it takes time for the pressure to build up. I expect to be hit by the full force of *Hurricane Liz* some time tonight.'

Perhaps the bachelor life does have its advantages, she reflected. 'Have you seen the Captain?'

'I don't think you'll be seeing much of him today, ma'am. He was poured out of three boozers and a Balti House during the night.'

'Grant and Raybould?'

'They were last seen doing the Highland Fling at the Thistle Club. Stan Raybould can't take the pressure of rank, ma'am. The only thing he's ever been in charge of before is his racing pigeons.'

Some time later, Grant, like a living corpse, sidled through the door and collapsed into a chair.

'Have you seen the Captain?' she asked, sensing that something was wrong.

He brushed back his ginger hair. 'When I came

round this morning, his bed was empty and his civvy clothes were missing. I think he's gone *AWOL.* In the Army that's desertion under fire, so to speak; they'll line him up against a bloody wall.'

'Not if they don't find out,' she said. 'We'll have to make excuses and hope he comes to his senses. You're sure he hadn't got a genuine reason for leaving?'

Grant groaned and reached for a cup of cold coffee someone hadn't had time to drink. Unsteadily lifting it to his mouth, he emptied it in one big swallow. '...No, ma'am. Your whole family could have been murdered in their beds and the Army wouldn't allow you to leave a job like this. I'm just praying to God we don't find another IED.'

She cursed under her breath, wishing she'd let the Captain into her room last night. 'Bill,' she said quietly. 'Go walkabout. Try and find out where the Captain's got to. Let me know the minute you have anything useful; we must get him back soon.'

The telephone buzzed. It was Chief Inspector Black returning an earlier call. 'Has anyone claimed responsibility for the letter bombs?' she asked.

There was no answer and she repeated the question.

'...It's Superintendent Davidson,' he said finally. 'We've all been given strict instructions not to tell you anything about the enquiries.'

'What?' she shouted down the telephone. 'I'm in charge of the force Bomb Squad, for Christ's sake.'

'I know, Molly. And a lot of us are very pleased for

you, but he's put up the shutters.'

Typical, she thought. 'Roger, surely you can answer my one little question?'

His voice was barely audible. 'No one has claimed responsibility.'

'And have we got any more on Gina Jones?'

'No.'

'Where is she now?'

'I'll have to end this conversation.'

'Please, Roger - give me a break.'

He chuckled. 'You're a hustler, Molly Watson. The Queen Elizabeth Military Hospital in Woolwich, southeast London.'

She put down the handset, pleased Bannister hadn't mentioned the call from Gloucester to anyone else. If Davidson could put up the shutters, then so could she.

The telephone buzzed again. 'I've spoken to a friend who was on the switchboard last night, ma'am,' Bannister began. 'At five o'clock this morning, a Lieutenant Reynolds, Northern Ireland Army Intelligence, rang and asked for the Captain. Said he had to speak to him urgently on a matter of great importance.'

'Go on.'

'That's it, ma'am. She passed the message to a squaddie but can't remember his name. He promised to tell the Captain.'

'Did he return Lieutenant Reynolds's call?'

'Not through the switchboard, he didn't.'

No, she thought, that was the last thing he would

have done. 'Thank you, Bill, I'll see what I can find out.' Now they were a team, she'd have to start sharing information with him. She'd always been a loner but had never under-estimated the strength of a good partnership.

The next call was from the Chief's staff officer who, in his usual snobbish manner, ordered her to be at Headquarters at 2 p.m. He refused to say what it was about.

'Ah, there you are, Watson,' the Chief said as she walked into his office. 'Take a pew, I've just been speaking to an Assistant Commissioner at New Scotland Yard. They need your help, it seems.'

She remained standing. 'Me, sir?'

'Yes, and your sergeant. My staff officer is contacting him right now.'

She sat down. For once in her life she didn't know what to say.

'It's the letter bombs,' the Chief continued. 'They seem to believe you're the only one who has a full picture concerning the incident at the Letter Office.'

There was a grunt of indignation from the corner of the room and for the first time she noticed Davidson.

The Chief spoke again. 'Sorry you must leave in the middle of the mail search, Watson. But I take it as a compliment to the force that one of my detective inspectors has been called in to assist the Met.' He glanced at his CID Chief. 'Makes us all very proud, doesn't it, Superintendent?' Davidson pulled a face but

149

nodded dutifully.

She found her voice. 'When, sir?'

'My car will pick you up at your home in four hours
time. They're expecting you at the Yard at around ten
o'clock this evening.'

'Thank you, sir,' she said, turning to leave.

'There's one more thing,' said the Chief, stopping
her in mid-stride. 'I think you know the man who's
waiting to see you. He's Detective Superintendent Cran-
something-Smythe, with a Y.'

She put together a few essentials and selected suitable
clothes from her crowded wardrobe. But her mind was
elsewhere. James Cranleigh-Smythe, a detective
superintendent, no less. He'd helped her and Bannister
to arrest a team of villains in the West End. Then he'd
put his career at risk by unofficially sending his
undercover squad to the Midlands when she was having
difficulty setting up Sergeant Conrad.

Afterwards, mentally and physically exhausted
following the most horrendous two weeks of her life,
she'd run to him for support and they'd shared a
wonderful few days at his Cotswold cottage.

Later, back in her Staffordshire home and suspended
from duty, her dreams of a more permanent relationship
were shattered by his long, rambling letter which could
have been reduced to two words: *it's over*.

Handing a bulging travel bag to the driver, she jumped

into the front passenger seat of the Chief's Jaguar.

'All right, ma'am,' Bannister said from the back seat of the car as it shot through Coovers Wood and headed south.

She looked over her shoulder and could see he was not a happy man. 'Cheer up, Bill. We're travelling to the big city in style this time.'

'I prefer trains.'

'What's put your nose out?'

'It's the missus. Rang the Chief himself, she did. Really bent his ear. Said he'd got no right to work people day and night, then send them all over the universe at a moment's notice. *How are me and the kids supposed to manage?* she screamed at him.'

'She wasn't happy, you mean?'

'It's no joke, ma'am. We were just getting it together. Now it's like the bloody Drug Squad all over again.'

She smiled to herself. The Chief had done well to win Liz over, even grudgingly. 'We'll be back in a couple of days. You can buy her something nice from Harrods.'

'It'll have to be the whole bloody shop.'

'Any news about the Captain?'

'Afraid not, ma'am, he's vanished.'

'And his car?'

'Hasn't got one. He came in an army Landrover with Joe Grant.'

Resting her head on soft leather, she closed her eyes,

151

cursing herself again for not answering the Captain's plea for help.

Now she was going to London to see another man in her life, one who abandoned her when she'd needed him.

22

'Good luck, ma'am,' said the chief's driver before he drove off.

Molly looked briefly at the dreary office block novelists referred to as the birth place of modern crime detection. Aware that *New* Scotland Yard was the third and least inspiring London building to house the headquarters and specialist departments of the Metropolitan Police, she was not impressed.

Bannister, carrying her sheepskin coat and travel bag, followed her into the building. The creamy marble foyer was cold and unfriendly and their footsteps echoed in its emptiness. Glancing up from the racing pages of the Evening Standard, a security guard checked their warrant cards and directed them to the fifth floor.

Leading Bannister past abandoned offices, she noticed her reflection in dark windows, flicked back a rebellious strand of fair hair, and fastened the top button of her navy blue jacket. Despite James's sudden ending of their relationship, she was looking forward to meeting him again.

She knocked on an unmarked door and strode into a small, featureless room, furnished with a scratched mahogany table and metal-framed chairs.

James, and a man he introduced as Richard, stood up. Their greetings were formal and James's handshake was as cold as the marble foyer.

They all sat down and she was reminded of dreary, Monday morning crime conferences with Davidson.

But one of these men was James, the man she had once loved. His face was now lined with fatigue and his narrow shoulders were rounded so that he looked older than his forty years.

He held up a fax. 'This anonymous message you received on the night of the explosion at the Westhampton Letter Office,' he said stiffly. *'The letter bombs are only the beginning: a diversion to keep MI5 chasing their tails. They're moving south to take out the town.* What does it mean?'

'The first part is clear enough,' she replied in a neutral voice, trying to hide her disappointment and come to terms with his frostiness. 'It's the final sentence that's the mystery.'

'You *must* know the caller.'

She felt her anger rising. Who the hell did he think he was talking to? 'Yes,' she replied. 'As a matter of fact, I did.'

'Then why didn't you say so?'

'I had my reasons,' she replied curtly. If he wanted to play the hardened detective she would oblige by being the bloody-minded interviewee.

'Circulation was limited; don't you trust us?'

'In a word - no.' He may be a Scotland Yard

detective superintendent but she hadn't left Westhampton in the middle of an important operation to be cross-examined by him or anyone else. 'I didn't want my informant's name flashed around the country. As it turned out, I was right.'

IIis sombre expression did not change. 'Right about what?'

She sighed, wanting to escape from the oppressive room. 'His body was found on waste ground in Belfast the next morning. He obviously knew what the bombers were planning and was about to tell me.'

'It's a great pity...'

'That he's dead or that he was unable give me any more information?'

James looked at his feet, seemingly unsure of himself. 'Both I suppose.'

'He was a good snout.'

'How good?'

She told him about Mad Mick; he didn't need her protection now.

'Have you any other contacts in Northern Ireland?' James asked when she had finished.

'No.'

'Where's this town he spoke of?'

'If I knew, I wouldn't be here.'

James brought his hands together, like a man in prayer. His long, slender fingers were topped with manicured nails she remembered so well.

'What do you know about Captain Standish?' he

155

asked.

Alarm bells sounded. Why the sudden change of direction? Her perplexity showed and the men seated across the table exchanged glances.

Richard intervened with a polite cough. 'I'd be grateful if you'd tell your sergeant to wait in the next office.'

Tempted to walk out herself, but needing to know why they were interested in the Captain, she faced James. 'Is this really necessary?'

'Yes, I'm afraid it is,' he replied.

Bannister left, slamming the door shut behind him.

'My Chief Constable said you wanted both of us,' she said angrily. 'The man you've just insulted gave up a lot to be here.'

'I'm sorry,' James said wearily. 'This enquiry goes beyond the explosions and is particularly sensitive.'

'So am I,' she retorted. 'If it isn't the letter bombs, then why *did* you send for us?'

'To answer some questions.'

'About what, for Christ's sake?'

'Captain Standish.'

'We worked together at the Letter Office,' she snapped back, cursing herself for sounding too defensive.

'How well did you know each other?'

'We shared toothpicks and went to the same aerobics class,' she exploded. 'What the hell are you implying?'

'We need to know if he confided in you. Did he talk

about his family or any particular worries he might have had?'

She looked at the two men, convinced they were not being straight with her. They must already know of the Captain's drink problem and his hate of the IRA. What were they really after?

Richard spoke. 'You'll have to tell us eventually.'

Now she was sure she didn't like the man. Older than James, his grey worsted suit hung loosely on his sparsely covered frame and his red woollen tie appeared to have been squeezed over his head rather than knotted at the neck. But it was his light grey eyes that worried her; they were completely expressionless.

'What are you going to use - thumbscrews?'

'We're talking Government business.'

'And who's *we* - MI5?'

'Something like that,' he replied.

His patronising smile was as false as the rest of him, she decided.

James, a vague image of his former self, gave her a weak smile and took over. 'All right, Molly,' he said. 'It's getting late. I'll have you taken to your hotel. The expenses are better this time around and you'll find the accommodation more agreeable.' Richard seemed about to argue but James stopped him with a warning look.

Agreeable turned out to be an understatement. The hotel was luxurious, each room furnished with a three piece suite and a king sized bed. A vase of carnations stood on a polished table and beside it, the manager's gilt-edged welcome card was propped against a bottle of red wine

When she left Bannister, he had recovered his spirits and was watching a Western on the television, having already asked room service for a plate of ham sandwiches and a basket of chips.

In her own room, on the floor above, she kicked off her shoes and sank into an easy chair. She had some serious thinking to do. Why were Scotland Yard and the mysterious Richard so interested in the Captain?

A knock on the door interrupted her thoughts. It was James and, judging by the way he looked up and down the corridor, he didn't want to be seen.

'Can I have a quick word, please?' he whispered.

She let him through the door but barred his way when he tried to walk around her. 'What did you want to talk about?' she asked, her emotions in a state of turmoil.

He faced her, his eyes earnest; pleading almost. 'We must talk.'

'About the Stock Market or the Police Gay Society?'

'I thought we were friends.'

'Some *friend*. The whole flaming police force was ganging up on me and the one person I thought I could turn to, sent a letter on mummy's crested notepaper - telling me to go and kiss the monkeys.'

'Mother was against us from the start.'

'I bet. I can hear her now. *James darling, have your little bit of fun with the silly bitch then settle down and find a nice girl of our own class...*'

James pushed past her and flung himself into a chair. 'That's a bit over the top.'

'Over the top! You and Snake Eyes make the Commandant of Belsen seem like the Archangel Gabriel.'

He grinned, showing perfect white teeth. 'You should be on the stage, Molly. You're a star turn when you're in full flow.'

She sat on the edge of the double bed. She didn't really want to fight this man. His eyes locked onto hers and his smile started to work its magic. Knowing her cheeks were about to colour up, and not wishing to give him the encouragement of a smile, she retreated to the privacy of the bathroom.

She sat at the dressing table and refreshed her lipstick, giving herself time to think. Events had pushed her along at such a hectic pace since Friday, she was losing control of her personal life. First the surprising night with the Captain. Then her former lover had treated her like a stranger. Now he was in her bedroom in the middle of the night. She'd never been very strong when he turned on the charm. She felt trapped and vulnerable, and was not sure she would cope with it.

Returning to the bedroom, she found James sitting on the settee, the manager's wine and two glasses on a small table in front of him.

He poured the drinks and offered one to her. She shook her head, conscious of what he was trying to do.

Their first date had been at an Italian restaurant in Soho and he knew how mellow she was likely to become after a few drinks of red wine.

He held out his hand. 'Please, Molly, for old time's sake.'

'No,' she said quietly, resuming her former position on the edge of the bed. 'I think you should leave.'

'When you've had a drink.'

This time she accepted the glass.

'That's better,' he said. 'We can be pals again.'

She put the glass down, determined not give way. 'I'm here to catch a gang of bombers; no other reason.'

He stood up and walked across the room, stopping directly in front of her. Smiling, he moved closer. She felt his legs pressing against hers. A sudden sense of foreboding overcame her. Her arms felt cold and the hairs on the back of her neck stood up.

'Don't look so startled, my pet,' he said softly.

She pushed against his chest but it was too late. He grabbed the back of her head, his lips crushing hers and his tongue trying to force open her mouth.

Holding back the tears, she tried to fight him but he was too strong. He pushed her onto the bed, his body on top of her so that she was trapped.

How could he do this to her? she kept asking herself as she struggled to escape from under him.

Tears now streaming down her cheeks, she called out his name and begged him to stop. Instead, he gripped her legs, his fingers sinking into soft flesh as he forced them apart. Face contorted and eyes glazed, he held her legs open with his knees and she felt his hands again; not gentle and caressing as they had once been but rough and probing. Breathing heavily, like a man possessed, he snatched at her pants, trying to drag them over her hips but ripping the crotch so that she was completely exposed to him.

A door crashed open. Dark shadows merged above her. The weight was lifted from her body. Men fought and cursed. Fists smacked and thudded around her, furniture toppled and the room shook. It was like a bad dream. Her mind swam and the pink lamp above the bed seemed to disappear into the eye of a whirlpool as she lost consciousness.

It was two hours later before she felt able to ask Bannister to leave.

'I can stay,' he offered. 'Sleep on the chair.'

Lying in bed, a duvet up to her chin, she looked up at him. 'No, thanks, Bill. You've done enough, we've got another big day tomorrow.'

'You should see a doctor, and we should go back to Westhampton.'

'I'm all right, Bill. It was just the shock.'

'You should turn him in, he's a nutter.'

'We've been through all that, Bill. I've got my reasons.'

'The job's not worth it, neither is he.'

She sank deeper into the pillow. 'You're probably

right; we'll talk some more later. Right now, I'm so tired, I hardly know what I'm saying.'

23

Molly peered through the October mist at the small park beneath her window. A man was stretched out on a wooden bench, newspapers protecting him from the pigeons roosting on the bare branches above. Beyond the trees, rising out of the murk like an airship, was the dome of St. Paul's Cathedral. Despite the paracetamol given to her by Bannister, she had slept fitfully, her head crowded with distressing images and difficult decisions.

Getting up early, she'd stuffed last night's clothing into a laundry bag and hurled it into the bottom of the wardrobe.

She'd then had a shower, scrubbing her bruised legs until they were sore.

After drying her hair, she ironed the denim dress she'd packed in such a hurry.

She picked up a glossy magazine but did it lay unopened on her lap. What was she going to do about James? He'd lost control of himself and had gone berserk. Thank goodness for Bannister who'd called to ask what time they were starting in the morning. When she questioned him about the fight, he'd clammed up, saying James must have accidentally bounced into a wall. James was probably in his apartment right now, she thought. Nursing a sore head and waiting to be arrested for attempted rape.

A man commits rape if he has unlawful sexual intercourse with a woman who at the time of the intercourse does not consent to it and at the time he knows that she does not consent to it or he is reckless as to whether she consents to it. She'd recited the definition at the police training centre years ago and she had never forgotten it.

Now that it had almost happened to her, she felt dirty and abused. She also, for the first time, really understood the emotional shock of the scores of victims she'd cross-examined.

If details of the incident got out, press and public would clamour for the maximum retribution and demand that a man in James's position should be sent to prison for a long time, even for the lesser offence of attempted rape.

But what did she want? They'd been lovers, who had willingly and enthusiastically shared their bodies so many times. Solicitors would call it attempted *date rape* and practically every victim of this offence subsequently withdrew her allegations.

Why had she let him into her room in the middle of the night, friends, the court and the press would ask. Was she scheming for the resumption of her relationship with a very desirable senior detective from Scotland Yard?

And what about James? The moment they met it had

been obvious to her that he was not his normal, relaxed and charming self, and she had wondered what kind of pressure he was under. People tried to cope with stress in their own inadequate ways. He may have come to her for help and simply lost control of is emotions. It was a very human thing to do.

Was she constructing a defence for him because she couldn't face the trauma of being a rape victim? Interviewing officers demanding a full, descriptive account of the crime and lurid, intimate details of her past relationship with James. The police doctor staring up her vagina and taking swabs. The young police photographer aiming his flashgun at her private parts and showing the pictures around the lab. A CID man with a sick sense of humour, or her old enemy, Davidson, flashing them around at Divisional functions or to groups of detectives in pub corners. Then the court appearances; sniggers and innuendoes as her sex life became public property and her moral standards were made out to be those of the gutter by the Sunday tabloids.

She'd seen it happen to so many women and, even though the press would not be allowed to publish her name, she knew it would ruin her life as surely as it would destroy James. She wouldn't be able to stay in the force and there was nothing else she wanted to do.

Rising from her chair and putting down the magazine, she saw the early morning sun shining weakly on the dome of St. Paul's.

She had no alternative, she decided, she must try to

put the terrible experience to the back of her mind and get on with her life. She had a team of terrorists to catch and she could tough it out with James, confident he wouldn't do anything like it again. In fact, if she knew him at all, he would come crawling, asking forgiveness and claiming loss of memory or a blackout. It wouldn't be easy but life never had been easy and she'd never expected it to be.

She didn't have to guess who it was when Bannister knocked. 'I thought for a minute you were going to smash the door open again,' she said, letting him in.

'How are you feeling?'

'I'm all right, Bill - thanks to you.'

He examined his repair work on the lock and was apparently satisfied.

'I don't know what normally goes on in five star places like this, ma'am, but why no one came to see what was happening in here last night beats me.'

She tried to smile but guessed it was more like a grimace. 'In this city it probably pays to keep out of other people's business. Have you had any breakfast?'

'First in the dining room, ma'am. With these help-yourself-jobs it's the only way. I told the head waiter you wouldn't be needing any breakfast.'

He glanced around the room. 'You would never have known last night's fracas had taken place,' he murmured.

She fixed her eyes on him. 'It never did, Bill, remember that.'

166

He looked at the bed, then the door. 'I shall never forget it, ma'am. The dirty bastard wants locking up, I don't care if he is a superintendent.'

'It's my decision, Bill.' She perched on the edge of the bed, then changed her mind and settled into an easy chair. 'You've probably punished him enough already.'

'Last night I wanted to kill him.'

'I'm glad you didn't, we need him to help us catch the bombers.'

'He tried to rape you. I'm surprised you want to be on the same planet as him. Can't we do our own enquiries?'

She looked at the door and frowned, certain she had heard the clink of cutlery. 'I'd like to but unfortunately we need his local knowledge and his contacts with MI5. Let's just play him along and see what happens. There's nothing he can come up with which we can't handle.'

'Before last night I might have agreed with you,' Bannister said, before going into the bathroom.

The door of the bedroom opened and a man with a smiling black face and gold buttons on his blue uniform wheeled in a hot food trolley. James, carrying a worn briefcase, followed. He walked awkwardly, as if in considerable pain, but there were no obvious marks from his fight last night. Bannister must have had enough sense to hit him in the body, she decided.

'I hope you don't mind,' James said warily. 'I thought you might prefer to eat in your own room.' Feeling faint, she gripped the arms of the chair to stop herself shaking. She couldn't bear to look at him and realised how difficult working with him was going to be. Perhaps Bannister was right.

James stood quietly in the centre of the room until the waiter had left.

'I'm sorry,' he cried, as soon as they were alone. 'I don't know what came over me.' She didn't move. 'I'd missed you - wanted you.' he went on. 'I know what I did was wrong but it was because you're something special to me.' He paused, as if hoping for some response that would ease his guilt.

Forcing herself to look at him, she said nothing; he deserved to suffer.

'I would never have hurt you for the world, Molly. We were friends, more than friends, we were lov...' The toilet flushed and Bannister filled the bathroom door.

James stepped backwards. 'I didn't...'

'...Realise he was here?' she asked.

'Yes.'

'You sent for us both. As you now know, we're a team.'

'I'm sorry,' croaked James.

She gestured to Bannister and he sat on the edge of the bed, watching his adversary with obvious contempt.

'Sit down,' she said to James. 'I have something to say to you.'

Hands gripping his chest, like a man suffering from cracked ribs, he leant forward and pulled a hard chair from under a writing bureau. He was wearing smart grey

168

flannels, a blue blazer, white shirt and a ruby red silk tie. Despite his obvious discomfort, he looked more like the Scotland Yard detective she remembered.

She was distracted by the sound of teeth crunching through fried bread and watched for a moment as Bannister filled a plate with his second breakfast.

'Shame to waste it, ma'am,' he said, piling scrambled egg onto rashers of bacon.

She turned her attention back to James who was perched apprehensively on the hard chair, like a sixth former expecting a bad report. 'I'll never forget last night,' she began, marvelling at her calmness. 'You defiled me, disgusted me, and destroyed any respect I had for you.' She caught her breath. 'But I've decided to take matters no further, at the moment, because it's no one else's damn business.'

Bannister burped loudly in the background and she silently cursed him for spoiling the dramatic impact of her words. 'I want to leave this place,' she continued, 'and never see you again. But I've a job to do here and I intend to carry on, with or without your help.'

James looked side-ways at Bannister, clearly not at ease in his company. 'I'll do my best to make it up to you, Molly.'

'That won't be necessary,' she said firmly. 'I don't need any favours from you, just co-operation of Scotland Yard.'

Some of the colour had returned to his face. She assumed it was because he realised she wasn't going to report him to the Police Complaints Bureau.

'I'll help in any way I can,' he said quietly.

Bannister noisily dropped his plate onto the trolley and burped again.

James, undoubtedly in pain, gasped as he picked up his worn briefcase. '...An urgent meeting, I'm afraid.' He stopped at the door. 'I should be back in an hour or so. There's something important I have to tell you - about Captain Standish.'

24

Bannister, protesting loudly at having to leave her alone, had gone to do some enquiries at the Criminal Record Office when James returned.

Having decided to blank out everything that had ever happened between them so she could treat him as a virtual stranger, Molly told him to sit on the hard chair some distance away from her.

'You said you had to discuss Captain Standish with me.'

He bit his lower lip, something she hadn't seen him do before. 'It's bad news, I'm afraid, Molly.'

'Go on,' she said, anxiety overriding her anger.

He avoided her eyes. 'I wanted to tell you before but was advised not to.'

'By *Snake Eyes,* I suppose.'

'If you mean Richard, yes. He's some kind of expert; interviewing, interrogation, that sort of thing.'

'MI5?'

He nodded.

'What's the bad news?'

'Standish is dead.' Now the words came in a rush. 'It happened mid-morning yesterday. People in the street heard shots. Four men ran from a house, raced across the road, then dived into a tube station. He was found in the hallway, near to the door.'

Feeling as though she'd been kicked in the stomach by a horse, she held her mouth and fled to the bathroom.

When she returned, James told her what he knew about the shooting. The premises, an IRA safe house in north London, had been under surveillance for a week. According to intelligence reports, something big was coming up and Lagan was expected to arrive at any time. *Lagan,* he explained, was a title the Anti-Terrorist Branch had given to the IRA Mainland Commander.

'Why didn't your surveillance team pick up the four men?' she asked.

'They were some distance away - in a high-rise flat. If we had known someone was going to storm the place we would have staked it out.'

'The Captain was a good man,' she said, suddenly realising she didn't even know his first name. Tears filled her eyes and she lowered her head, unwilling to share her distress. She wanted to hide in a dark cupboard and sob her heart out. She felt guilty. She'd used him, and when he had called out for help, she'd ignored him. What kind of a woman was she, for heaven's sake?

She wiped her eyes and looked up. She would grieve later, in the solitude. Right now, she needed answers.

'Has anyone been in touch with the Army?'

'No, we're keeping it tight. You're the only one I can trust who's been close to him recently.'

'I don't understand any of this,' she said. 'My

instincts tell me the letter bomb campaign is a classic IRA operation but no one is allowed to say so. My own Chief has spirited away evidence and said we must not even suggest they are involved.'

James shifted in his chair. 'The peace process moves on.'

'Like hell, it does; people are being blasted to bits all over the place.'

'I'm just doing my job, Molly. I had to obtain a full intelligence profile on Standish.'

'Why?'

'There were several reasons.'

'Was the information vital to you, or to Snake Eyes?'

'Both. Richard is one of the best men in MI5.'

'Is he married?'

'Why do you ask?'

She shrugged. 'It's a woman's question, I suppose. I'd feel safer if I knew he had a normal home life.'

'What's normal these days? He's a confirmed bachelor, and he breeds bull terriers with his brother. They do quite well at the dog shows, so I'm told.'

'I still don't trust him. Does he know anything about you and me?' The moment she spoke she realised her carefully thought out strategy for dealing with James had fallen to pieces already. There were too many memories and the past could not be wiped away so easily.

'Richard isn't aware of our few days in the Cotswolds, if that's what you're getting at,' he replied.

She glanced at the large bed with the blue patterned

duvet. 'You didn't answer my question.'

'I doubt it,' he said lamely. Still suffering from Bannister's punches, he rose stiffly from his chair and walked over to the pseudo Victorian fireplace. 'This enquiry is so hush hush my department doesn't even have a name. Anyone who wants to contact us has to ask for Room Six. We'll have to change that soon - before it becomes a label.'

'What's so important?'

He looked down at the glass coals in the brass fire basket. She didn't know whether he was searching for the right words or undecided how much to tell her.

'We have a mole at Scotland Yard,' he said. 'A very senior police officer who's been feeding information to the IRA for some time.'

'Good God,' she exclaimed, understanding his reluctance to tell her earlier. 'But what has this got to do with the Captain?'

'He knew about the safe house and probably that Lagan was expected. I have to find out how he obtained such highly classified information?'

'...Which could only have come from the Mole?'

'Right. Whoever he is - it's my job to catch him. He's the reason why control of IRA investigations was taken away from Special Branch and given to MI5.'

'So the Government can use MI5 to play their dirty political games, more likely. Many people believe that's why our illustrious leaders engineered the release of the Guildford Four and the Birmingham six. It was the only way they could get Sinn Fein around the table.'

She took a deep breath, warming to her subject. 'It's all a big con. We're being duped because the powers-that-be can no longer afford Northern Ireland and want to get out by any means they can, including cosy chats with convicted killers.'

James looked her directly in the eye for the first time since he had entered the room. 'Tell me why Standish came to London?'

'I don't think it would take a super-brain to work that one out.'

'But he must have been told him where the safe house was.'

'All I know is at about five am yesterday, a Lieutenant Reynolds, Army Security at Lisburn, telephoned the Incident Post and asked the Captain to get back to him. He said it was important.'

'And did he?'

'I assume so.'

'Where did he go?'

'Somewhere on Army business.' It was the first thing she thought of, but it would do - for the moment.

'Tell me about him - please?'

She repeated Joe Grant's story of the torture and death of the Captain's girlfriend. She also mentioned his courage and his need for a drink after he had dis-armed a letter bomb.

'You liked him, didn't you?'

'If you must know, I felt sorry for him. He was a

175

lonely man and his world had crashed. No one could have known what was going on inside his head.'

'He certainly ruined our show; weeks of observations for nothing.'

'Is that all you care about?' she cried, rising to her feet and going to the window. The man who had been sleeping in the park had gone, leaving a newspaper flapping in a rose bush. She looked at the bench and visualised another man lying there, a man dressed in a khaki jumper with its colourful cartoon cat and three gold stars on each shoulder.

'You look dreadful,' James said when she turned to face him.

'That's how I feel.'

'Last night you said you were in the middle of an enquiry. Have you got a lead on the bombers?'

She glared at him, shocked that he could mention last night so casually when the very thought of it sent shivers down her back. 'I'm not sure.'

'Tell me?'

She studied his handsome face. He'd entered the room as the timid miscreant, begging forgiveness. Slowly, his confidence growing, he'd changed so that now he was the shrewd investigator again. But she still saw the contorted face and the glazed eyes. Fortunately the fear had gone; she simply despised him.

She sighed, deeply; working with him was going to be more difficult than she'd imagined.

'Tell me?' he repeated.

She described the incident at the Gloucester service station.

'What makes you think the same men were involved with the letter bombs?' he asked when she had finished.

'Just a hunch. The timings are right. Their car looked lived in. Snippets of info' I picked up from the Murder Enquiry Room at Gloucester. Tomorrow, me and Bill Bannister are going to see the Office Manager. He should have received the lab reports by now.'

'You'd do better staying here,' James said. 'Lagan dropped the four men off near to the safe house.'

'Who told you that?'

'A Dublin informant. He also told us that after they shot Standish, the gang holed up at another place in the city.'

'Where?'

'We're still searching for them.'

'How did they get from the service station to London?'

'We're not sure.'

'What do you mean?'

'We followed the Rover from Belfast. It had been tagged. GCHQ Cheltenham, NSA satellites; you know the system. Unfortunately, because of a technical fault, we lost the car north of Westhampton and didn't pick it up again until they were driving past Stratford upon Avon. After their long stop at the service station, the suspects switched vehicles and we followed four stooges in the Rover as far as Torquay before we realised it was a decoy.'

It took her some time to find her voice. 'You lost them *twice*?' she exclaimed.

'The Anti-Terrorist Squad did, yes.'

'And are you now telling me that you allowed the bombers to smuggle letter bombs onto the mainland and post them in Westhampton?'

'Yes.'

'D'you know how many people they've killed and maimed?' she shouted at him. 'Christ, a little baby was shredded and at least a dozen bodies are laid out in mortuaries all over the country.'

His composure cracked. 'I keep telling you, woman,' he shouted back at her. 'If we don't get to Lagan soon, there'll be many more. We must stop him and find out who his contact is at Scotland Yard.'

'Who decides? Come on, *God!* When are you going to stop the killings?' She knew she was screaming but she didn't care any more. 'Go on, tell me: is it twenty lives, thirty lives or how many flaming lives?'

'You're distraught.'

'Of course I'm distraught. Not only are you a rapist, you're a mass bloody murderer; what the hell do you do for an encore?'

'Molly,' he said, rising to his feet.

'Go away - I hate you!'

25

'Four days stuck in a stinking car; now we're locked up in a pissing ice box,' Coster grumbled. His unshaven face was ashen and he blew on his hands in a hopeless attempt to warm them. The dingy bedsit had no heating and wood rot had jammed open the top half of the sash window, leaving a space big enough for a cat to crawl through.

Sean McKindon leaned against the pink door. All the woodwork was pink, as if to divert attention from the mould colonising the tattered brown wallpaper.

'You didn't have to empty a whole magazine into the man. He was history; a head shot from Danny.'

Coster used the back of his hand to wipe bread crumbs from the corners of his mouth. 'Danny, Danny, fucking Danny! That's all I ever hear.'

'He clocked the crazy man's gun as he charged through the door.'

'Who the hell was he?' Coster asked. 'And how come he knew where to find us?'

Sean glared at his explosives expert. 'All I know is you nearly brought the cops down on us.'

Coster rose stiffly from the rickety old card table where he had eaten a late breakfast of bread and jam. 'I need some hot food and a drink, this place is doing my head in.' He kicked the wall, knocking a hole in the plaster. 'The West End and Piccadilly, with all the booze and hairy pie a man could wish for, is just down the sodding road.' He gave the wall another kick.

'Stop that!' Sean ordered. 'D'you want the landlady poking about?'

'Poking.' Coster laughed derisively. 'That's it, I need to poke the silly cow in the gob.' He gave the wall another kick. 'And she wasn't too happy about letting us stay here either. Not until she saw the size of your roll, she wasn't.'

'She'll be okay, if we don't cause her any bother.'

Coster returned to his seat, digging Danny McKindon in the ribs as he passed the cast iron bed.

'Ger'off,' cried Danny, rolling over and burying his head under a grubby pillow.

Mahmoud, lying on the other half of the bed, stared at the ceiling as if in a trance.

'I can't stay in this dump much longer,' Coster moaned. 'We may as well be locked up in pissing H Block.'

Sean moved away from the door to look out of the window. 'Lagan said we're to sit tight until he makes contact again.'

'Yeah. And who's he, I'd like to know? And how come we're being bossed about by a bloody Brit? He's a right pillock if you ask me.'

'He's in charge. Remember that if you want to get

out of this lot alive.'

Sean returned to the door. 'We've just got to wait until we know what the next job is.'

'And how are we supposed to get out of this lousy country? A load of dough is no fucking use if we're dead.'

'A motor boat will be moored near to the target. We'll be down the Thames and on our way to Buenos Aires within hours.'

'In a *motor boat*?'

'No, idiot. A container ship will pick us up in the English Channel.'

Coster's top lip curled. 'How come you know so much all of a bleedin' sudden?'

'I told you, I'm clued into some of it.'

'Yeah, a fucking lot, if you ask me. Enough to make sure you and your half-brained fucking brother are all right.'

Sean lunged across the room and held Coster by the throat, tightening his grip until the man's face turned puce and his eyes bulged. 'One more crack like that and I'll choke the miserable life out of you.'

Less than a mile away, Molly opened her eyes and saw the gold drapes and pink carnations of her hotel room. She checked the clock-radio: it was twelve noon. James must have stopped the cleaners.

What a disaster her trip to London had turned out to be. The horror of last night, the shock of the Captain's death, then the realisation that James could have prevented so many deaths. She'd cried herself to sleep; something she hadn't done since the day her parents were murdered.

Did she break down because the man she once loved had attacked her and later admitted to being partly responsible for the letter bomb explosions or because she felt guilty about the Captain's death?

Restless, and in need of air, she opened the door of her room. Leaning against the corridor wall was a slim, blonde haired young woman with a pretty face and a figure that would have won a beauty contest in most small towns. She was wearing faded jeans and a black leather jacket; the uniform, or so it seemed, of all Met women detectives.

She invited her inside.

Stuffing a grubby paperback into a canvas duffle bag, the young woman walked past her into the room.

'I'm sure you know who I am,' Molly said, shaking her hand. 'Are you my bodyguard or my keeper?'

'Detective Hartley, ma'am. Cran - Mr Cranleigh-Smythe asked me to keep an eye on you until he came back.'

'Did he say when that was likely to be?' The detective's expression made it plain he hadn't. 'Good. I need to get out of this room,' she continued. 'Where do all the best tourists go?'

'I think he expected you to stay here, ma'am.'

'Tough! You can either follow me and use it as a

surveillance exercise or we can go walk-about together and enjoy ourselves.'

DC Hartley smiled. 'The day out will be easier, thank you, ma'am.'

'What's your first name?' she asked, knowing she was going to like the detective.

'Lynda, ma'am. A trip along the Thames is nice at this time of the day. The catamaran from Charing Cross Pier to Greenwich is the best.'

They sat at the back of the lower deck, where they could see everyone but not be disturbed. The other passengers, cam corders held shoulder high, scrambled eagerly up the steps to the top deck.

As the boat pulled away from the pier, spots of rain pebbled the portholes.

Soon they were passing the Tower of London, its Union Jack billowing in a light breeze. She'd always been fascinated by the Tower's history and knew that many nobles, mostly accused of treason, had been incarcerated and tortured in its dungeons. Anne Boleyn, Queen of England, had spent her last days there before she was beheaded on Tower Green.

Lynda, too familiar with London's landmarks to be interested in the Tower of London, went to the bar and bought large gin and tonics.

A cockney accent boomed over the loudspeakers as the First Mate described interesting public houses on both sides of the river whilst paying scant regard to other buildings of historical interest.

'Tell me about your work,' she said to the detective during a break in the commentary.

'I've only recently joined the department, ma'am - if you can call it that. I moved over from Obscene Publications. It's mostly hanging about and none of us know what's happening. Which is the way it's going to stay, according to Cranny.'

'What's he like?'

'He's a nice enough bloke,' Lynda replied guardedly.

'I knew him once,' Molly said, realising she'd have to open up a bit if she was going to find out anything else about James. 'Only he's changed.'

'I can't talk about my work, ma'am, but the guys at the office say he didn't volunteer for this job and he's had a shitty deal. The top brass don't like him because his old man's stinking rich and a big wheel at the Stock Exchange. Cranny's also having a load of grief from MI5. Ruthless bastards they are, ma'am. The guy you met last night would have been over qualified for Hitler's SS.'

When they returned to the hotel, Bannister was waiting for them in the foyer. A head taller than the chattering Far Eastern visitors milling around him, he was easy to spot.

'I've been looking everywhere for you, ma'am. The Yard denied any knowledge of you, even when I told them that they were paying the bill.'

She smiled. The river trip and the gin had refreshed her. '*Especially* when you told them they were paying the bill. Have you eaten yet?'

'No, ma'am. I was waiting for you,'

'Good. Take Lynda to dinner, please, Bill; she's earned it. And don't forget to charge it to our account.'

Chest expanding like a bullfrog's in the mating season, a wide grin split his face. 'Anything for the job, ma'am.'

26

Molly returned to her hotel room and found James sleeping soundly in an easy chair. Things must be catching up with him, she decided.

He shivered violently and woke up.

Too late to slip away unnoticed, she made hot drinks.

'I'll have to go,' she said, handing him a steaming cup.

Sleepy-eyed, he stood up and stretched. 'Why?'

'Because I don't want to be in this room with you a moment longer than I have to, and I've got to find a gang of bombers.'

'They're in this city; I told you.'

'You've said a lot of things. Where are they?'

'We're still trying to find out. Whatever they've got planned, it's going to happen on Friday.'

'How do you know?'

'It was mentioned in the service station restaurant. We taped their conversation.'

She sat down next to the writing desk. 'Is this Lagan chap worth so much grief?'

'In retrospect, of course not. We simply have no other way of getting to the Mole.'

Nothing was said for a few moments and for the first time since she'd entered the hotel she heard the hum of London's traffic. 'Do you trust Richard?'

'Some. We're both after Lagan and the Mole. He's trying to sneak in ahead of me but I can live with that. It's all part of the power struggle; MI5 trying to prove they're better at dealing with terrorists than we are.'

She rose, her mind made up. 'If the bombers are going to strike on Friday we've still got the rest of today and tomorrow to catch them. I think we should get things moving.'

'Yes,' he replied, clearly still unsure of himself. 'Why don't we go to my HQ. I'll show you the set up?'

'Why not? It might take my mind off something I want to forget.'

James parked his car outside a Georgian style house in a small square of similar properties. Black iron railings protected paved areas on both sides of the front doorstep. Plants trailing from window boxes cast shadows on whitewashed brickwork.

'Unobtrusive I think you'd call it,' he said, working hard to repair their fragile relationship. It's surely that, she thought.

They entered the Operations Room and she was introduced to busy detectives and computer operators.

Lynda Hartley was using a monitor to call up pictures of known terrorists and Bill Bannister, sitting unnecessarily close, was being very attentive.

The dinner must have been a success, she decided, suspecting Bill Bannister was about to have another complication in his stormy sex life.

Two hours later, she was in a taxi heading towards Woolwich and the Queen Elizabeth Military Hospital. She was dropped off at the back door where Sister Parker, a robust, grey haired woman with apple-red cheeks and friendly eyes was waiting for her.

The Sister helped her to change into a nurses uniform. 'It's the men's ward you should be visiting,' she said. 'You'd make them feel a lot better - or worse maybe.'

Molly was more concerned about her own feelings. She'd posed as a prostitute, thief, receiver and drug dealer but never as a nurse. Plumping up pillows, taking temperatures and fixing drips was not what she did; and the very thought of a mucky bedpan made her cringe.

'What's Gina's condition?' she asked.

'Not too bad. But her face is an unholy mess and it's affecting her mind.'

'What are you doing about it - her mind?'

'That's up to the psychiatrist. It's going to be a long haul and she'll need a lot of support from family and friends.'

'Can she speak?'

'No.'

Taking a deep breath, she prepared for the worst.

'Come on, *Nurse Smith*. You'll do just fine,' said

the Sister. 'Let's go and fool those big buffoons who are cluttering up my nice clean hospital. Keep your mouth shut and let me do the talking.'

Crossing a deserted lobby, they approached a door guarded by two uniformed police officers wearing body armour and carrying 9mm Browning pistols. Both officers acknowledged them and stood aside as they passed through the door.

Now in a short corridor, the Sister spoke to two MI5 guards, telling them that they were making too much noise and disturbing her patient.

They glanced briefly at the new night nurse, murmured an apology, then moved further down the corridor.

After the Sister had left her in Gina's small, dimly-lit room, she approached the bed. It wasn't a person she had to interview, but a red-eyed ball of bandage.

'Gina,' she said quietly. 'Can you hear me?'

The blood-shot eyes moved, and a hand on the bedcover signalled that she could. She then picked up a pencil and scribbled on a note pad: *Who are you?*

'A friend.'

The pencil moved erratically across lined paper: *I don't talk to the filth.*

'I might be able to help you,' she said cautiously.

Gina shifted slightly in the bed and there was a stifled scream. Her eyes closed and then opened. Tears with nowhere else to go, soaked into bandage.

Bannister and Hartley, arm in arm and slightly the worse for drink, stepped out of Shutter's Bar into the garish bright lights of Piccadilly Circus. Huge illuminated advertising signs gave the whole area an unreal, every-day-is-Christmas atmosphere. It was the West End's busiest hour. Theatre-goers spilled onto the pavements and headed for their favourite restaurants, nightclubs or casinos.

'Hub of the universe,' Lynda yelled cheerfully above the roar of the traffic.

Bannister gripped a parking meter to steady himself, slipping his other hand around her waist. 'Where next, my beautiful, sensuous Isabella?'

'Fool,' she laughed. 'Let's go back to your swank hotel.' Hands in the air, she stood on her toes to catch the attention of a passing taxi driver. The black cab pulled up but Bannister yanked her away from the kerb. 'Hey!' she cried. 'I've got us wheels.'

'Shut it,' he hissed, suddenly cold sober. 'The three guys who just passed us are Irish.'

She laughed in his face. 'So are half the drinkers in London.'

'I'm sure one of them was the big guy you showed me at your HQ,' he persisted, holding onto her arm.

She stared at him for a moment, her joyous mood evaporating in the cold night air. 'You'd better be right, Bill Bannister...I'd got plans for you. I'll take the other side of the road, we'll alternate at the junctions.'

One of the men they were following stopped to light

190

a cigarette and Bannister saw his face for the first time. There were long scratch marks down his right cheek. *The service station*, he thought excitedly. He started to sweat. Molly Watson was right; the four men were the Westhampton bombers and one of them was a rapist.

A mile further on, the three men drifted into narrow back streets fed by a network of dark passages. Prostitutes loitered on corners. Punters, wary of vice patrols, cruised by in their company cars. This must be the old London, he thought, glancing across the road to make sure that Lynda was all right. Could Jack the Ripper have prowled these same street in search of his next victim?

He closed up to the targets in time to see them turn down a narrow entry at the side of an old terraced house.

Sean, in a darkened bedroom, looked through a gap in the curtains at the street below. 'It's the filth, I'm sure of it,' he said to the men behind him. 'The bird's gone for backup.'

Danny groaned. 'How did they know we were here?'

'It's got to be that cowin' landlady,' Coster said. 'I saw her at tea time. Eying us up, so she was. There'd been a bit on the news about Westhampton and four dangerous Irishmen.'

Sean asked his brother to switch on the light. The bed springs creaked as Mahmoud sat up and rubbed his eyes.

'Why fuck have you put the light on?' Coster yelled in alarm.

'Because that's what we're supposed to be doing,' Sean replied. 'We'll put it out in a few minutes and they'll think we've turned in for the night. That way they won't raid the place until dawn.'

'We're trapped,' Danny whined.

'Not if we get a move on,' Sean said. 'We can nip out of the back while the cops are still sorting themselves out.'

'After I've silenced that fucking landlady,' Coster muttered.

Sean looked doubtful. 'There's no need. She probably didn't hear us come in and, if we're quiet, she won't hear us leave.'

'The rotten bastard tipped off the filth, didn't she? When she's finished watching the box she'll be up here to check the rooms.'

Sean glanced at the door, he didn't have time to argue. 'All right. Just keep her quiet long enough for us to get well away from here. Danny, you go with him while me and Mahmoud watch the street.'

Coster and Danny stopped outside the landlady's room. They could hear the television.

'Stay!' Coster hissed, pointing to the side of the door.

'Sean said I was to be with you,' Danny whispered.

Coster pushed him against the wall, then pressed the

flat of his divers knife across Danny's lips. 'Now, fat pig,' he snarled, 'if I have one more squeak out of you, I'll cut off your skinny cock. Stand here and wait for me.'

Eyes wide with fright, he nodded. Coster released him.

'Come in,' called the landlady in answer to his sharp tap on the door. 'It ain't locked.'

27

Molly's taxi sped through London's quiet streets. Lofty red buses had not picked up their first passengers and newsagents were still removing metal grills from their shop fronts.

Before leaving the hotel, she'd knocked on Bannister's door but there had been no reply. Did he spend the night at Lynda Hartley's place, she wondered.

Entering James's Headquarters, she knew immediately that she was wrong; the two detectives were in the Operations Room.

'The terrorists are holed up in a house!' Bannister called out as soon as he saw her.

'How come?'

'We caught them; me and Lynda.'

Hartley shook her head. 'It's all down to, Bill.'

'You always said I was a jammy so-and-so, ma'am.'

'Why, it's fabulous!' she beamed, a flood of euphoria sweeping through her as she realised their job was almost done. What a triumph to take back to Westhampton. She shook Hartley's hand, then playfully thumped Bannister's broad chest. 'I said you'd never look back once you joined the Bomb Squad.'

He laughed happily, then explained what had

happened since they followed the three men from Piccadilly Circus.

'Everybody's geared up and ready to jump the place, ma'am,' he said finally.

She looked at a large wall map of London. A house in the top half was flagged, **Stronghold**. Around the stronghold someone had drawn a red circle and marked it, **Inner Cordon**. Further out, and encompassing the inner cordon, a blue circle was labelled, **Outer Cordon**. Men in combat kit stood in front of the map and argued tactics.

A row of constables dealt with incoming telephone calls. Food and drink was being ferried between work stations by a cadet who kept bumping into people. Messages spewed out of the fax machine. An inspector and a sergeant crowded the computer operator and followed the progress of the incident as actions flicked across the monitor screen.

In the centre of the room, a superintendent held a microphone to his mouth and spoke to the ground commander outside the stronghold.

'You've been up all night, Bill,' she said thoughtfully. 'I think you and Lynda should go and get some rest.'

Lynda's tired eyes brightened but Bill was plainly shocked by the suggestion. 'The gov'nor said we could stay,' he protested. 'As long as we keep our heads down when the shooting starts.'

'There'll be no shooting,' said James as he strode

into the room with Richard. 'The raid's off.' The Superintendent seemed about to argue but James handed him a slip of paper. 'I'm sorry,' he said. 'Ring that number if you need confirmation.'

Groans of disappointment sounded around the room. Everyone had been called out in the middle of the night and now their hard work was for nothing.

At 8 am control of the Operations Room reverted to James's people.

He approached her. 'Sorry, Molly. We've got to let the men inside that house lead us to Lagan and, ultimately, the Mole.'

'Stuff them!' she shouted. 'You've already let my bombers escape twice. If they get away again, it'll be for keeps.' She was too angry to notice the startled looks of the people around her; some hardly able to conceal their delight, others embarrassed for James.

His voice was ice cold. 'Come with me, Inspector.' Grabbing her arm, he frog-marched her out of the building.

'Let go of me!' she protested, pulling away from him.

'No,' he said sternly. Tightening his grip, he bundled her into his car, then drove into Thursday morning's commuter traffic.

'It's time you learnt to button it,' he said angrily. 'That temper of yours could get a lot of people into serious trouble.'

Shaking with indignation, she dropped back into her seat. He could be God Almighty in the Met, but he wasn't her boss.

He left the car on a meter, then ushered her into Hyde Park. She didn't object, she had plenty to say to him.

He hurried along a narrow pathway and she matched him stride for stride. He'd soon recovered from his beating, she decided, wishing Bannister had hit him harder.

They stopped at a small paved square surrounded by empty bench seats.

'You were out of order back there and I think you know it,' he said between clenched teeth. A man wearing a flat cap approached and James set off across the grass. She fell in beside him, not caring that the dew soaked into her shoes.

When they had distanced themselves from the flat cap, he stopped again.

'I'm about to tell you something that's so incredible few people would believe it,' he said. 'Captain Standish was brought back to the mainland during a tour of Northern Ireland to lead a covert operation. Something that would cause the press to scream *Whitehallgate* and our partners in Europe to boot us out of the Union...'

'The Captain was a better man than y...'

'He packed tons of Semtex behind the walls of the Channel Tunnel.'

She caught her breath. 'It's mined, you mean?'

He glanced at a park patrolman, then nodded.

'The Captain would never do such a stupid thing, for goodness sake?'

'He was a soldier; trained to follow orders.'

'Who's orders?'

'Who was running the country when the Tunnel was being dug out?'

'Maggie Thatcher.'

'And who's now expressing fears about Europe being dominated by Germany?'

'Maggie Thatcher.'

'That's right, and she would have mentioned her concern to others; close friends, Cabinet colleagues, those sort of people.'

'And you think they authorised the Semtex?'

'That's my guess, and without telling the Prime Minister. They would want to protect her in case it got out.'

'And these friends of the PM would have given instructions to MI5?'

'Verbally, yes. I doubt whether more that a handful of people in the whole country know about it.'

'Why did they do it, for goodness sake?'

'So they can cut the umbilical cord in the event of another war. Their fathers and grandfathers fought, and in many cases died, to stop Germans crossing the Channel and invading this country.'

'That's ridiculous,' she exclaimed. 'There couldn't possibly be another war in Europe.'

'Couldn't there? Look what's happened in former Yugoslavia.'

'That's different.'

James looked around him again before speaking. '...Chancellor Kohl has already warned of the possibility of another major war in Europe if the opportunity to build a permanent political and monetary union isn't seized in the next two years.'

'He's just trying to frighten us into agreeing with his policies.' Her face coloured and then paled as she grappled with the implications of what James had told her. 'Do you really think Germany is trying to take over Europe for a third time?'

'I don't know, but it makes you wonder. If they have their way, by the turn of the century, the pound and its nine hundred years history will have been ditched so that this country's finances can be controlled from a bank in Frankfurt.'

'Which will reduce this country to a bit player.'

'Something like that.'

'He looked at her closely. 'Now do you understand when I tell you it's a matter of national security.'

Her legs felt weak and she sat on a bench. 'Why was Captain Standish involved?'

He sat beside her. 'He was the best explosives expert in the country. Two soldiers helped him but they were killed in a road accident shortly after the work had been completed.'

'How convenient. Why didn't MI5 take out the

Captain at the same time?'

'You're being paranoid again, Molly. I'm trying to be straight with you.'

'Like the last time?'

'I wanted to protect you.'

'I don't need protecting.'

'Yes, you do. We all do. By telling you about the Channel Tunnel I might have signed your death warrant.'

'Bit dramatic, aren't we?'

'I'm being serious, Molly. These people play for real; murder's not a problem.'

She shook her head, it was an amazing story. 'What has all this got to do with Lagan and the Mole and, come to think of it, my letter bombs?'

'It's been suggested that Standish had been in touch with an IRA agent with whom he did a trade - the team who killed his girlfriend for details of the Channel Tunnel Operation. With that kind of information Sinn Fein could crucify John Major at the peace talks. Army Intelligence have never heard of a Lieutenant Reynolds. We think the telephone call to your Incident Post was the IRA agent keeping up his end of the bargain.'

'It could have been one of the Captain's army buddies doing him a favour.'

'That's another possibility.'

She watched a man who was picking up litter, certain he had passed them a few minutes earlier. 'The Captain would never betray his country and he hated the IRA.'

'He was out of his mind with grief. In that state, a

man is capable of anything.'

'Are you still going to let the bombers walk out of that house?'

'They're our only lead to Lagan. It's vital we get to him.'

'To stop the killing or because of your precious Mole?'

A pained expression distorted James's features. 'Can't you get it into your stubborn, bolshy head - it's all the same problem.'

'Now the Captain's dead, you'll never know if he talked about the Tunnel.'

'Richard has a man inside the Sinn Fein HQ. Nothing has reached them yet. Either we're wrong or the IRA agent hasn't had an opportunity to pass on the information. He could, of course, be Lagan; Lagan or the Mole.'

They stood up together and walked on, her mind still working furiously. 'What triggered off the enquiry?'

'Several weeks ago, Standish was drunk in a Hereford bar, shouting his mouth off about the IRA. He said that he would stuff them all into the Channel Tunnel, block off both ends, then press the button. Your Captain was quite an act when his vocal cords were well oiled.'

'He wasn't *my* Captain,' she protested.

James stared at the dull leather of his wet shoes. 'I had to assess his reliability, MI5 thought he was a security risk.'

'And you dragged me down to Scotland Yard and

tried to screw me in the hope that I'd tell you something about him. As my old DI used to say, *there's three ways to get information, someone gives it to you, you pay for it, or you fuck for it.*'

'That's unfair.'

'Too flaming right it's unfair; it's despicable. I thought you were better than that - once.'

'Molly, listen to me, please...I didn't want you involved in all this. I had to do it. The orders came from the very top.'

'That's your trouble, James, you're too ready to do what other people tell you. We had something good going but to please your mother you wrote that letter and ruined it all.'

Looking cold and wretched, he scanned the park, then concentrated on a man using binoculars to study a holly tree. 'Someone else has been asking questions about Standish's involvement in a secret Government operation; someone in the civil service gay community.'

'I didn't know there was such a thing.'

'They're very well organised. Partly self-protection, mostly self-interest. It's a better way of climbing the ladder than the Masons these days.'

'Not another gang of men dressing up in aprons and reciting gobbledygook?'

'That isn't funny, Molly.'

'I didn't mean it to be. Did MI5 set up the Captain?'

'What do you mean?'

'Had him tipped him off that the men he was after

were in the safe house, knowing full well he would high-tail it down here and get himself killed.'

'Surrogate murderers? I don't think so. You've been reading too many thrillers.'

'After this lot, I'll write my own.'

He continued to watch the man with the binoculars.

'Bird watcher?' she asked.

'You can never be sure, there's more fruit and nut cases around here than in California.' A group of yelling school children skipped past them. 'Do you understand everything now?' he asked.

She looked at the man she had once loved and surprised herself by feeling some sympathy for him. He wasn't an evil man, she knew that. Like the rest of us, she thought, he's being used. Manipulated by powerful people so they can sleep at night, sure that their reputations were intact.

'I never imagined... ' she said quietly.

'How could you?' He reached for her hand, then changed his mind. 'Just be on my side, please.'

She watched two dogs fighting and their agitated owners trying to separate them. 'One thing still bothers me. Why is the Government talking peace when they must know a murdering IRA active service unit is loose on the mainland?'

James moved forward a few paces and kicked at the gravel. 'The official word is they're not IRA.'

'Then who the hell are they?'

'I don't know,' he replied, leading the way through

Albert Gate and into Knightsbridge where his car was parked.

She spoke to James as he pulled away from the kerb. 'After I left your Operations Room last night, I went to the hospital to see Gina Jones.'

'The woman who was injured in the MP's place?'

'Yes.'

'Richard wouldn't even tell me where she was being treated. How did you find out?'

'I have my sources.'

'Another informant no one knows about?'

'Perhaps.'

'How is Gina?'

'She should be on her feet soon enough, but it will be years before she feels the sun on her cheeks.'

'What do you mean?'

'Her face will have to be completely rebuilt.'

'Can she talk?'

'She can write. She's an IRA undercover agent and has been working in Whitehall offices and the Houses of Parliament for two years. She wouldn't admit it but I think she had something to do with getting the names and addresses for the letter bombs.'

'One of which nearly killed her.'

'Yes. She's convinced her controller tried to get rid of her at the same time as the MP.'

'Did she say why?'

'Because she's of no further use to the IRA, they

didn't want to pay the huge bonus they'd promised her, and she's a security risk.'

'Who is this nice controller?'

'She doesn't know. He only spoke to her over the phone. Stolen or copied documents were dropped through letterboxes at different addresses.'

'She must know something about him.'

'She describes him as a cold, sarcastic devil who spoke like the men she worked for in Whitehall.'

'It isn't much.'

'Give me time and I'll get closer to her. Apparently she was due to go home on the day of the explosion and has a large sum of money and some jewellery stashed away.'

They drove down the ramp into Scotland Yard's car park, then went to Room Six.

James made several telephone calls, checked his messages, fed information into the computer, then switched them to coded terminals elsewhere in the building.

'Right, breakfast,' he said, more like his old self.

The telephone buzzed. He picked it up and listened intently for a few moments.

Without warning, he cried out and leaned across his desk, open hands covering his face. The telephone dangled beside him.

She waited, resisting a natural urge to put a comforting arm around his shoulders.

When he sat up and spoke, she could hardly hear

him. 'The terrorists have escaped...' His voice broke and she waited again. '...My team found the house empty, except for the landlady. She was in bed - floating in a pool of blood.'

28

Molly referred to her pocket book, then told the driver of
the un-marked police car to stop outside a large house.

The red bricks were weathered and needed pointing
but a row of splendid chimneys and a walled garden gave
notice that the property had once belonged to someone
wealthy.

Walking past a neglected rose bed and an over-
grown lawn, she reached the entrance. The illuminated
list of residents included the name **G Jones.**

She took a Mickey Mouse keyring out of her bag,
guessing rightly which key opened the front door. After
the drab exterior she was surprised to find the inside of
the building bright and well cared for. Moving swiftly up
a wide curving staircase to the first floor, she let herself
into Gina's apartment.

'Christ!' she exclaimed. The room was a shambles;
ornaments smashed, clothing torn, pictures ripped out of
frames; nothing had been spared. Floorboards were
propped against the walls and holes had been poked into
the ceiling so that plaster dust covered everything.

'Don't move!' ordered a gravelly voice.

She turned and faced a grey-haired man who had
once been tall and straight but was now bent and twisted

with arthritis, the pain written large in the lines of his face.

'Who are you?'

He stepped closer. 'That's my question.'

'I'm a friend of Gina's.'

'So's the butcher, but he doesn't walk into her apartment when he feels like it.'

She produced her warrant card.

He studied her photograph, then squinted at the small print. 'Strayed off your patch, haven't you, Inspector? I was at an RAF camp near to Westhampton in the war.'

'I'm investigating a serious crime and need some answers. We can talk here or go down to the local police station.'

He straightened his RAF tie. 'My apartment's on the ground floor. It comes rent free because I look after the other tenants. My old squadron leader owns most of the street.'

She looked at the mess around her. 'Have you reported this?'

'No. Gina made me promise I'd never talk about her to anyone, not even you people. I keep watch on her place when she's away; water the pot plants, that sort of thing. She's very kind. Always giving me presents. Gilbey's mostly. I started drinking after we'd flattened Dresden and haven't been able to give it up since. I flew Wellington bombers, you see, miss.'

'Tell me about her?'

He shook his head. 'Sorry. You can take me down

to the station it won't make any difference. A chap's already been asking questions.'

'What about?' she demanded, trying to keep the excitement out of her voice.

'I can't tell you,' he replied doggedly.

'Not about Gina, the man asking the questions?'

'Oh, him. He wanted to have a look at this apartment.'

'What was he like?'

'Ordinary looking sort of a bloke. A bit intense and not very pleasant. Beggin' your pardon, miss but he had a face like an old turd. One of my rear gunner's favourite expressions - before he was blasted by a Fokker-Wolf over the North Sea.'

'What happened?'

'Spitfire got the Jerry and we limped home...'

'The man asking about Gina?'

'I sent him packing. That was before this room was blitzed. Feel terrible about it, I do. As if I've let her down. I should have suspected something like this was going to happen and doubled my rounds.' He scanned the wreckage. 'It's got to be the same chap; shifty-eyed bugger he was. I never trust a man who can't look you in the eye. Very important, the eyes, miss. That's how I could tell when one of my air crew had got the jitters and wouldn't last another bombing mission. You could always see it in their eyes.'

'Can you remember anything else about him?'

'Like I said, he was an ordinary looking chap.

Londoner but not East End. Middle-aged. Asked questions like a surgeon cutting out a brain tumour. We had his kind in the RAF; pain in the arse efficiency and no soul. Not the type of bloke you'd go to a Bombay brothel with.'

'What kind of questions?'

'Had anyone been here since Saturday morning? Did I know any of her close friends? What was the name of her bank? Yes, and this should have put me on my guard, did she have a safe deposit box?'

'When did he call?'

'Last Saturday - no - Sunday. I'd been to chapel and it was in the afternoon; while I was watching the Arsenal match.'

'Gina's not been home for five days, did that worry you?'

'Of course, she usually lets me know if she's going to be away for some time.'

'Did the other visitor ask where she was?'

'I didn't tell him anything; even when he got stroppy. Said the ack-ack had affected my brain so I got all mixed up about things, especially under interrogation. He didn't like that; thought I was taking the you-know-what. When I kept on about night raids over Germany, he stormed off in a huff. I thought Gina might want to know who he was so I slipped out after him and got the number of his car.'

Bored with his war stories, she had turned him off. Now her heart was racing. 'Did you keep it - the car number?'

He scratched his head. 'You know, that's the strange thing, I wrote it down on a fag packet but it seems to have gone missing.'

'Have you looked for it?'

'Not really had the time. But I might - if I knew where Gina had got to. Just to have a chat, if you know what I mean.'

She made a quick decision. 'I think I can arrange that. It'll do her good to see a friend.'

'Where is she?'

'In hospital.'

'What happened?'

'It was an accident. Her injuries are serious but she's out of intensive care.'

He started down the stairs. 'I'll get my coat.'

Forty minutes later, when they arrived at the hospital, they were on first name terms and she'd had to listen to Henry *Cats-Eyes* Taylor's entire war record.

'I've cleared your visit with the Sister but you'll have to get past some armed police officers and Government people before you can see Gina,' she said as he climbed out of the car. 'They're worried about security because of the way she was injured.'

He gave her a devilish grin. 'If I put my mind to it, I could con my way into Buckingham Palace.'

'Be careful,' she warned. 'It's her face mostly; burned up in an explosion.'

Henry's eyes blanked for a moment. 'Some of my crew had those kind of injuries. In those days the lucky ones were killed outright.'

He slammed shut the passenger door then opened it again. 'I've just remembered. The man asking questions about Gina; he had three fingers missing from his left hand.'

29

'Really hit the big time, we have,' Coster moaned. 'First the *safe* house stormed by an armed madman, then a flea pit run by a dirty old tart who turned us in, now Gunga Din's fucking curry house.'

Sean wiped condensation off the dirty window and looked out. Storm clouds were moving away, leaving large swathes of blue sky. He glanced across the road. People in the bus queue, representing every race in the world, were still sheltering under a variety of umbrellas and plastic bags. 'This is Brick Lane,' he said. 'A short stroll from the target.'

'Yeah, and that's another thing,' said Coster. 'You tell us it's the most important job we've ever done and now you're saying we've got to leg it. We should go in Cadillacs like the Chicago hats did.'

'They were mobsters - we're soldiers.'

'I bet they knew which fucking target they were going to hit.'

'The boss will be here soon, he'll lead us in.'

'If the Ayatollah downstairs doesn't grass on us first.'

Sean glanced through the window again, then hurried to the door and slid open the bolts at the top and bottom. A medium sized man wearing a dark striped suit strode into the room. Strands of wet hair hung around his ears. It was Lagan.

They were late for lunch and Scotland Yard's self-service canteen was empty.

James, recovering from the shock of losing the terrorists again, pushed away his plate. 'How did it go, Molly?'

She told him about her visit to Gina's apartment and meeting Henry.

James picked up a table knife and idly studied the maker's name. 'The other visitor sounds interesting. Who do you think he was?'

Convinced he was the same man who visited the Queen's Hotel and Bernie's bar on the day of the letter bomb explosions, she didn't trust James enough to tell him yet. 'I don't know, but Henry's got the number of his car.'

James's knife bounced off the table and clattered to the floor. 'Have you checked it out?'

'No. He jotted the number down on the back of a cigarette packet and claims to have mislaid it.'

'I can send a team to turn his place over.'

Her eyes narrowed, perhaps she was wrong. 'Was it one of your lot who broke into Gina's?'

'Now I know you're paranoid.'

'If DVLC refuse to disclose the owner's details, It must be you or MI5.'

His laugh was hollow and insincere. 'If we had searched the place, you wouldn't have known we had been anywhere near. I need that car number, Molly - urgently.'

'Henry has promised to give it to me. He's now at the hospital; seeing Gina.'

'How did he get past MI5?'

'The Sister in charge of the wards could talk her way through a forest fire.'

'Does Henry know Gina well?'

'Like father and daughter. I'd hate to think what a flag waver like him would say if he knew Gina was an IRA spy.'

Her name was called and she went to the telephone. 'Detective Inspector Watson, Scotland Yard.'

A woman laughed. 'Bless my itchy arse, if it isn't our Molly putting on the airs and graces. How are you, cocker?'

Listening to the familiar voice, she felt better. 'Things are not what they seemed to be before I arrived, but I'm getting by.'

'I told you about men, my girl. They'll fuck you and leave you every time. Come back to your old Aunt Bernie and I'll put your mind right, so I will.'

'Why have you rung?'

'Because I said I would.'

'Did you?'

'Hail Mary Mother of God, you've gone and bleedin' forgot. No wonder the other side's taking the piss out of you lot. The queer fellow with the missing fingers.'

'What about him?'

'The big-eared bugger in my place; the one who might have heard what he was gobbing off about.'

'Well?'

'He's back and he's in the bar.'

Her hand tightened around the handset. 'Did he hear anything?'

Bernie laughed. 'Well now, she's back in the land of the living.'

'Tell me!'

'I'm going to, aren't I. There's no need to lose your rag with me, Molly Watson.'

'Sorry.'

'He didn't hear much because three fingers had his tongue down his bum boy's ear most of the time. All he can say is that they both mentioned a tower.'

'A town?' she asked, thinking of Mad Mick's message.

'No, dummy, a tower.'

She stared at the wall for a moment then dropped the handset and shouted across the room - 'It's *THE TOWER*.'

30

Sean and Danny McKindon entered the Tower of London at 3 pm.

Coster and Mahmoud followed ten minutes later.

They were all searched by diligent security guards wielding explosive and metal detectors like magic wands.

Lagan, who had been in the Tower for some time, was seated on a wooden bench in the shadow of the *White Tower*, the limestone central keep that dominated the surrounding buildings.

He didn't need to refer to his well-thumbed guide book. He already knew that the grey stone, castellated building in front of him was the *Waterloo Block* which had once been the barracks for a thousand soldiers. The first and second floors were now offices and the ground floor contained the world's most valuable collection of jewellery.

Between the White Tower and the Waterloo Block, there was a tarmac quadrangle the size of two football pitches end on. This was called the *Broad Walk* and it was lightly peopled by visitors enjoying the mid-afternoon sun.

A group of Beefeaters had gathered outside the Chapel next to the west end of the Waterloo block. They were looking across Tower Green to the Thames and appeared to be waiting for four-thirty, when they could lock up and return to their homes inside the Tower grounds. They were early, Lagan thought, checking his watch: it was three twenty-five.

Sean and Danny McKindon sat down beside him. Keeping an eye on the Beefeaters, he reached under the bench and pulled his holdall closer to him. He then opened it and took out four Pepsi cans and two lunch boxes, dividing them equally between the two men.

The brothers quickly emptied the lunch boxes, rose to their feet and drifted towards the Fusiliers Museum at the east end of the Broad Walk.

Five minutes later, Coster and Mahmoud took their places next to Lagan.

He handed them Pepsi cans and lunch boxes.

Giving Coster a final look of concern, Lagan picked up the holdall and wandered across the Broad Walk to the Waterloo Block where he stood close to the entrance of the Jewel House.

Coster opened his lunch box. Inside, wrapped in wax paper, was a nine millimetre snub-nosed Beretta. Looking around him to make sure he was not being watched, he checked the magazine, then slipped the pistol into his waistband. Alongside him, Mahmoud did the same.

Coster's mouth was dry but he didn't open a can. He knew they were packed with Semtex and releasing the ring-pulls would start the timers.

He felt ill. He always did when he was stressed out. His mind was back in Falkland's Port Stanley harbour. He was ten feet below the surface, defusing mines left by the Argies. There'd been a problem. He and his mate both knew the mine they were working on was about to blow. He'd kicked out and tried to escape while his mate - they had gone to school together, shared the same girl, and played in the same village football team - continued to work on the mechanism. His mate's body saved him, and his mate's blood coloured the boiling water around him. He hadn't been seriously injured but there was a noise in his head that would stay with him until he died. A gentle, humming sound mostly, but at times like this, it was a high-pitched scream.

The Navy invalided him out of the mob because of a perforated ear drum and tinnitus. The compensation award had all gone within a few months, most of it spent on booze. To get money to buy more, he'd offered his services to the IRA.

Telling them what they needed to know about explosives was easy and he'd done well out of it. This was different. He was scared. His insides were churning like butter in a tub and his back was wet with sweat. Only drink or a woman steadied his shattered nerves and reduced the noise in his head. The landlady had helped but there hadn't been time to work on her properly.

A young woman taking pictures of the Waterloo Block backed towards him. She dropped the lens hood of her camera and bent forward to pick it up.

He saw the lines of her pants inside her tight jeans and he wanted her. He also felt the urge to put his hands around her neck and choke her, so that at the exact time he shot his load, she would die. That would give him peace. Terminal sex; *the supreme joy*, he'd read somewhere. It worked in the woods at the service station when his timing had been perfect and the ecstasy totally and absolutely mind-blowing.

The woman with the camera rejoined her pal in the Jewel House queue.

The noise in his head was starting to hurt.

Sean, now without his Pepsi cans, emerged from the Fusiliers Museum and Danny passed him on the way in.

Lagan had briefed them thoroughly, going over the plan repeatedly until they could answer all his questions. He said they would have no trouble planting their bombs beneath the radiators without being seen because the museum closed to visitors half an hour before the Tower itself and only a few people would be in the building. More importantly, there were no spy cameras or guards in the museum, just a cashier. Soldiers from the barracks preferred to swank around the Tower grounds, posing for tourists.

The bombs were timed to detonate at eleven tomorrow morning, when the museum would be packed with visitors, Friday being the busiest day of the week. The Brits would pay a high price for the arrogance of their beloved Army, he thought. They were better at spilling blood on the streets of Belfast than protecting the public in the heart of their capital city.

He saw Danny, also without his Pepsi cans, appear on the steps of the museum, pause, then walk towards his brother who was standing in the centre of the Broad Walk, opposite Lagan.

Next it was Mahmoud's turn and then it would be his. His hands shook and the Beretta felt ice cold against his burning skin. Why was he always the last? They needed him, he was the explosives expert. The others should have planted the bombs and the boss should have kept him back for the more complicated jobs.

Mahmoud stood up. Without saying a word, he walked towards the museum. Coster watched him, wondering how he could be so calm and casual at such a moment; he may well have been going to the corner shop to buy a packet of Benson's.

31

Molly waited for James while he made a telephone call.

When he had finished, they took the lift down to the underground car park.

Hurtling up the ramp out of Scotland Yard, still fixing the blue light to the roof of his BMW, he forced his way into London's traffic, rounded the island at Parliament Square on two wheels, then raced along Victoria Embankment.

She held onto her armrest and checked the console clock: it was three forty-five.

Tyres screeched as the car turned right at Queen Victoria Street and sped along Thames Street, overtaking traffic and cutting up other drivers who shook their fists and sounded horns. Turning left into Tower Hill, James veered to the right and jammed on the brakes. The BMW skidded, marking the road with parallel lines of black rubber, before stopping outside the entrance to the Tower of London.

At the turnstiles, James flashed his warrant card. The attendant opened a side gate and stood aside to let the detectives pass. Running through the Middle Tower archway and crossing a bridge over a grassed area that had once been a moat, they dashed under the portcullis of the outer wall, Byward Tower.

A bemused group of tourists stopped listening to their Beefeater guide's stories of torture in the dungeons, and turned to gape at the tall man in the suit and the slim woman wearing a denim dress who was chasing him.

At the Bloody Tower they moved left into the Inner Court, skirting lawns and paved areas beside the White Tower.

James, leaping stone steps two at a time, caused a pair of flightless ravens to hop onto the remains of an ancient wall. Supremely fit after her recent long-distance walks, she kept up with him.

An untidy group of tourists at the top of the steps parted to let the detectives pass, then run onto the Broad Walk.

He stopped abruptly and she side-stepped to avoid a collision.

'Why here?'

James sucked air into his lungs. 'Just a guess. I'm going to have a word with those chaps in flat hats.' He grabbed her arm and pointed towards the Waterloo Block. 'The ground floor of that building is the *Jewel House*. Check out the queue but be careful. If you spot anything suspicious hold off and wait for assistance.'

'What then?' she asked, looking around to get her bearings.

'We'll wait for the cavalry. The initial back-up teams will be in plain clothes and they can mingle with the paying visitors. We'll keep the helmets in reserve until we need them.' He moved away from her. 'See you shortly,' he called, walking around the lawn of Tower Green and hurrying towards the group of Beefeaters.

She made her way across the Broad Walk and approached the Jewel House entrance. The people in the queue were mostly students dressed in jeans, T shirts and trainers, the exception being a small group of immaculate, camera-carrying Japanese who gazed in awe at the historic stew all around them.

Pocket book and pencil in hand, she wandered down the line, hoping to convince anyone interested she was a Tourist Board researcher taking a count.

She listened to the friendly banter. A young woman claimed Ohio was the finest place on God's earth and an Australian asked if it was the capital city of South Korea. Not to be out-smarted, a man with a Texas drawl said any Aussie convict who paid to re-enter the Tower of London needed a brain transplant. 'It's their boomerang mentality,' another American chipped in before a bush hat, complete with corks, was rammed onto his head. At the end of the queue two young women were standing behind bulging rucksacks almost as big as they were.

Her attention was diverted by a short, thin man who rose unsteadily from a seat at the foot of the White Tower. He looked around him, then set off towards the building at the eastern end of the Broad Walk. In each hand he was carrying a Pepsi can and he staggered from side to side. Was he ill, drunk or pilled-up?

Staring at the Pepsi cans, she had an uncomfortable

feeling they should mean something to her. Who had mentioned Pepsi cans?

He glanced over his shoulder and increased his pace. Instinctively, she followed. He looked back again and she noticed the long angry scratches down his right cheek. No, she thought, it couldn't be. They walked faster, breaking into a trot.

'Police!' she called out.

He stopped.

She drew close to him.

He tensed, feinted to his right, then turned towards her. She saw the fear and hate in his blue eyes, and knew he would put up a fight. His fist sank into her stomach. She doubled over, the breath forced out of her. His other hand rose into the air and she caught a glimpse of dark metal. She ducked and weaved, like a boxer, but he was quick on his feet and the pistol butt smashed into her jaw. A blinding flash of pain seared through her head. Darkness enveloped her. She was falling, falling, falling...

She heard someone calling her name. It was Bill Bannister. He was holding her upright and his arms gripped her so tightly, she could hardly breathe.

'Are you all right?' he asked.

She wasn't sure. She felt no pain. It was as though she was swimming through dark water. In the distance she heard shots and screams and running feet. Orders were shouted, then repeated.

'I'd feel better if you'd let get some air, Bill.'

He loosened his grip. 'Sorry, ma'am.'

Her head started to ache and her eyes wouldn't focus properly. She took deep breaths to fight off the nausea. 'I think I'm all right,' she murmured. 'It was the Gloucester rapist.' She fingered a graze on her cheekbone, wanting to look into a mirror.

'Can you stand by yourself now, ma'am?' Bannister asked, gently easing her away from him but not letting her go. Feeling as if her legs would buckle at any moment, she gritted her teeth and fought to stay on her feet. Gradually, her strength returned.

'Where's the bastard who hit me?'

'Holed up in the Jewel House with his mates. Can you walk?'

'Where did you spring from?'

'Lynda heard the coded signal on her radio and rang in. They told her to get over here smartish. She drives like a mad thing.'

He stood to one side and encouraged her to walk. 'Come on, ma'am, you can do it.'

She moved one leg, then the other, like someone learning to use artificial limbs.

Eventually, with much coaxing, she reached the alleyway between the Chapel and the Waterloo Block.

Turning, she looked across the Broad Walk. It was deserted but in the evening gloom she could make out the litter of rucksacks, shopping bags, hats and umbrellas. Where were the happy people from the queue? she wondered.

On the other side of the square, black figures moved furtively from cover, then disappeared again.

'Marksmen,' Bannister whispered. 'The inner cordon.' He signalled to someone in the distance. 'Are you fit enough to make it out of here?'

'I'm fine...Stop fussing.'

'Right. The marksmen will cover us. We'll make our way around the Chapel and go through the Devereux Tower.'

'How come you know so much about this place all of a sudden?'

'I'm ace at reading name-plates, ma'am.'

The men in the radio room were still arguing; James defending her. 'She's saved dozens of tourists who might have been blown to pieces.'

'What's she to you?'

32

It was two hours since Molly had arrived at the Tower.

She was seated in the back of a mobile police communications van parked outside the entrance turnstiles. Her head ached, she was still dazed, and every bone in her body felt like a lead weight.

A police surgeon had given her a brief examination and asked if she'd lost consciousness. Not wishing to spend twenty-four hours in hospital for observations, she had lied and he told her to rest.

Fat chance, she thought. For the last few minutes an almighty row had been going on behind closed doors in the radio room at the front of the van, James taking a lot of stick from an irate Yorkshireman who accused him of 'letting a female fucking rambett loose in a Tower full of bloody terrorists.'

She pressed her hands against a window and looked through them as if they were binoculars. All she could see under the street lights was a shifting mass of dark uniforms.

The men in the radio room were still arguing; James defending her. 'She's saved dozens of tourists who might have been blown to pieces.'

'What's she to you?'

'It's not what I believe you're thinking; we're working on a case together.'

The Yorkshire voice boomed again. 'Thanks to your lady friend's stupid heroics, we've got a top-of-range siege, and a couple of Yank students holed up with four heavily armed terrorists.'

'Five,' James corrected. 'One of our snipers has seen another man in the Jewel House. He's in a suit and might be Lagan.'

'Who the bloody hell is he?'

'Mr Big, the IRA Mainland Commander.'

'I thought there was a peace on?'

'It's a bit complicated. I'm working with MI5.'

After a long silence, the Yorkshireman spoke. 'I don't trust MI5. What's the hidden agenda?'

'They don't have one. We'll keep you informed.'

'Hum, I bet you will. Tell me about the other terrorists?'

'Three are IRA from Armagh and we think number four is an Arab.'

'How do you know?'

'We've been tailing them for a week. They posted the letter bombs in Westhampton.'

'So that's why the Watson woman's causing havoc down here. A Detective Superintendent Davidson's been on the blower. He said she's trouble wherever she goes.'

'He would. His own enquiry team were getting nowhere until the chief put her on the case.'

The Yorkshireman snorted. 'I want her out of

229

here...' The sound of gun fire came from the Tower. 'What the hell's going on now?'

'The Jewel House monitors in Tower Control have blanked out, guv,' said a new voice. 'They think the terrorists have shot up the cameras.'

'Any news of the hostages?'

'No, guv. The inspector in charge of the inner cordon thinks they've been taken into the east wing.'

'I need more plans of that building and I also want to know about their weapons, particularly any explosives they might have.'

The van's emergency door opened and Bannister and Hartley climbed into the back.

'You okay, ma'am?' Bannister whispered.

She gestured for silence and pointed towards the radio room. Orders were being sent out on VHF and emergency UHF radio frequencies.

'I'll go and check out that firing,' she heard James say, before the front door shut behind him.

'What's it like outside?' she asked Bannister and Hartley as they sat down opposite to her.

'Pandemonium, I'd call it, ma'am,' Bannister replied. 'Half the Met are milling about; most of them seem to be gaffers.'

'They probably are.'

'It's great – like a film set,' Hartley exclaimed in a noisy whisper. 'Oh yes, ma'am, I nearly forgot. There's a message from a man called Henry. Said he's got something important for you.'

230

That's it, she thought smugly. They can't send me back. I'm the only person close to Gina Jones; the only link with the terrorists. 'Is your car outside?' she asked Hartley.

'Yes, ma'am.'

She turned to Bannister. 'Get me out of here, Bill.'

He grinned and nodded towards the emergency door. 'You and Lynda leave now. I'll deal with anyone who might cause problems while you get away. See you in a minute.'

Henry was watching the six o'clock news when they arrived at his apartment.

'Look at this lot?' he exclaimed after she had introduced Bannister and Hartley. 'It's better than the Iranian Embassy do; seventy-nine, wasn't it?'

She nodded, not sure when it was.

'I thought you would have been down there,' Henry continued. 'My old squadron leader used to say that if you want to get on you should always be where the action is.'

She took a seat. Her legs were still wobbly and the pain in her head wouldn't go away. Perhaps she did have concussion.

'I say, old girl, you look a bit peaky.'

She gave Henry a weak smile. 'I'd appreciate a drink of water, thank you.'

'Not in my hangar,' he said firmly. 'It's a drop of Martell's that you need. I used to smuggle it on board when we went on a raid. Best medicine in the world I always told the chaps.' His leaned closer to her. 'And you've fallen over. You should put something on that cheek before it turns nasty.'

She accepted a large measure of brandy. 'I'll get it seen to. Have you got some news for me?'

He glanced at the detectives. 'I might have.'

'What's the problem?'

'One good turn deserves another, as my navigator always said. A right dandy he was; always after the ladies.'

She held her breath for a moment and told herself to stay calm. 'Come on, Henry, I haven't got much time.'

'Will you help Gina if I give you the number of the car?'

'If I can.'

'She's asking to go into the Tower. Said she'll help you. How, I can't imagine.'

'That's impossible. As you could see yourself, she's being guarded by armed police and men in suits. Are you sure that's what she wants?'

'Of course I am. Had a call from that bossy hospital Sister. I don't know what she means but Gina will write down everything that has happened during the last two years.'

He looked longingly at a photograph of a four engined, propeller-driven aircraft with faded RAF roundels. 'When we came back from a bombing mission we had to record every detail. We were so knackered we couldn't even hold a pen, let alone write a perishing report.'

'Henry,' she said, a little more forcefully. 'It's important I have that car number. As to Gina, you must trust me. First I have to find a way of getting her out of the hospital.'

He looked at her for a long moment and she felt sure he was about to give her the number.

They were distracted by a television news flash and watched fire engines and ambulances lining up on Tower Hill. She thought of the explosion at Westhampton's Letter Office. Was it only six days ago?

'The number please, Henry?'

He shook his head. 'Only when Gina goes into the Tower.'

33

Peter Fitzpatrick Finch, alias Lagan, eased his back down the wall until he was sitting on the stone floor. It was three hours since everything had gone wrong.

He looked around him. Display cases packed with priceless treasures. Gold and silver encrusted with precious stones; crowns, swords, sceptres, orbs and banqueting plate. The history of a nation written large in outrageous wealth, most of it stolen from distant parts of the world when maps were predominately British Empire red.

When he was five years old his parents emigrated from Belfast to find work. They settled in the north London suburb of Islington, alongside other families forced to leave the old country.

His father was sweated labour on road-building gangs. On the rare occasions when he was at home he spent his time in the nearest pub, returning late at night to smash up the furniture and his mother.

Peter was raised by his mother. His earliest memories were of her extolling the virtues of Ireland and vilifying the rapacious Brits. An active and vociferous supporter of the Cause, she never let him forget he was an Irishman forced to live with the very people who had turned his homeland into a battleground.

She had brain-washed him as only a mother could and on her death bed made him swear before a picture of the Pope that he would fight for a united Ireland, free from the yoke of British tyranny.

His father had got drunk at the wake and, after a couple of fist fights, spent the night in the matrimonial bed with two sisters from Dungannon.

The following morning he left without a word and never returned. Peter was just twelve years old.

Plain and withdrawn at school, the other kids called him, *The Pape* and regularly beat him. After a bomb exploded at a local shopping arcade, killing a child in a pushchair, he was frog-marched into the washroom where his head was rammed down a dirty toilet by a gang of cheering boys and girls.

Too frightened to complain, he promised himself that his tormentors, and many other Brits, would pay a high price for their cruelty.

His first sexual experience occurred when he was sixteen. Bored and lonely, he'd drifted into a Hackney pub used by expatriate Irishmen.

A man from Belfast poured gin into his orange juice and insisted he shared his good fortune at the races. Having sworn during one of his mother's regular beatings he would never touch alcohol, he refused at first.

He didn't remember leaving the premises and when he woke up the following morning he was shocked to find himself sharing the man's bed.

Christopher was twenty years older than himself but he was a good friend and an attentive lover who plied him with presents and took him to all the West End shows. Afterwards they went to parties which didn't break up until first light.

They stopped seeing each other when Christopher started going out with a younger boy he picked up in an amusement parlour. There'd been other men since then, but none so intense and exciting as Christopher.

During his early working life, he was employed as a clerk at the local Social Security office, his hatred of all things British being reinforced by his colleagues' coarse jokes about *thick paddys*.

To occupy himself in the evenings, he'd studied at the local polytechnic and obtained a degree in business administration.

Worn down by the form-filling drudgery of DHSS work, he was attracted by an administrative post at the Home Office. It was the rider at the bottom of the advertisement that first grabbed his attention. **We welcome applications from candidates regardless of ethnic origin, religious belief, sex, sexual orientation, disability or any other irrelevant factor. People with disability and those from the ethnic minorities are currently under-represented and their applications are particularly welcome.**

Being Irish, gay, and disabled - his left hand had

been damaged when a petrol tanker ploughed into a bus he was sitting in - he believed he had definite advantage over the other candidates. Vetting by MI5 and MOD's security department was thorough and unpleasant. It had taken considerable will-power to restrain himself when they goaded him about his mother's *crackpot crusade* for a united Ireland.

Certain they had gone against him, he'd been ecstatic when the personnel manager said the job was his.

Five years later he was promoted to a more senior position at the Police Department in Whitehall's, Queen Anne's Gate.

At a concert the following Spring, he met Christopher again and was introduced to United Irishman, the English arm of the Irish Republican movement.

He attended some of their meetings but was disappointed. Members of the committee were more interested in protecting their easy life styles than fighting the Brits. Anyone suggesting violence was regarded as a trouble maker and asked to leave.

Several months after they resumed their friendship, Christopher visited his Lambeth apartment with an IRA official from Dublin. Following that meeting, the Republican Army Council, aware of his position at the Home Office, invited him to join them as an undercover agent and he accepted.

That was seven years ago. Since then he'd built up a network of civil service contacts who provided information from other Government departments, some of which he passed on to GHQ at Dublin. Delighted with his contribution, the Chief of Staff gave him the title *Mainland Commander,* even though there was no such post in the IRA hierarchy.

Many times he wondered if his luck would run out and it was almost a relief when a memo crossed his desk suggesting there was a highly placed mole at Scotland Yard.

Believing the Republican cause could only be achieved through armed conflict, he'd been disillusioned when the IRA used Sinn Fein to announce a ceasefire. But this feeling did not compare with his surprise when they asked him to organise a letter bomb campaign against British Jews and a spectacular explosion in London. He was to be paid one million pounds if he succeeded but the IRA would deny any knowledge of him and his active service unit.

Now he was trapped in the Tower of London, the largest mediaeval fortress in Europe and a place soaked in the blood of history, much of it Irish. In his eagerness to command his own team, he had made the mistake of working with people he didn't know.

He moved and felt a sharp pain in his leg. Leaning to one side he pulled a shard of video camera lens out of his trousers.

Sean guarded the entrance door and Mahmoud the door at the east end of the building. Coster was in the Beefeaters' kitchen looking after the students and Danny was resting.

It was stalemate. But for how long? And how had he got himself into this mess? A woman challenged Coster. But who was she? The connection must be Westhampton and the only woman involved in that operational had been the detective inspector who took over the Letter Office during the search. The Chief Constable sent a glowing report about her to the Head of the Home Office Police Department and had put her in charge of his Bomb Squad. Molly was her first name; ironically the Irish equivalent of Mary.

Yes, he remembered now; Detective Inspector Molly Watson. She was in London because Detective Superintendent Cranleigh-Smythe had sent for her. She must be the woman who challenged Coster.

But how the dickens had she known about the operation at the Tower? He stared at the old stone walls and the fog in his mind slowly cleared. Captain Standish was the Bomb Disposal Officer at Westhampton. They must have worked together. Had she been waiting outside when he stormed the safe house and got himself killed? She could then have followed his team to their next digs, Brick Lane, and now this place.

His reasons for choosing Westhampton has been valid. It was a convenient place for McKindon's unit to post the letter bombs, there were frequent mail trains to London, and Jimmy was a student there.

Dear Jimmy, so sweet and so good in bed. Would he ever see him again? They'd met in a cinema when Jimmy was fifteen and still a virgin. But now he was at Westhampton University and they only saw each other during the holidays.

Jimmy's family lived within the walls of the Tower, his father, a former Royal Marine, being a Yeoman Warder. This gave him the idea of staging the IRA's spectacular in the Tower. It had been difficult to persuade Jimmy to smuggle in the guns and explosives. In desperation, he'd taken him to one of Christopher's all night parties, introduced him to crack cocaine, then filmed him as he went wild and tried to satisfy everyone in the room, mostly two or three at a time. Jimmy would have done anything to prevent his parents seeing that film.

Westhampton had punished him for being cruel to Jimmy. It was where the Watson bitch worked and where she'd met Standish, the bomb disposal captain.

He was already making enquiries about Standish. During his third tour in Northern Ireland, MI5 had used Standish for a secret assignment. He'd seen letters between ministers; members of the Cabinet who were quietly shitting themselves. *Whatever happens the facts of this matter must never become public knowledge,* the last letter read. They hadn't said what the operation was but they were worried because Standish was drinking heavily and shouting his mouth off. One minister suggested alcohol poisoning might be a convenient solution if MI5 could make the necessary arrangements. A posthumous medal for past services would make things more bearable for Standish's regiment and distant relatives, he concluded.

Making enquiries about Standish had been the last thing he'd wanted to do while he was planning two mainland operations but it was obviously so important, he couldn't afford to ignore it. He'd seen his most highly placed contacts in an effort to discover what the panic was all about but without success. Checking through police and MI5 reports on Standish's death, he was struck by an apparent lack of commitment to find those responsible. There was no murder investigation team and the preliminary papers were marked for the special attention of Detective Superintendent Cranleigh-Smythe. It was almost as if the authorities didn't want to catch the killers and have the embarrassment of a trial.

He stood up and walked stiffly into the central corridor. 'We'll be out of here soon,' he said to Sean.

'No one's getting out of this place alive,' grumbled the active service unit leader. 'The SAS will arrive shortly and it'll be Gibraltar all over again; we'll be blood stains on the pavement.'

'You're wrong. We've got the students.'

'Will the filth negotiate?'

'Where have you been for the last ten years? Every school kid knows how to run a siege. They always negotiate; they'll be setting things up right now. First there'll be the usual chat and we'll all pretend we're the best of pals while secretly working out plans to kill each other. Then, when each side thinks they've won the verbal battle, a deal will be struck. We get out, the students are released, and everyone lives happily ever after.'

'That's a bloody fairy tale,' Sean growled. 'The last film I saw, they called in the Air Force who used laser-guided bombs to vaporise the house and everyone inside, including the hostages.'

'It must have been an Italian director, they're born pessimists.'

'So am I,' Sean murmured.

'Your man panicked. Up to that moment it was going well.'

'Coster wasn't my choice. The man has been trouble from day one.'

Lagan studied the big Irishman. He was very good after Coster downed the policewoman. When soldiers, police and Beefeaters closed in from three sides, he called his team together, grabbed the two students, and led the retreat into the Jewel House. 'If Coster was jeopardising the mission you should have got rid of him.'

'I needed someone who knows about explosives. Brigade should never have sent him; unless they wanted this mission to fail.'

Lagan snatched off his civil service tie and opened the top button of his cream shirt. The possibility had crossed his mind; the IRA saving themselves a load of money and eliminating a potential security risk at the same time. 'Why should they want to do that?'

Sean shuffled his feet. 'Just a feeling.'

'You worry too much. When the police negotiators arrive we'll make our demands.'

'They'll tell us to fuck off.'

'No they won't.'

'How come?'

'I helped to write the book, didn't I. They'll want to give us a land line and food because the boxes have built-in listening devices which will enable them to assess the situation in here. They will only launch an attack if they believe they can release the students before we have an opportunity to kill them.'

'Will we?'

'Depends on the Brits.'

Sean glanced at his watch. 'It's eight o'clock. The lads are hungry and soon they'll need some sleep.'

Lagan sat down on an empty wooden crate. 'I'll keep it in mind.'

He took a filing card from the inside pocket of his jacket and pretended to make notes. Working for the civil service had taught him how to conceal his true feelings but he couldn't hide from himself. Physically he was a coward who had never fought anyone in his life. He was a pen-pusher, a schemer and a planner. How could he deal with this situation when he felt as if his guts were in a vice and his mind was immobilised by fear?

34

Expecting a tongue-lashing, Molly walked into the radio room of the communications van in Tower Hill.

James looked up from his desk. 'I thought you'd deserted ship and headed north?'

'I've been doing some ground work for you,' she said brightly. He was her ticket into the Tower and she would use him as he had used her.

'Where's Yorky?' she asked.

'Don't let him hear you say that. Superintendent Joe Nelson's been in the Met for thirty-six years. He thinks he's a cockney. They've stuck him in the White Tower, in charge of the Forward Control Point.' Like Henry, he looked hard at her face. 'You look bushed.'

'It's the light,' she replied, not wanting his sympathy.

'Joe's said you must return to your force.'

'What's happening?' she asked, determined to reverse the decision.

'Things have settled down. All units are in place and a cordon has been thrown right around the Castle.'

'*Castle*?'

'Scotland Yard have decided it will cause less confusion. There's twenty-two towers in the outer and inner walls.'

James stood up and offered her his chair. 'People living inside the Castle have been moved out. The Chief Yeoman Warder went spare. Said he would personally complain to the Queen. The *Ceremony of the Keys* - held each night when the gates are locked - is a tradition that has gone on uninterrupted for hundreds of years and he didn't see why a gang of terrorists should be allowed to stop it.'

She thanked James for the chair and sat down.

'Anything else?'

'We've doubled the inner cordon and the Special Operations Room has been opened up at the Yard.' He leant over a radio operator's shoulder and read a message. 'It seems the Cabinet Office Briefing Room is also on line.'

'*COBRA*! They must be worried about the nation's precious baubles.'

'If those hostages are harmed, London's three billion pound tourist trade will sink into the Thames mud faster than Florida's sank into its swamps.'

He turned away for a moment to deal with a resource problem raised by the Incident Commander.

'You need me here, James,' she said, when she had his full attention again. 'And I'm staying put.'

'I doubt it. They don't call Joe Nelson *Stonewall* for nothing.'

She spoke very quietly. 'James, I'm not asking, I'm telling you.'

He paled, patently aware that she had the power to break him. 'It will be difficult.'

'Life's a bitch, and then you're dead.'

'You're hitting below the belt, Molly.'

'That's rich, coming from you.'

He sat down and rubbed his brow, a look of desperation in his eyes.

'There's something else I need,' she said.

He looked up at her, waiting. 'Gina wants to come here and the only person who can authorise that is probably Richard.'

James laughed without mirth. 'That's impossible and you know it.'

'Do I? It's the only way we're going to get that car number out of Henry.'

'Why does Gina want to come here?'

'Does it matter?'

Sean McKindon felt a cold draft on his back; the corridor separating the two halves of the Jewel House was like a wind tunnel. He didn't mind, it helped him to stay awake. He was guarding the entrance doors of the Jewel House. Metal-studded solid oak, they opened inwards leaving a hole big enough to drive a furniture van through. Above the doors was a fanlight of small windows.

The heavy iron door latch rattled and he raised his Uzi, one of the sub-machine guns Lagan had produced from his holdall. If an attack came it must be through

246

these doors or the exit door. Steel bars, set close together, protected the windows and armoured glass was bolted on the inside. He glanced up at the high ceiling and wondered whether there was a third possibility.

Several long minutes passed before he breathed more easily and lowered his weapon. He wiped a hand across his face then reached for a bar of chocolate taken from one of the students' bum-bags. It wasn't hunger, simply a matter of storing energy for whatever lay ahead.

Bright light streamed through the fanlight, startling him. Reacting instinctively, he poured shots into the door, emptying half of his magazine.

'Stop firing!' Lagan shouted as he ran into the corridor. 'They're only floodlighting the place.'

Sean shook his head, as if to clear it. Points of light marked a crooked line of holes in the door. 'Sorry,' he said. 'Must be more jumpy than I thought.'

The older man gripped his shoulder. 'No matter, it will give those idiots out there something to think about.'

'What's up?'

Lagan spun round and faced Coster. 'Our keepers have given us some light. Who's watching the women?'

'Danny.'

Lagan's anger showed. 'I told you to look after the students while Danny had some rest. Get out!' Coster, a wicked look in his eyes, backed off, then left the corridor.

'What happens now?' Sean asked.

'They'll be in touch soon. Worried in case we've

hurt the students. Those shots must have been heard all over the city and the media will be giving the Scotland Yard press office hell.'

'Where are they - the filth?'

Lagan pointed to the fanlight above the door. 'In the tower across the Broad Walk. Before the floods were switched on you could see the lights in the windows.'

'Who makes the decision to attack?'

'The Home Secretary. But only if he's convinced the students' lives are in immediate danger. The police will then sign the operation over to the Army.'

'Which regiment?'

'Special Air Services.'

35

Visitors to the Jewel House rarely notice the door between the coronation robes and the banqueting plate. It is the entrance to the Beefeaters' rest rooms.

Beyond this door, Ingrid Mestrovic lay on the floor of the kitchen. Cold and miserable, she tried to move into a more comfortable position. Her hands were tied behind her back and her feet were tied together, the tender skin of her wrists and ankles already rubbed raw.

She thought of relatives and friends at home, they wouldn't know she was a hostage in the Tower of London. Perhaps it was best, her mother had always been against the trip to Europe.

Lying on the floor a short distance away, her friend cried out in her sleep. She'd fought like a wild cat when they'd been dragged into the building and bundled into the kitchen.

Forced to lie face down, with revolvers pushed into the back of their necks, Nancy Price had screamed and screamed until the small guy with the scratches down his face had lost his temper and kicked her in the head. Even so, she'd managed to break free, dash across the room, and jump up at one of the windows. He'd pulled her down and beat her with his fists until the big Irish guy had pulled him away.

Like herself, it was the first time Nancy had left California. She'd been raised with five brothers and could scrap as well as any of them, but nothing could have prepared her for this.

The door opened and the guy in the suit who the others called Lagan sidled into the kitchen. Behind him, through the open doorway, she caught a glimpse of gold and silver and precious stones sparkling in their display cases.

She'd decided Lagan was the leader because he was different from the other guys. He had soft white hands and his voice was the same as the manager's at their hotel. At home she'd always liked English visitors with their cute voices; now she hated them.

He walked over to her and dropped onto his haunches, turning her onto her side and testing the ropes around her wrists and ankles. The pain was excruciating and she screamed through her gag.

Apparently unmoved by her distress, he studied her for some time and she wondered what he was thinking about. She could feel the tears running down her cheeks but she forced herself to smile at him with her eyes. He had the power of life and death: there was nothing she wouldn't do to stay alive.

Detective Inspector M Watson. Please meet me at the FCP in the White Tower. You'll need an escort to get through the outer cordon, began the note James had left

250

for her in the communications van. She'd been back to the hotel for a quick shower and a change of clothes.

Following his instructions, she crossed the old moat with a uniformed PC.

At the top of the wooden steps leading into the back of the White Tower, she paused. It was a moonless night and across the Thames she could see the lights of South London. Ferries glided along the river below her, late night revellers dancing in the saloon bars.

A guard checked her warrant card and another man took her through the Royal Armouries, the national collection of arms and armour. The lights had been turned off and the beam of his torch danced between the burnished helmets of giant metal men holding lances as long as flag poles in one hand and huge battle swords in the other. She looked about her, as if expecting Henry VIII's army to march out of the walls and trample her underfoot.

She moved closer to her escort and they climbed stone steps to the second floor, walking between lines of longbows that helped the English to rout the French at Agincourt.

Passing through a gap in a temporary partition, they were back in the twentieth century of computers, printers, fax machines, copiers and telephones; trained staff jostling for space in which to work.

James was arguing with Superintendent Nelson who reminded her of Bert Tallis. He had the same thick grey hair and puffed himself up when he was annoyed.

Cigarette ash laid a white trail down the front of his uniform. Both men turned to face her.

'So, you're the woman who's caused all this bloody chaos,' the Yorkshireman said angrily. Seething with indignation, she was about to respond when he beat her to it. 'I don't want your opinions, Watson. Just keep quiet and we'll get along nicely.'

'He's not too bad,' James said a few minutes later, as they stood outside the Forward Control Point. 'There's been some shooting inside the Jewel House and he's worried about the hostages.'

'What happened?'

'We can only speculate. My guess is that one of the terrorists panicked when the floodlights were switched on. The ninjas - our firearms people - wanted to storm the place. It was quite hairy for a moment but Joe managed to hold them off. He's due to retire next week and doesn't want to spend the rest of his life attending public enquiries.'

'I take it, you've got me a stay of execution?'

'Yes,' he said quietly.

'Was it difficult?'

'No; surprisingly enough, it wasn't. You're something of a star at the Yard. The Press Office have asked Westhampton for your photograph. They're still working out the publicity angle. Something like *Fearless woman police inspector tackles gang of international terrorists single-handed*. Only to be issued to the media if the siege is resolved successfully, mind you.'

'What about Bill and yourself, and everyone else who's had a hand in it?'

'We don't matter. It's the decade of the woman and they need a role model.'

'They've got the wrong woman,' she protested. 'I just want to be left alone to do my job. What did Nelson say?'

'Something about being lucky he was born sixty years ago.'

'Typical. Have you spoken to Richard about Gina'a request to come here yet?'

'Yes. They're prepared to play. It seems they've got nothing out of her and are happy to let her run and see what happens. They will, of course, put a tail on her.'

'Even in this place?'

'I doubt it. Not while we're protected by two cordons of heavily armed soldiers and ninjas.'

'Have we made contact with the stronghold yet?'

'We're waiting for the negotiators. They're on a job at Wormwood Scrubs prison. A group of lifers are holed up in the Governor's office and have threatened to cut his head off with a bread knife if they don't get a written promise of more toilet rolls, toothpaste and telephone cards.'

James intercepted two mugs of tea on their way into the Forward Control Point, handing one to her.

'Will you tell me about the Jewel House?' she asked, sipping at her drink.

He carefully balanced his mug on a box of stationery. 'Let me see...it contains twenty thousand gems, including the world's largest diamond. All together they're known as the *Crown Jewels*.' A woman carrying a notebook computer pushed past them and he waited until she was out of hearing.

'The Government has recently spent millions of pounds modernising the place so it can process hordes of tourists and bring in more cash,' he went on. 'They've even fitted a travelling walkway to keep the dawdlers on the move and increase the flow of visitors to twenty thousand a day.'

He drank some of his tea, thought for a moment, then continued. 'The Jewel House has two halves separated by a large central corridor. The west side contains state of the art technology which introduces the exhibition and explains the history of the Crown Jewels. The east side is where the goodies are on display in their glass cases lit up by fibre-optics.'

'Is that where the terrorists are camped out with the hostages?'

'Yes, or so it would appear.'

'What's security like?'

'The jewel cases are bomb-proof and it goes on from there; security devices overlapping like onion rings. Protection extends to the far walls of the Castle and beyond the moat.'

'They can't be that good.'

James gave her a sickly smile. 'Armed terrorists may

have got in, but one's thing's for certain - they're not going to get out.'

36

The SAS sergeant dressed in a black balaclava and jump suit waited until thirty minutes past midnight. He then ordered his corporal to close up. They were opposite the rear wall of the floodlit Waterloo Block and close to the west end of the building. After a brief exchange of hand signals, they dashed across a bright path and ran down the dark alleyway next to the Chapel.

Seconds later, they emerged from the other end of the alleyway and into the glare of more floodlights. Sprinting along the front of the Waterloo Block to the entrance of the Jewel House, they ducked into an alcove.

Waiting for a moment, the Sergeant then moved forward and clamped four magnetic explosive charges onto the hinges of the Jewel House door.

Dangerously exposed in blinding light once more, the two soldiers then ran towards the east end of the Waterloo Block and around the corner to the safety of the only unlit side of the building.

When their eyes had grown accustomed to the dark, they attached explosive charges to the exit door.

Other men in black, carrying weapons, CS gas canisters, stun grenades, smoke bombs and climbing ropes, stood in line. A silent order was given and they scaled scaffolding left by builders. Scrambling over the parapet on to the flat roof, the soldiers then dispersed to prearranged positions.

A quiet whirring sound woke Nancy Price. Her head had been resting against the wall and when she moved it away she could no longer hear the noise. Someone was drilling and they didn't want the terrorists to know about it, she decided, feeling less isolated from the outside world.

Strong beams of light penetrated the kitchen and enabled her to see a small cooker, a table and two chairs. A painting of cavalry officers charging at canons hung on the far wall. A wicker basket stood in one corner; it was full of carpenters' tools.

She raised her arm so she could see her wrist watch: it was exactly one am. They should be clubbing in Covent Garden now, after their planned trip to see Les Miserables at the Palace Theatre.

Ingrid, trussed up like an oven-ready turkey, lay on the floor near to the table. The small guy with the scratched face was flat out on a blanket placed across the doorway.

She moved her arms and legs, feeling the slack in the ropes. Luckily, the fat guy hadn't tied her wrists and ankles properly. She'd often been bound with the family clothes line by her brothers. In their small world only girls were captured; boys fought to the death. Keeping her eye on the guy at the door, she freed her wrists.

Suddenly, he sat up and looked around him. She closed her eyes, breathing steadily and hoping he'd think she was sleep.

When she dared to look, she saw him bend over Ingrid and lift her onto his shoulder like a fireman. He then carried her into a small storeroom, laying her on the floor before closing the door behind him.

Christ! What could she do now, Nancy wondered. She'd intended to release Ingrid so they could make the dash for freedom together. Thinking furiously and trying not to panic, she quickly removed her gag and untied her ankles. She then rubbed her arms and legs to ease the stiffness. A short distance champion at UCLA, she knew how to prepare herself mentally and physically for a sprint.

Muffled sounds came from behind the door of the storeroom. What the hell was happening? If she tried to save Ingrid now she would probably lose her only chance to escape. Should she make a break on her own and get some help? More noise came from the storeroom, followed by what she thought was a gagged scream.

Nancy sweated more than she'd ever done on the track and her clothes clung to her. She couldn't fight the man; he was a terrorist. She must get help, she decided, wondering if the true arbiter was self-preservation.

She crept across the kitchen and took a heavy wooden mallet from the tool basket. Her head hurt, her mouth was dry and she felt terrible. Fortunately, her clothing was light and ideal for running. She carefully re-tied her trainers. She'd run the hundred metres in twelve seconds but on an uneven surface, and without a starting block, she knew it would take her at least another three seconds to reach the safety of the buildings on the far side of the square.

Feeling dreadful at having to abandon her friend, she took one last look at the storeroom door, then crept out of the kitchen.

Ducking beneath the bright beams of light that pierced the windows, she moved forward between a maze of display cases, trying to find a path to the corridor with the big doors. After several dead-ends and retracing her steps, she finally made it.

Near to the entrance door, sitting in a chair, was the fat guy. A sub machine gun lay across his lap. She tip-toed forward until she could hear his regular breathing. He was asleep. As she drew level with him he snorted and changed his position on the hard seat. Wide-eyed with fear and experiencing a whole gamut of new emotions, her hand tightened around the handle of the mallet.

There was a commotion at the other end of the building and she guessed someone had discovered she was missing. She ran to the double doors and lifted the iron latch. The fat guy sat up and his gun clattered onto the stone floor. Mallet raised, she turned and ran back, hitting him on the side of the head and knocking him off his chair. Picking up his gun, she slung it down the corridor, then fled through the door and out of the building.

Head back like an athlete and hair trailing in the wind, she sped across the tarmac towards Tower Green.

She heard shouts of anger behind her, followed by the sound of gunfire.

Cramp gripped the muscles of her legs, slowing her down. Tears blurred her vision and sobs of sheer panic broke the controlled rhythm of her breathing.

The gunfire behind her seemed louder, then she saw flashes of light in front of her. 'No! No! No!' she screamed, realising that she was in the middle of a fire-fight.

Fear released a flood of adrenaline. Her speed picked up and her brain started to work again. She zig-zagged, like she'd seen fugitives do in the escape films. But this was for real and she was terrified.

Glancing over her shoulder, she saw red light spitting from the dark recess of the Jewel House door and chips of white masonry from the archway around the door flying into the air as shots were returned.

Straining to push herself forward, she tripped, then regained her balance.

Again she glanced over her shoulder and again she screamed. Rushing towards her across the hard tarmac was a line of red and white sparks.

She summoned her last reserves of energy, her whole being concentrating on reaching the safety of the buildings only a short distance away. But now she could hear the bullets bouncing off the tarmac at her heels and she knew it was hopeless.

Still running, still weaving, she felt a sharp pain in her back and her eyes filled with blood.

37

Mahmoud slammed shut the large doors. Holes appeared in the woodwork. A bullet grazed his temple and another took off the tip of an ear. More bullets ripped open the shoulder of his jacket. Cursing in his own language, he moved away from the door and fired a volley of shots into the air, killing an SAS sergeant who was stretched out on the floor above and inserting an endoscope into a small hole next to a light fitting.

Danny, nursing his head, lay on the floor.

Lagan, shocked and sickened by the brutal reality of armed combat, was crouched in a recess in the corridor wall, sheltering from ricochetting bullets.

He'd planned and caused many deaths but had never bloodied his own hands or been in any danger himself.

Mahmoud's face showed his contempt for the frightened man. 'Why wasn't Coster looking after the women?'

'He was, but he took one of them into the storeroom and allowed the other to escape.'

'Where is he now?'

'Still in the storeroom with the student. Sean's told him to come out but he won't.'

Mahmoud clipped a full magazine into his Uzi and

stood over the cringing civil servant. 'I will deal with him. From this moment, I am in charge. You will all do exactly as I say. My brother is paying you well and I am here to see that his wishes are carried out.'

Lagan gave a weak nod of compliance and stared up at the tall Arab. Blood from his ear ran down the side of his face and he held the Uzi across his chest like a symbol of absolute power.

In the Forward Control Point Nelson was venting his feelings. 'I don't give a pig's arse whether the Home Secretary's dining in Beijing or on Hampstead Heath,' he bellowed over the telephone. 'It's two o'clock in the bloody morning and they're shooting up the Jewel House. They've already shot one hostage...God knows what they're doing to the other. I need a decision now!'

Red in the face, he slammed down the handset. 'They couldn't manage shit. Kill those bloody lights,' he bawled at his Inspector.

Before he had an opportunity to reply the floodlights went out. 'Firearms are recovering the body, guv.'

'What d'you mean - body?' Nelson shouted at him. 'Until the doctor tells us otherwise, that's a young woman out there. He walked across the room. 'All right, Watson?'

Staring at a blank message pad on the desk in front of her, she nodded without looking up, unable to drive from her mind the picture of the fleeing woman, a crooked trail of bullets chasing her across the square as the marksman used sparks from the tarmac to line her up in his sights. Then the horror of the woman being hit; her whole body jerking and dancing in the air, as if she were running on molten metal.

The SAS commander glanced at his watch.

Nelson, who rarely missed anything, caught the movement. 'You'll have to wait until those idiots at the Yard get their act together. They won't budge until COBRA gives the word. If we do get a decision, when will you be ready to go in?'

'Thirty minutes.'

Nelson lit a cigarette and threw the empty packet into a bin. 'Can't you speed it up?'

The soldier shook his head. 'We only get one go; it must be right.'

'*Right* is five dead terrorists and a live hostage in my book.'

'We don't shoot to kill - unless there's no alternative.'

'The doctor says the woman's dead,' interrupted the Inspector from a safe distance.

His boss glared at him as if he were personally responsible, then turned his attention back to the SAS man. 'Get your men tooled up.'

The soldier strode towards the door. No badges of rank decorated his jump-suit, but if he had walked past any squaddy in the British Army they would have thrown up a salute without even thinking about it.

The floodlights came on again. Six white wooden

pegs now marked the spot where Nancy Price's broken body had lain on Tower Green. Close by a raised metal plate informed visitors that it was the site of the scaffold where two Queens of England and four members of the nobility had been executed in the sixteenth century.

Danny, a large plaster stuck untidily onto the side of his head, was back in his chair, watching the entrance door of the Jewel House and occasionally glancing over his shoulder. Above him in a dark attic, moving a few centimeters at a time, soldiers dragged their dead colleague away. The man who took his place did not need the smell of blood to remind him that the slightest sound might be fatal.

There was no fear in Sean's eyes as he faced Mahmoud in the kitchen. 'You've killed the student, haven't you?'

'Yes, where is the other woman?'

Sean gestured towards a door. 'In the storeroom with Coster.'

Mahmoud gripped the barrel of Sean's gun. 'You are a good fighter, my friend. Go and see Lagan who will tell you about the new situation. I will deal with Coster.'

Sean stared into the dark, unflinching eyes of the Arab. A few days ago he might have stood up to him. Now there was no point. He was sick of war and Coster wasn't worth arguing about. Pulling his gun from Mahmoud's grip, he left the kitchen.

Mahmoud looked around him; men like Coster were

dangerous when cornered. He needed a plan if he was to reach him without hurting the woman.

Approaching the storeroom door with his back to the wall, he stopped and listened: nothing. The student must be gagged and Coster, who would have heard him talking to Sean, must be waiting for him.

He examined the door, noting the standard mortise lock and the soft wooden panels. Using his shoulder or his boot would only break the door where he struck it.

He laid his gun beside the skirting board and retreated.

Picking up the kitchen table, he gripped a metal leg in each hand, testing the table for weight and balance. Satisfied, he aimed the formica top at the storeroom door. Swaying backwards and forwards, like a high jumper preparing to launch himself at the bar, he psyched himself up for the charge.

Someone started shouting in the distance. He guessed it was Lagan and Sean arguing about his take-over.

Blanking it out of his mind, he took a deep breath, then threw himself and his improvised battering across the room.

Several things happened at once. The storeroom door collapsed. The woman Coster was using as a shield bounced back into him. The barrel of his Uzi was knocked into the air. His finger tightened around the trigger. Bullets peppered the ceiling, smashed the overhead light, and showered the darkened room with broken glass.

Lagan, walking into the kitchen with a message for his new leader, swerved to one side as Mahmoud hurled the table and remains of the storeroom door across the floor. Coster's body followed, a leather bound knife handle sticking out of his chest.

Feet crunching on broken glass, Mahmoud carried Ingrid Mestrovic into the kitchen and gently laid her down.

'Get me the first aid kit,' he said, wiping blood from her battered and swollen face.

Orders from the Incident Commander flooded into the Forward Control Point and Molly kept herself busy, trying to put the horror of Nancy Price's violent death at the back of her mind.

'Message from COBRA, sir.'

'Thank you, Watson,' he said, taking it from her.

Knowing the contents of the message, she watched his expression change as he read.

'The stupid idiots!' he bellowed, looking around the room for the SAS leader. 'They say we can attack the stronghold but not until first light; when's that, for Christ's sake?'

The man in black took a moment to work it out, then gave a precise time.

'Eight am.'

Nelson glared at the clock. 'Another four and a half hours for that poor kid in the Jewel House.'

The SAS leader showed no emotion. 'We have a better chance of taking the terrorists without injuring her in a dawn raid.'

'If there's anything left.'

'Having survived the night, the terrorists will feel safer in the daylight. They'll also be at their lowest ebb, physically and mentally.'

Nelson thumped the table. 'Just make sure we don't have to serve the bastards breakfast.'

38

Friday, Molly mused, breakfasting at one of the picnic tables set up in the Royal Armouries by the Metropolitan Police Catering Department. At Westhampton, the Chief would be calling it *Day Eight*. Had they found any more letter bombs, she wondered. And was Tallis still tearing his hair out about his mail being held up? She'd have to pop in and see him when she got back.

Feeling remarkably fresh after three hours sleep on a camp bed, she looked around her, noticing a milk bottle stuck in the mailed metal gauntlet of Henry V's suit of armour and a burnt piece of toast sticking out of his visor.

The ninjas, she guessed, looking at a group of men and women sitting at the next table. Wearing black jump suits and stripped of their bullet proof jackets, they reminded her of council dustmen. They were loading cholesterol and their laughter had a nervous edge to it. Most of their time was spent on tedious training exercises; today could be the real thing and some of them might be killed.

Finishing her bacon butty, she got up and walked past them, ignoring cracks from the men about black dresses and red knickers.

She was not surprised by the high level of activity in the Forward Control Point. Final preparations were being made to storm the Jewel House.

'Morning, Watson,' murmured Nelson, pointing at an empty chair. 'Make yourself useful and man that phone.'

'Small explosion in the Jewel House,' announced the Inspector. 'The officer in charge of the inner cordon thinks they're blowing open the display cases.'

Nelson leapt to the window and looked across the Broad Walk. A light mist drifting up from the river shrouded the Waterloo Block but he could make out the large front doors and the windows of the Jewel House.

'I thought the bloody things were supposed to be bomb proof.'

'Lob a bomb into the place and they'd probably hold. Put in an explosives expert and things are different,' replied the SAS leader.

'Didn't you say that the windows and ceiling panels would burst open and disperse the blast?'

'Normally, yes. But this man knows his stuff. He's only used a small amount of Semey and would have smothered the target area with curtains or something.'

Nelson, his face showing signs of a night without sleep, sighed wearily.

'Don't tell me the silly buggers are after the Crown Jewels?'

'Inner cordon on the line, guv,' called the inspector. 'They think the terrorists are coming out.'

'Why?'

'The Jewel House door has opened.'

Mahmoud, working on the wooden crate in the corridor, made a final adjustment to the anti-probe switch and checked the binding that held Coster's second Pepsi can in place. He had used Semtex from the first can to open the display case, surprising the others with his dexterity and expertise.

Making bombs in his father's basement factory had been his job after school, whilst other boys earned their pocket money distributing anti-jewish leaflets in the West Bank villages.

Pleased with his handiwork, he nodded to Lagan who obediently pushed one of the double doors further open.

Standing in shadow, Mahmoud looked across the Broad Walk. Early morning sun penetrated the mist. Bending his right knee, he took aim and carefully bowled a round object, the size of a football, across the tarmac.

The man in charge of the inner cordon watched it roll towards him, then stop in the centre of the square. An agitated voice shouted in his ear piece, demanding to know what he could see.

He raised his binoculars. 'I think it's a mine, guv.'

'A what?'

'It's the same shape...no...wait a minute...it's

sparkling. Yes, guv, it's something shiny. Precious stones - it's a crown with a Pepsi can inside.'

'A bloody crown?'

A voice called from the darkness inside the half open doorway of the Jewel House. '...We want to talk.'

The man in charge of the inner cordon exchanged his binoculars for a loud hailer. 'An unarmed officer will walk towards you. He'll leave a land line at the entrance. Is that understood?'

There was a pause before the voice in the doorway answered. 'If there's any trouble, he'll be shot.'

In the Forward Control Point, the Inspector was flicking through a Tower of London guide. 'Got it guv,' he called. 'It's the Imperial State Crown, used by the Monarch at major occasion such as the opening of Parliament. It has nearly three thousand diamonds, including the Second Star of Africa.'

'I'm not bidding for the bloody thing' Nelson retorted. He picked up a handset and spoke to the man in charge of the inner cordon. 'Have they said what the crown is doing on the Broad Walk?'

'Yes, guv. If we attack, they'll blow it up.'

Nelson issued a stream of orders. Activity in the room had increased to fever pitch and tempers had started to fray; the attack on the Jewel House was only fifteen minutes away.

He wanted things right and he checked and checked

again to ensure that everything was in place, giving particular attention to the paramedics and their ambulance. 'The woman must not be hurt,' he kept mumbling to himself as the minutes ticked by.

'A flag's hanging on the Jewel House door, guv,' called his Inspector.

'What kind of flag?'

'I don't know, guv.'

'Then bloody-well find out.'

'Yard on the line, guv,' Molly said, deciding that Met speak was in order.

He snatched the telephone from her hand and glanced at the clock. It was seven fifty-seven. 'What the bloody hell are you bothering me for now?' he bellowed into the mouthpiece. He coughed, coloured slightly, and was quiet for a moment.

'Yes, Commissioner' he said. 'I'll see to it.' Slowly, he replaced the handset, then spoke to his Inspector. 'Tell Arnold Schwarzenegger to stop the clock.'

Bewildered, the Inspector gaped at his boss. 'You want everything on hold, guv?'

'Are you bloody deaf or something?'

39

James stood behind three middle-ranking detectives seated at a long wooden table covered with an orderly array of communications equipment and blocks of message pads.

'How are you feeling today, Molly?'

'Fine,' she replied. 'Did you get some sleep?'

He shook his head. 'No - but I'm good for another twenty four hours.' She looked at his dilated pupils and wondered what he had taken.

'The man on your right is Negotiator 1,' he said quietly. 'He's the only person who can speak to the terrorists' spokesman. Negotiator 2, in the middle, monitors their conversation. Negotiator 3, on your left, can't hear what the terrorist is saying - like the rest of us - but he has a separate telephone link to the Incident Commander in the Special Operations Room at Scotland Yard. Whilst Negotiator 1 and the terrorists' spokesman are talking, all contact between the negotiators is by way of written notes so that the concentration of Negotiator 1 isn't broken.'

'What about Nelson next door?'

'Strictly speaking, the FCP commander isn't supposed to interfere but he's insisted on having a line and can hear both sides of the conversation.' James turned towards the door. 'The man at the back is the *Go For*. He must be ready to provide anything the negotiators need. There's also a guard outside and no one comes in here without my say so.'

She looked at the notice board in front of the negotiators. It covered most of the wall, the terrorists being listed as **A B C D** and **E.** Columns below the titles already contained partial descriptions. Columns were also headed **DEMANDS** and **TIMES.** In a space at the top of the board, someone had scrawled *THE LIFE OF THE HOSTAGE IS IN YOUR HANDS - HANDLE WITH CARE.*

Above the notice board there was a large, white-faced clock which reminded her of the one PC Raybould had acquired for the Incident Post at Westhampton.

Negotiator 1 raised his hand for silence and adjusted his headphones.

'What shall I call you?' he asked quietly.

'-----------------'

'Yes, I can understand that. But it would be better if we used some kind of handle. My name is John.'

'-----------------------'

'Colin. I'm pleased to meet you. What's happening in there?'

'-----------------------------------'

'I agree. The welfare of the student and the safety of the crown will always be our over-riding concern.'

'-----------'

'No, of course we won't do anything silly. We only want things sorted out. Perhaps you can tell me what this is all about?'

'--

-----------------------'

'Yes, I'll pass them on to the Chief at Scotland Yard.'

Negotiator 2 scribbled on his message pad and passed the top copy to Negotiator 3 who picked up the direct line to the Special Operations Room.

Negotiator 2 then walked over to the notice board and wrote:

TIME 0915
DEMANDS
1. SAFE ESCORT OUT OF THE TOWER.
2. POLICE LAUNCH AT TOWER PIER TO TAKE THE PARTY DOWN THE THAMES TO INTERNATIONAL WATERS.
DEADLINE - 1115

'I can't make any promises, Colin,' Negotiator 1 continued. 'Your demands have been passed to the Chief, the only person who can make these kind of decisions.'

'----------------------------'

'He's unable to speak to you, Colin. He's up to his neck with all kinds of problems. Is there anything you

276

need?'

'----------------------------------'

Negotiator 3 slid a note along the table and Negotiator 1 read it before speaking again.

'Colin. The Chief wants to know if the young woman is all right?'

'------------'

'Is there anything you have to tell me about her? Does she want to give her family a message?'

'----------------'

'No, Colin, I'm not stalling. You'll get an answer soon.'

'----------------------------------'

'Yes, I realise that and I'm doing my best.'

'-----'

'The food shouldn't take long. Colin, do you need any medicines for the young woman?'

'----------------'

'No, Colin. I'm not causing delays.'

'------------------------'

'I heard what you said about the crown and understand what you're saying.'

Negotiator 2 slid a second message to Negotiator 1 who read it.

'...Colin. the food's ready. It's in containers on a trolley. Can someone push it across the Broad Walk to the door?'

'------------------------'

'No tricks, I promise, Colin...'

Nelson burst into the room. 'Who the bloody hell do they think they're talking to?' he roared. James opened his mouth to answer but the furious Yorkshireman continued, 'And what's all this deadline crap?' He glanced at the clock. 'We've only got one hour forty-five minutes and it takes COBRA that long to decide how many lumps of sugar they want in their sodding coffee.'

The man guarding the door, tapped her shoulder. 'Inspector Watson,' he whispered. 'Someone outside wishes to see you.'

Reluctantly, she left the negotiators' room.

Bannister and Hartley were waiting for her and she wondered briefly where they had spent the night.

'Gina's here,' Bannister announced.

'Did Henry give you the car number?'

'Yes, but I've done a quick check with DVLC and there's an official stop on it.'

'Check with Special Branch. They're the only people who can tell you which Government department owns the vehicle.'

'Yes, ma'am.'

'How's Gina?'

'Not too bad. Her face is still in bandages but she can walk all right.'

Where do you want her, ma'am?'

'Find her a room on the ground floor so that she can see the Jewel House. And make sure she has everything she needs. That includes a desk, writing materials and a couch or something to rest on.'

Bannister grinned. 'You've made a thief of me, ma'am.'

His cheerfulness was infectious and she had difficulty not smiling back at him. 'It's all a matter of priorities. Have you noticed anyone following you recently?'

He looked behind him. 'A car seemed to be tailing us for a couple of miles after we left the hospital but nothing since. Why do you ask, ma'am.'

'Oh, just a thought,' she said, wondering if MI5 had followed Gina into the Castle.

Bannister exchanged glances with Hartley. 'Any chance of going into the negotiators room or the FCP?' he asked. 'We're missing the action.'

'Sorry,' she replied. 'In the first place I want you to keep Gina well away from Superintendent Nelson and, secondly, one of you must remain with her at all times. I suggest you take it in turns.'

'Thanks,' said a disheartened Bannister.

'Any developments?' she whispered, rejoining James.

Before he could answer, the room shook, telephones fell off tables, and the window shattered. Stepping over broken glass, they ran to the window and looked towards a building on their right. Masonry and brick dust was scattered over a wide area. Red and yellow flames licked exposed woodwork, and clouds of thick black smoke billowed into London's blue sky. Several black clad figures from the inner cordon lay still on the tarmac. Others knelt or staggered about holding their ears or other parts of their body where they had obviously been injured.

'The Fusiliers Museum,' cried James. 'They came to blow it up.'

'No,' Molly cried angrily. 'They came to stage a spectacular - to murder innocent people.'

40

Lagan and Sean, cheering loudly, shook hands as they watched the destruction of the Fusiliers Museum.

Mahmoud, standing apart, gave them an enigmatic smile. It was only a partial success and not the result he and his brothers had been planning for so many months. Many foreign tourists should have been killed and the news should have reverberated around a shocked world so that *Hamas* was on everyones lips.

The three men returned to the central corridor, Sean resuming guard at the entrance, Mahmoud leading Lagan to the wooden crate which was now the telephone table.

Boxes of fruit juice and biscuits, supplied by the police, were stacked against a wall. Empty tinfoil food packets littered the floor.

The containers they arrived in had been thrown out after Lagan found what he presumed to be listening devices, cleverly concealed in the handles.

Taking instructions from Mahmoud, Lagan picked up the telephone handset.

He swallowed hard, like a radio announcer about to make his first broadcast. 'Now do we get out of this stinking jewellery shop, Johnny boy?' he asked with a toughness he didn't feel. He was trying to win favour with Mahmoud. Since the man's cynical killing of the student, and his ruthless elimination of Coster, he'd been terrified of him.

'----------------------------------'

'Fig off. If we don't get a decision by eleven fifteen the student will be dog meat and the tin hat on the square so much scrap metal.'

Nelson, back in the Forward Control Point, wrenched off his headphones and flung them across the room, hitting a detective on the back of the neck. 'I'll kill the bastard with my own hands,' he roared, striding over to the detective to make sure he was not hurt.

'Inspector!' he called. 'Any information from the museum?'

'Afraid so, guv. A PC from the inner cordon is dead and three are seriously injured. Inside, the receptionist and a soldier have been killed.'

'What do you mean, *inside*? The museum's a no go area?'

The inspector made a clicking sound in the back of his throat, a sure sign he was wilting under the pressure. 'The receptionist got permission to visit the museum to empty the cash box. The squaddy was her *friend*.'

Nelson scowled. 'Whatever they were doing, they've paid a cruel price.'

'The terrorists are asking for hot coffee, guv,' said a sergeant, reading from a negotiator's message form.

Nelson's neck seemed to swell as it reddened. 'Hot

coffee - I'll piss on them first.'

Later, Nelson stood in front of the negotiators' notice board. 'It's thirty minutes before the deadline and still no word from COBRA.' He directed his gaze at Negotiator 1. 'Anything from the stronghold?'

'No, guv. Shall I give Colin a call?'

Nelson's scowl deepened. 'If I hear you call that murdering swine *Colin* once more you can pack your bags, understood?'

Negotiator 1 indicated that he did but the Superintendent went on anyway. 'And cut out that niceness crap the FBI taught you; it's a load of bullshit.'

Eyes raw from lack of sleep, he looked at the people around him. 'Right, what've we got?'

James answered. 'The museum is completely gutted. Relatives of the casualties are being informed before we tell the press. Like everyone else within ten miles, they heard the explosion and are demanding to know what's going on.'

'Why a military museum?'

'It's the only soft target in the Castle,' Richard replied. 'Everywhere else inside these walls is bristling with security devices and patrolled by wardens.'

'Wouldn't you know it. Who's behind it all?'

'Hamas. Militant fundamentalists, religious fanatics - call them what you will. It's the Palestine flag hanging on the Jewel House door. We had been tipped off by Mossad that they would be targeting Jews and high profile property in this country.'

Molly looked hard at James. How long had he known about this?

Shrugging his shoulders, he showed his palms in an elaborate gesture of innocence.

'What's their beef?' asked Nelson.

Richard looked at the door, as if to make sure it was shut. 'Autonomy in the Gaza and Jericho enclaves is a joke to them. They want the whole of Palestine for the Muslims and are trying to wreck the peace agreement signed by the late Yitzhak Rabin and Yasser Arafat. The Westhampton letter bombs were meant to kill high-ranking Jews living the London area. The attack on the museum was to attract world-wide attention to their cause.'

'How are the IRA involved?'

'Ostensibly, they're not. We're dealing with mercenaries - gunmen for hire.'

Nelson lit another cigarette and sat down. 'And who's hiring out?'

'The IRA has been offering its expertise in death and destruction to the highest bidder. They're desperate for cash to support their new political position. If this job had come off, Sinn Fein could have travelled to Stormont in limos instead of battered black taxis.'

'Did the IRA sell the letter bombs to Hamas?'

Richard glanced furtively at the door. 'Yes. They'd been put together in a secret Dublin arms factory.'

Nelson lit another cigarette. 'No wonder the bastards

don't want to hand in their weapons, they stand to make a fortune by selling them. Where does Hamas get its money from?'

'Iran, if you believe our Defence Secretary. He claims they're trying to destabilise the Middle East by giving huge sums to terrorist groups opposed to the peace process. But there's more. In 1988, America shot down their Airbus and killed two hundred and ninety people. The Iranians believe the Lockerbie aircraft bombing squared things with the Americans but, because we gave our cousins moral support, they still owe us. It may be they're now exacting revenge on this country by financing the Hamas operations here.'

Ash from Nelson's cigarette dusted his long service and good conduct medal ribbon. 'What's the going price for murder and destruction these days?'

Richard studied his hands for a moment. It was not MI5 policy to give so much top secret information. 'Twenty million pounds.'

41

It was eleven-fifteen - the deadline. Nelson glowered at the clock, then his wrist watch. 'If that dumb Home Secretary of ours doesn't do something soon, we'll lose the hostage and the crown, and he'll lose his precious peerage.'

James crossed and uncrossed his arms. 'Don't you think we should ask for a decision?'

'I've already been on to them half a dozen times,' Nelson chuntered. 'They're grown up boys; it's down to them.' He gestured towards the notice board. 'Tell me about those bastards.'

Richard took a deep breath. 'As the endoscope photographs are developed and more information comes in from the voice recordings, my backroom boys are putting together more precise intelligence profiles.

Terrorist **B** is now the leader. He's the Arab, Mahmoud Abdel Rahim, a distant relative of Sheik Ahmad Ayish, one of the founders of Hamas. He's been busy planning and organising suicide missions in Israel for some time, including last year when one of his group blew up a bus in Tel Aviv, killing forty-three people.'

'And he, no doubt, hung the bunting on the door,' said Nelson.

'Most likely,' Richard replied, glancing across the room. 'Are you all right, Molly? You look a little green around the gills.'

Still unable to get the shooting on Tower Green out of her mind, she looked up at him. 'Long days and short nights. Is he also the man who killed Nancy Price?'

'Yes. He's fighting a holy war and regards anyone who gets in his way as fair game.'

'Don't try to justify murder too me,' she retorted. 'He's a cold-blooded killer.'

Nelson brushed past her on his way to the window. 'Steady, Molly,' he said softly.

Surprised - it was the first time he had spoken to her in a civil manner - she watched his back as he gazed at the crown bomb in the centre of the Broad Walk.

Returning to his former position, he checked his watch and spoke to Negotiator 3. 'Advise the Incident Commander that it's seven minutes past the deadline. Then pass the word to the SAS leader and the man in charge of the inner cordon. Tell them they must be ready to act instantly.'

He glanced out of the window again before facing James. 'Go on,' he said heavily, 'Fill me in on the rest of the gang.'

'The small, good looking terrorist, **D** is James Andrew Coster, an ex-Navy underwater munitions expert. His friend was killed during the Falklands war but he survived the same incident and was decorated for bravery.'

287

Richard took up the story. 'Army Intelligence at Lisburn have him on file. He never really recovered from the Falklands episode and is regarded by some as more unstable than the stuff he handles. Informant was surprised he'd been used for such an important job and suggested internal politics might be at work.'

'As if they wanted the operation to go wrong, you mean?' asked Molly.

'Only after they've completed their mission.'

'I think that **D** was responsible for the rape and murder at the Gloucester service station,' she said.

Richard nodded. 'Yes, you're probably right. We believe he also sexually assaulted the landlady and slit her throat. A real psychopath, if ever there was one.'

Her surprised showed. 'What do you mean, *was*?'

Richard gave an apologetic little cough and glanced at James. 'Coster's dead. Mahmoud killed him after he had assaulted the remaining hostage.'

'Good God!' she exclaimed. 'Is Ingrid all right?'

'It seems so. She's been heard on the tapes - hobbling about.'

Nelson looked at the clock, as he had done every few minutes for the past hour: it was eleven twenty-eight. 'At least one of them is off the screen. But if he was their explosives expert, who wired up the crown?'

'Mahmoud,' replied Richard. 'Thanks to Molly, **D** wasn't able to plant his bombs in the museum. The downside is the Arab used Semtex from one of the bombs to break into the display case and he fixed the other one inside the Imperial State Crown.'

'The Pepsi can. How's the bloody thing supposed to explode?' asked Nelson.

'We're not sure. He could have rigged an anti-handling device or a simple triggering mechanism that can be activated by a single shot.'

'Have they got a good marksman?'

'**C** - the fat one - is a former IRA sniper,' Richard replied.

'Take him out and we just might save Lizzy's best tin hat,' Nelson speculated, his eyes now permanently locked onto the clock.

'**A**, his brother, is one of the IRA's most experienced active service unit leaders,' said Richard.

'That leaves **E**,' said Nelson. 'What do you know about him?'

James spoke. 'He master-minded all the IRA mainland bombings during the last five years. Earnings from these last two jobs were to be his golden handshake. According to intelligence reports, he's being replaced by a younger man.'

'What do you mean - replaced? I thought they'd given up the so-called, armed struggle.'

'So did a lot of people, but they haven't kept their guns and bombs for souvenirs. It was just a ruse to give themselves time to re-organise and retrain. We were winning the battle and could have finished them off. Those not in prison, were under constant surveillance.'

Nelson glowered. 'And our brilliant Government fell

for it. Look at all the convicted IRA killers they've let out. Most of them had only done a few years inside.'

'Yes, ' said Richard. 'The very people they need to organise the next London bombings.'

'When's that likely to be?'

'When they've got their sleepers in place and we've dropped our guard.'

'*Sleepers*?' asked Nelson.

'Newly trained terrorists with no obvious IRA connections. They're given fresh identities and settled quietly in various mainland communities. It may be years before they're called into service in some role or other.'

Nelson brushed ash off the front of his uniform. 'You were telling me about **E.**'

'We call him Lagan,' said James. 'He was the leader when they entered the Jewel House. Mahmoud took over after he'd killed the girl and the team's explosives expert.'

'It all fits,' Nelson muttered. 'This bloody castle has been an executioners playground for centuries.'

'There's another fatality you should know about,' said James.

'After Mahmoud had shot the hostage and shut the Jewel House door, he fired into the ceiling and killed a soldier fitting the overhead camera and listening device.'

'How the hell did he know the army was up there?'

Richard chipped in. 'He didn't. It was an accident. He was letting off steam because Coster had let the student escape.'

42

Negotiator 2 called for silence and everyone turned towards the long table.

'I'm sorry for the delay and I'm ready to take down what you say,' said Negotiator 1.

'---

--'

Negotiator 2 scribbled on his message pad.

Negotiator 1 spoke to the caller. 'Yes, I've got your latest demands. They'll be passed to the proper authority immediately.'

Negotiator 3 passed the demands to the Incident Commander.

Negotiator 2 took the second copy of his notes to the notice board and started to write:

Time 1149
ADDITIONAL DEMANDS
1. A BBC WORLD SERVICE BROADCAST
SUPPORTING HAMAS'S CLAIM TO ALL
THE LAND NOW OCCUPIED BY ISRAEL.
2. £20 MILLION POUNDS TO BE PAID IN
CASH.
NEW DEADLINE - 1330

'Mahmoud!' Richard gasped.

Nelson kicked the leg of a desk. An old jam jar shook, balanced precariously on the edge, toppled onto the floor and smashed, sending broken glass and ball point pens flying in every direction. Coughing in the back of his throat, part apology, mostly satisfaction, he found his voice. 'Filling the IRA's bloody coffers. Did the Incident Commander get the new demands?'

'Yes, guv,' replied Negotiator 3.

'He'd better tell those bastards to piss off.'

'It's COBRA's decision, guv.'

'Don't you lecture me, son...I'm thinking aloud.'

'Sorry, guv.'

Nelson faced Richard. 'What have we got on the hostage?'

'We found a letter on Nancy Price's body and have been in touch with both girls' parents in California. They were Environmental Studies students at UCLA and this is the first time they've been outside the States. Ingrid Mestrovic is eighteen and, according to mum, a bright, precocious girl. Highly strung, she's given to fits of depression but doesn't lack courage. Her doctor says she's had all the usual growing up illnesses and is strong for her age. Her hobbies - mum again - are boyfriends, pop music and TV soaps,'

'Sounds familiar,' mumbled Negotiator 3.

Nelson made eye contact with the SAS leader at the back of the room. 'Not even our half-baked Government will accept these new demands. Are your men tooled up and ready to go in? They've had a long night and no sleep.'

'They're used to it.'

'What notice do you need?'

'Five minutes.'

'That's an improvement. I'm relying on you to get the young woman out safely. What weapons have the terrorists got?'

'Each man has an Uzi sub machine gun and a pistol of some kind. They seem to have plenty of ammunition.'

'Any Semtex left?'

'Possibly.'

'Are you satisfied with your plan of attack?'

'We've practised in the mock-up rooms so often we could do it blindfolded. It's the unexpected we have to watch out for. An eighty percent chance of success, I should say.'

'Just remember the student.'

Face deadpan, so that no one could guess what he thought about Nelson's prompting, the SAS leader simply nodded.

'Have you liaised fully with our firearms people? I'd hate you to start putting holes in each other.'

Another nod.

'Good,' said Nelson. 'You'll have all the necessary back-up. Ambulances, medics, hostage reception, prisoner processing, fire brigade, debriefing unit, forensic, enquiry and evidence gathering teams.' He frowned and looked around the office. 'What's that I hear, Watson?'

'Chopper overhead!' she called from the window. 'Looks like a television crew.'

Nelson joined her. 'That's one advantage of being at the FCP; we've got two bloody great walls between us and the media.' He looked at James. 'Get one of our fly boys to buzz them or shoot the buggers down.'

Negotiator 1 picked up his telephone.

'Yes,' he said.

'----------------------'

'I'll see what I can do.'

'------------------------------'

'Yes. I told you.'

Negotiator 2 passed the message to Nelson.

'The cheeky bastards are asking for travelling clothes and packed lunches,' he growled.

Negotiator 3 handed him another message. He read it once and then again, more slowly. It was only two sentences but he needed time to digest the contents:

Time 1201
From Incident Commander.
Negotiate for an extension of one hour past the deadline. We undertake to give them a decision not later than 1430.

43

Five people inside the Jewel House were preoccupied with their own thoughts.

Lagan, crouched in the recess he had made his own, silently cursed himself. The cunning negotiator had talked him into allowing them another hour and Mahmoud had shouted at him for giving in.

'Oh, God in Heaven,' he moaned. 'Why Westhampton, and why the police bitch who had ruined it all?' Without her, everything would have been fine and he'd be on his way to Buenos Aires.

Sean McKindon, guarding the front entrance, shifted his exhausted body in the hard chair. He too, thought of getting away. He wanted to start a new life with his brother, free of guns and fighting.

Danny, a sparkling crown on his head, dreamed of giving it to his ma.

In the kitchen, Ingrid, arms and legs numb, eyes swollen and bowels out of control had given up hope. Nancy Price was already dead and if the terrorists didn't shoot her, a stray bullet from the raiding party would. *The SAS is something else - no one stops those guys*, her boyfriend had said as they'd watched an old war movie.

Only Mahmoud was content. He stood beside the wooden crate in the corridor, cleaning his sub-machine gun. Fatique was etched into the smooth lines of his face, but his clear brown eyes shone with anticipation. Soon he would be revered by all the people of Palestine.

'Inspector Watson!' called a uniformed PC. 'They want to see you in the Security Services office.'

She glanced at her watch: it was two o'clock. 'Who does?'

'Detective Superintendent Cranleigh-Smythe and a chap in civvies, ma.'am.'

She walked into an office on the second floor and was surprised by the number of people, including men in dark suits she hadn't seen before. There was also a man tuning a receiver and picking up the conversation between Negotiator 1 and the terrorists. In a glass-fronted annex James was seated at a table with Richard.

'Sit down,' invited Richard as she joined them. His eyes had a look of respect she hadn't seen before. 'You've done a first rate job,' he said, leaning close, as if about to kiss her. Instead he handed her a photograph. 'This was taken by one of our endoscope cameras. It's Lagan, the IRA Mainland Commander and formerly the leader of that bunch of terrorists across the square.'

She looked at the grainy picture of a middle-aged man with a plain face and dark, receding hair. 'How can you be certain he's the Mainland Commander?'

'It fits his intelligence profile perfectly - all we

needed was a name.'

James chipped in. 'The car Henry Taylor saw is a Saab allocated to the Home Office Pool. Only two people used it on the afternoon someone visited Gina Jones's apartment. A woman from accounts and this man.'

She frowned. 'How did you get the car's number?'

'From Special Branch. Your Sergeant Bannister made an enquiry and they passed it on to us.'

'Without giving him the information he asked for?'

'Of course not. If needs be, they can stall forever.'

She shook her head. 'I want to go back to Westhampton. The air may be full of shit but it's cleaner than what I'm having to breathe down here.'

Richard smiled and showed her the back of a photograph.

She read the neat writing: **Peter Fitzpatrick Finch. 44 years. Born Northern Ireland. Moved to London with his parents when he was five. Catholic. Senior Civil Servant, Home Office Police Department.**

She turned the photograph over and her expression was suddenly one of incredulity. 'It's the same man,' she gasped. 'It's Lagan.' Both men grinned, the weariness wiped from their faces so that even Richard seemed youthful.

'We didn't have to dig very deep into his antecedents to start making the connection,' he said. 'His mother would have blown up the Houses of Parliament single handed if someone had given her the gunpowder. Born in the Divis Flats, Lower Falls, Belfast, she came from a well-known family of active Republicans. Fighting the British was in her blood, a tradition. Although this country gave her a good living for most of her life she never stopped hating it. She also made sure her son felt the same way.'

Richard sat back in his chair. 'Yes, the Mainland Commander and the Mole are the same person, and he's trapped inside the Jewel House.'

'Great,' she said, understanding their jubilation but still trying to get things straight in her mind. 'Are you telling me the Mole was not from Scotland Yard?'

'Yes, but we were close. He would have seen a lot of important Scotland Yard reports addressed to the Home Secretary, other ministers, and Police Department heads.'

'Is there anything wrong with his left hand?'

Richard frowned. 'There is, actually; three of his fingers are missing. Why do you ask?'

'He was in Westhampton on the day of the letter bomb explosions and it confirms that he was the man who visited Gina's apartment and spoke to Henry Taylor.'

'The man with the missing fingers?'

'Yes.'

'Why didn't you say so before?'

'My job was to catch the Westhampton bombers. I wasn't going to be side-tracked by your capers.' She glanced at James. 'Nor Scotland Yard's.'

Richard shook his head. 'You're a deep one, Molly Watson. You couldn't tell me how Lagan and his men smuggled enough explosives and weapons into this place to equip a small army by any chance?'

'Yes, I think I can.' She then described Lagan's meeting with the student in Bernie's place.

'Before they parted, he gave him a heavy holdall. It was open and the lady who runs the pub saw that it contained Pepsi cans,' she concluded.

'It might have helped if you had told us about this sooner.'

Her back straightened. 'And it might have helped if you two had been honest with me from the very beginning.'

James coughed in his throat. 'What matters, is we've now cornered the man who is both Lagan and the Mole.'

'Did Lagan have access to information about the Channel Tunnel operation?' she asked.

Richard sprang to his feet. 'What did you say?'

She glanced at James. The blood had drained from his face so that his eyes looked black and baggy and his lips were straight white lines.

Richard stared at her, his voice low and threatening. 'You must never, never, never, repeat what you've just said.' She looked from one man to the other. The camaraderie of the last few minutes had been replaced by an awesome tension.

A man in a check sports shirt and faded jeans handed

Richard a message. He read it, then passed it to James.
She peered over his shoulder.

Time 1413

**From Incident Commander to Officer in
charge of Forward Control Point,
information MI5.**

**COBRA has instructed that the terrorists'
demands are to be met in full.**

**A police launch will be at the Tower Pier
at 1600 hours to take five persons down the
Thames to the sea and international waters.**

**A man from the Home Office will be on
board the launch and will hand over the
twenty million pounds.**

**Liaise with the terrorist leader and make
plans for a peaceful and orderly evacuation
from the Jewel House to the Tower Pier,
commencing at 1530.**

She struggled to find a reason for the madness of it
all. Who but the British Government would make deals
with multiple murderers? People who had callously and
indiscriminately killed men, women and children.

James stood up and walked around the small annex.
Richard dropped into his seat and stared at the wall in
front of him.

'If the Government lets that gang of murderers go
free,' said James, 'I'm going to tell the press they've

packed the Channel Tunnel with Semtex.'

'No you won't,' snapped Richard. 'They'll destroy you.'

'I don't care.'

'But you care about Miss Watson.'

She rounded on him. 'What's that supposed to mean?'

The MI5 man's reply was barely audible. 'You're both on file - with pictures.'

'The Cotswolds?' James asked hoarsely.

Some of the strength returned to Richard's voice. 'Yes.'

She glared at him. 'You dirty bastard.'

'Dirt is better than dead. I'm doing you a favour.'

'That's what the Nazis said when they herded eight million Jews into the gas chambers.' She laughed without humour. 'If I'd known you were watching, I would've got out my leather gear and put on a special show.'

'Molly!' said James firmly, 'that's enough.'

She stared at him, confused by the note of desperation in his voice. Then she understood. It wasn't only their steamy weekend in his cottage that he was worried about, it was his attempt to rape her at the hotel; he couldn't be sure that incident hadn't been filmed by MI5.

'It's enough for me,' she yelled, picking up her shoulder bag, her arms shaking as she fought off a powerful urge to beat Richard around the head with it.

301

James stood up. 'I'll see you later, Molly.'

She took one last look at the MI5 man. 'You should be behind bars - in a zoo!' she screamed, before striding through the outer office, past his startled staff.

44

The terrorists and their hostage were standing in the Jewel House corridor.

'Watch out for the woman who stopped Coster yesterday,' Mahmoud warned. 'We may be walking into an ambush.'

'They said they'd let us go - they prommised?' whined Danny, face ashen as he hugged his gun close to his chest.

'Just keep your mouth shut and do as I say,' Mahmoud said quietly. 'They would like nothing better than an excuse to kill us off before we cross the moat into Tower Hill where the press and the TV cameras will be waiting.'

He pulled his national flag from the door and hung it on the barrel of his Uzi. Today he might die but it did not matter. He had completed two important missions, killed the enemies of his people, and gained world wide publicity for their just cause. He would be a hero of Palestine. In Qalqilyah and all the other towns and villages of Gaza and Jericho there would be rejoicing and dancing in the streets. His mother and his sisters would boast of his exploits and show everyone his Hamas farewell video in which he had read a saying of the prophet Muhammad: *The Judgment Day will not come until Muslims will fight Jews and kill them and, even if a Jew hides behind a stone or a tree, the tree or stone will say, "Muslim, slave of God, there is a Jew hiding behind me."*

At three-thirty Sean McKindon stepped out of the Jewel House onto the Broad Walk. Big and strong, his heavy jaw was darkened by several days of growth, and his pale forehead was topped by a thatch of black hair. His bloodshot eyes squinted against the daylight. In his right hand, his Uzi was pointed menacingly across the Broad Walk. His left hand held Ingrid Mestrovic's arm above the elbow. She had a brown army blanket draped over her shoulders and walked awkwardly, as if in pain.

Danny, face streaked with black dust, and seemingly fatter than ever, was close behind his brother, using him as a shield.

Mahmoud followed. Only his rough clothing identified him with the other men. He was tall and majestic, and he carried himself with calm assurance. But those close enough to see his intelligent, restless eyes and his firm grip on the sub machine gun, were patently aware that his brain was racing and every muscle in his lithe body was ready for action.

Lagan came out last. Stooped, with shoulders rounded, as if to protect his puny chest, the barrel of his gun waved about like a stick in a storm.

Black-suited SAS troops and police marksmen, like

304

so many fearsome gargoyles, lined the tops of the towers and the castle walls all around them.

Blue **POLICE** tape marked the terrorists' exit route across the Broad Walk, past the White Tower, and under the portcullis of the Bloody Tower.

On Tower Hill sightseers were packed tight behind solid lines of policemen dressed in full riot gear. An expectant, carnival atmosphere had taken hold and a heaving mass of excited people was waiting for something extraordinary to happen; an event that would bring colour and excitement to their dull lives.What a story they would have to tell their friends back at the office or wherever.

Hot dog and ice-cream sellers, charging extortionate prices, were unable to cope with demand. 'They should bring back public hangings on Tower Hill,' one of them said cheerfully as he stuffed a bundle of notes into his pocket.

Battalions of the press, herded into their own compound, pushed and jostled to get the best viewpoints. Television newscasters, supported by the terrorist experts who always appeared on these occasions, had been reporting the siege hourly to viewers around the world; some hoping for the safe release of the hostage and the return of the crown, others eagerly looking forward to a bloodbath of *Waco* proportions.

As the terrorists and their captive neared the centre of

the Broad Walk Mahmoud called his party to a halt, and sent Danny to retrieve the crown with the bomb strapped inside.

Looking about him, as if he expected to be shot dead at any moment, Danny scampered across the Broad Walk. Nervously, he picked up the crown and carried it back to Mahmoud.

The Arab eased it into a Tower of London gift bag which he tucked under one arm. Satisfied, he took time to study the scene around him before shouting an order over his shoulder.

Lagan, dishevelled and dirty, straightened up. He then raised his left hand, jabbing his thumb and little finger at the numerous guns trained on them.

Joe Nelson, looking down from the Forward Control Point, issued orders.

The guns around the Broad Walk were withdrawn from view.

'Molly,' James whispered in her ear. 'That's Lagan.'

She nodded. They were standing on Tower Green with observers from Scotland Yard. She shivered. It was not the cold but seeing Lagan's hand with three fingers missing for the first time. To her it was the symbol of evil; the killings, the rapes, and the bloodshed. It had been a catalogue of violence. Now she must stand aside and watch the perpetrators walk free.

Another person saw the deformed hand. She'd seen it once before; when she passed photocopies of

Government documents around a door with no letter box. It was the hand of the man who caused the blast that took away her face and her will to live. She hated him with all her being. If she'd had the choice, he would have suffered a long, lingering death and she would have laughed in his face as he begged for mercy.

She moved cautiously around the furniture to a window broken by the blast from the Fusiliers Museum. With slow, deliberate movements she raised a Heckler Koch MP5 carbine to her shoulder. The effort made her feel faint and she leaned against the wall for support.

Giving herself time to recover, she adjusted her arm until she felt more comfortable. Her hand steadied and she squinted through the telescopic laser sight until she found Lagan. The leading terrorist with the hostage started to turn and she knew that in another minute she would lose sight of her target at the rear of the column. The pain in her face was excruciating but she forced herself to concentrate, fixing the red spot of the laser on Lagan's chest. She swayed slightly, losing him, then finding him again. Her right forefinger squeezed a fraction and stopped. She waited until the red spot was perfectly still, then squeezed again.

Peter Fitzpatrick Finch, alias Lagan, was dead before he hit the ground but reflex action caused his finger to tighten around the trigger of his Uzi. Bullets sprayed the wall of the White Tower and two soldiers were hit, one falling silently onto the tarmac, the other doubling up and letting out a terrible scream which echoed around the battlements.

Marksmen in the inner cordon, and those on the towers and lining the battlements, returned the fire.

Sean grabbed student and pitched forward, crushing her to the ground. His back was shredded by a fusillade of high velocity shots.

Danny McKindon raised his gun and staggered backwards as a hail of bullets hammered into his chest and ripped open his neck.

Miraculously, Mahmoud remained standing. Seeing Molly for the first time, he clutched the gift bag to his chest, raised his gun in the air and charged towards her, the Palestine flag trailing above his head.

The noise of so many guns firing at once was deafening. His body twisted and turned as lead poured into him from three sides. His own momentum and the impact of the bullets carried him forward so that he crashed to the ground in front of her. The plastic bag was partly hidden beneath his body but she could see his hand inside the crown - gripping the Pepsi can bomb.

Terrified and expecting to be blown to pieces, she closed her eyes and said a silent prayer.

But there was no explosion; only a moment of stunned silence. She opened her eyes and looked down. The mutilated remains of Mahmoud's once-proud body lay at her feet, his head beside the barrel of his sub-machine gun, his blood soaking into the Palestinian flag that was now his pillow. Amongst the horror of sudden death his face seemed strangely peaceful; like that of a sleeping child.

Strong hands gripped her shoulders and she heard a familiar voice behind her.

'Careful,' James whispered urgently. 'I'll guide you. Slide your feet backwards.'

She looked at Mahmoud's dark hand inside the crown. The knuckles were white and she wondered what powerful force still held the bomb. She felt her body starting to shake and couldn't stop it; neither could she move her legs.

James spun her around, picked her up, and carried her in his arms; across Tower Green towards the Broad Walk.

Stopping at a bench, he gently put her down. Holding her close, he soothed her, as a father might calm an hysterical child.

Slowly, she recovered, broke free from him and sat up. She gazed in awe at the gruesome battle scene all around her. Blood found shallows in the tarmac, formed pools, then snaked off like meandering streams making their way to the sea. A lone raven hopped a few paces onto the square, pecked at a piece of gleaming red flesh, then swallowed it in one gulp.

She simply stared. It was as though nothing could shock her any more. An inspector wearing a baseball cap back-to-front fired a shot into the air and the flightless bird hopped away.

Men and women from the inner cordon, who had been lying on the ground in prone positions, stood up

309

one after the other. Some took tentative steps towards the carnage on the Broad Walk. A pitiful cry for help caused those nearest to the mangled remains of Sean McKindon to run forward. Beneath him, her clothing soaked with his blood, they found Ingrid Mestrovic.

'Are you fit to walk, Molly?' James asked a short time later.

She stood up and moved mechanically towards the White Tower. When they reached it her legs lost their strength and she sat on the same wooden bench that Lagan had used to arm his men with bombs and guns twenty-four hours earlier.

'Parking ticket?' she asked, as soon as she started to feel better.

He glanced at the piece of paper in his hand. 'It was Gina.'

'What was?'

'She fired the first shot; the one that killed Lagan. Somehow she got into the temporary armoury next to her room and took one of the ninja's weapons.'

'Where were Bannister and Hartley?'

'On the second floor, getting a better view of the action.'

'Damn. Why did Gina shoot Lagan?'

'When the ninjas burst into her room she'd collapsed. This is the top sheet of Gina's note pad.' He handed her the piece of paper. She read the single printed word: **CONTROLLER**.

It was six o'clock before she was alone with James again. They were seated on plastic boxes amongst what was left of the Catering Department's equipment.

'I'm sorry,' she said quietly. 'Bannister and Hartley shouldn't have left Gina alone.'

He scratched his chin and she noticed for the first time that he needed a shave. 'Don't blame yourself, Molly' he said. 'You can't keep coppers away from something this big. I don't suppose either of them had been that close to an armed siege before.'

'Bill doesn't usually let me down,' she said quietly.

James studied his hands for a moment. 'He didn't, DC Hartley fouled up. It was her turn to guard Gina.'

'How do you know?'

'She had the decency to tell me.'

'At the end of the day Gina was my responsibility. How she got into the other room, let alone fire a gun and hit a target at that range, beats me.'

'There's no recoil with a Heckler Koch and my grandmother could hit a fly at a hundred metres with an infra-red sight.'

'It was still a remarkable effort.'

'She was driven by hate.'

'Like someone else we know. Did I really cause all these deaths, James?'

He put his arm around her. 'You've landed the most vicious gang of killers this country has seen for a long time. The IRA and Hamas would have made a deadly cocktail.'

She did not resist his embrace. 'And you've got the IRA Mainland Commander, the Mole, and the Controller. *Three for the price of one*, as my navigator used to say when we were dodging ack ack shells over Hamburg.'

'Pardon?'

She laughed. 'I was taking off Henry Cats-Eyes Taylor, World War II bomber pilot and a real gentleman.'

'I thought for a minute you'd had a relapse.'

'That will come later. Right now, I'm demob happy.'

He leaned closer to her. 'So am I, let's celebrate.'

'Perhaps. Do you think the big Irish chap tried to shield Ingrid with his body?'

'Does it matter? She's safe, that's the important thing.'

'There must be someone; a mother or a lover who needs to know that he wasn't all bad.'

James's gave her his special smile, the smile he had once reserved for the bedroom. 'You're a real softy, Molly Watson. Let's get off, my car's outside.'

She glanced at her watch, wondering where Bannister had got to. 'Tell me what's going to happen to Gina?'

'Nothing much. She'll be having plastic surgery for years.'

'Will she go to prison?'

'I doubt it. The Home Secretary will find a way of

keeping this lot out of the courts.'

James lowered his arm so that his hand was around her waist and she could feel his hot fingers through her dress. 'I shall never be able to prove it,' he went on, 'but I'm convinced that if she hadn't opened fire someone else would have done. The Government couldn't afford to let those men escape.'

'So Gina did them a favour?'

'I think so. I should have told you; Henry Taylor knew where she'd hidden her money. He's going to invest it for her. She should be a rich lady one day, Molly.'

She looked out of the window at the burnt-out shell of the Fusiliers Museum. 'And she'd gladly toss it all into the sea if she could have her face back.'

They watched men in white coats erecting covers over the bloody remains of the terrorists. On Tower Green an army bomb disposal team was preparing to disarm the Pepsi can bomb under Mahmoud's body.

'Why did the Arab attack me?' she asked.

James thought for a moment before he answered. 'I presume he saw you in action when the siege started and you were the only person of authority he knew. In his eyes you were the enemy.'

'And now he's dead. For what?'

'For God's sake, according to his creed. In his own country he will be a saint; a *living martyr*, as they call their suicide killers.'

'What makes young men give their lives so readily?'

313

'They believe the Jews took their land. How can people live without land to sustain them?'

'We shouldn't takes sides, should we?'

'That's what we were told when we joined the job.'

'Was I wrong about Richard? He didn't tell us Hamas were the real terrorists until the very end.'

'Who knows? He was under enormous pressure. The powers-that-be thought the Mole knew about the Channel Tunnel.'

'I still couldn't trust him.'

'He worked for the Government; all governments are corrupt.'

'Will we ever know why the Captain was killed?'

'No. The IRA and our side both had a motive.'

'I suppose they'll claim their lies and duplicity were necessary to keep the peace process moving. Anything that stops the killing must have some justification.'

'Let's hope so.'

She twisted in her seat. His arm was making her back ache but she didn't want to move it; not yet. 'Now that Finch, alias Lagan - the IRA Mainland Commander - the Mole - the Controller - call him what you will, is dead, your worries about the Channel Tunnel operation would seem to be over.'

He answered with a heavy voice. 'Professionally, maybe. Personally I agree with you. It was an ill-conceived and highly dangerous thing to do. I just hope future generations don't suffer as a consequence of such crass stupidity.'

She thought of the Captain and the legacy he had left.

'Standish was only doing his job,' James said.

'How did you know I was thinking about him?'

'You're pretty transparent at times.'

'It was your fault. I was lonely; left on the shelf by a pompous, no-good, Scotland Yard detective.'

'Now you're getting back to normal.'

'Thanks.'

His arm tightened around her. 'When this lot's over, and the Complaints Bureau has trampled all over us, do you fancy a short holiday at my cottage?'

'Will you stop Snake Eyes taking any more dirty pictures?'

He smiled and she thought how handsome he looked, even though his drugs were wearing off and he was plainly exhausted.

She slipped from his arm. In what dark recess of his mind had he hidden the night when he'd tried to rape her? She shuddered, knowing she would never forget or forgive.

'James,' she said, slowly, deliberately. 'After what you did to me, I'd die rather than go away with you.'

Shocked, his face paled and his mouth opened, lips quivering as he unsuccessfully fought for words.

Bannister strode into the temporary canteen. 'I've cleared your room, ma'am,' he said cheerfully. 'A taxi's waiting to take us to Euston Station.'

Ignoring the man slumped beside her, she stood up. 'Well done, Bill. When we get back to Westhampton

I'm going to treat you to the best meal in town and you can tell me what you and Lynda Hartley have been up to.'

He stepped aside to let her pass. 'Only if you keep your promise and let me return to uniform duties, ma'am.'